Feeling the room begin to spin, Tori closed her eyes tightly.

"Why would the investigator be asking questions about me?"

"You're new in town."

"So?"

"This is the first murder Sweet Briar's ever had."

Tori swallowed back the bile that threatened to gag her where she sat.

"And therefore *I* must be a *murderer*? Is that what he thinks?" She knew her voice sounded shrill, near hysterical even, but she couldn't stop. This had to be some sort of joke, didn't it?

"That's what a lot of people are going to think, Victoria."

Swiveling back toward the window, Tori stared out at the pockets of people standing around—virtually everyone either pointing or staring at her. They weren't curious about the new librarian. They didn't care about the changes she would bring to the library. And they couldn't care less whether she was from Chicago or Beijing. They were there for one reason and one reason only. To catch a glimpse of Tiffany Ann's murderer.

"But *you* don't think that . . . right, Leona?"

An awkward silence filled her ear as she waited, desperately, for the answer she needed to hear.

Sew
Deadly

Elizabeth Lynn Casey

BERKLEY PRIME CRIME, NEW YORK

THE BERKLEY PUBLISHING GROUP
Published by the Penguin Group
Penguin Group (USA) Inc.
375 Hudson Street, New York, New York 10014, USA
Penguin Group (Canada), 90 Eglinton Avenue East, Suite 700, Toronto, Ontario M4P 2Y3, Canada
(a division of Pearson Penguin Canada Inc.)
Penguin Books Ltd., 80 Strand, London WC2R 0RL, England
Penguin Group Ireland, 25 St. Stephen's Green, Dublin 2, Ireland (a division of Penguin Books Ltd.)
Penguin Group (Australia), 250 Camberwell Road, Camberwell, Victoria 3124, Australia
(a division of Pearson Australia Group Pty. Ltd.)
Penguin Books India Pvt. Ltd., 11 Community Centre, Panchsheel Park, New Delhi—110 017, India
Penguin Group (NZ), 67 Apollo Drive, Rosedale, North Shore 0632, New Zealand
(a division of Pearson New Zealand Ltd.)
Penguin Books (South Africa) (Pty.) Ltd., 24 Sturdee Avenue, Rosebank, Johannesburg 2196,
South Africa

Penguin Books Ltd., Registered Offices: 80 Strand, London WC2R 0RL, England

SEW DEADLY

A Berkley Prime Crime Book / published by arrangement with the author

PRINTING HISTORY
Berkley Prime Crime mass-market edition / August 2009

Copyright © 2009 by Penguin Group (USA) Inc.
Cover illustration by Mary Ann Lasher.
Cover design by Judith Lagerman.
Interior text design by Laura K. Corless.

ISBN: 978-0-425-22910-1

BERKLEY® PRIME CRIME
Berkley Prime Crime Books are published by The Berkley Publishing Group,
a division of Penguin Group (USA) Inc.,
375 Hudson Street, New York, New York 10014.
BERKLEY® PRIME CRIME and the PRIME CRIME logo are trademarks of Penguin Group (USA) Inc.

PRINTED IN THE UNITED STATES OF AMERICA

10 9 8 7 6 5 4 3 2 1

For my daughters,
who light my world each and every day.
I love you.

Acknowledgments

In many ways, writing is a one-person show. You sit in front of a computer screen day in and day out, crafting a world and its people entirely from your imagination. And while I love every moment of the process, I'm keenly aware of the people in my real world—the ones who love and support me long after the last word has been typed.

A huge thank-you goes out to my best friend and writing buddy, Heather Webber. Your constant support through all aspects of my life means more than you can ever know.

A teary-eyed thank-you to my agent, Jacky Sach, for handing me the ball and telling me to run. And to my editor, Emily Rapoport, for making one of my fondest childhood dreams a reality.

A huge thank-you goes to my assistant (and friend), Beth Thaemert. You took a load off my shoulders that allowed me to focus on the best part—the storytelling.

A special thank-you to the group of online sewing enthusiasts who took the time to answer some of my zany questions. Your sewing tips and funny stories helped the Sweet Briar Sewing Circle come to life!

And last but certainly not least . . . my heartfelt thanks and love to Jim. For walking beside me on some of my darkest days and loving me through to the other side.

Chapter 1

She wasn't entirely sure whether it was the pull of the mahogany sewing box in the window or a much-needed respite from the endless barrage of curious glances, but either way, Elkin Antiques and Collectibles seemed as good a place as any for a momentary escape.

Switching the paper sack of lightbulbs to her left hand, Tori Sinclair pushed the glass door open, her presence greeted by a wall-mounted bell and a cocked eyebrow from the sixty-something woman behind the counter.

"Yessss?"

"Oh, I'm sorry are-are you not open?" Tori glanced back at the door, the inward facing Closed sign in direct conflict with the irritation hovering above the clerk's shoulders like vapors off scorching hot pavement.

"Of course, I'm open." The woman stood statue-still as her gaze played across Tori's pale yellow sundress and white strappy sandals, lingered on her light brown shoulder-length hair and heart-shaped face. "Can I help you with something?"

"I—uh, wanted to take a closer look at the sewing box in your window." She pointed at the simple rectangular container that had piqued her curiosity from the sidewalk. "If I'm not mistaken, it's from the late 1800s, isn't it?"

The woman's mouth gaped open a hairbreadth. "Why yes, it is."

Tori closed the distance between the entryway and the display in a few small strides, looking over her shoulder as she stopped beside the box. "It was built by a company in Kansas that specialized in furniture but occasionally dabbled in keepsake pieces, yes?"

The woman nodded, the gap between her lips ever widening.

"I thought so." Tori ran a gentle finger across the backside of the box before coming to rest on the carved scene that adorned its lid. "My great-grandmother had one just like this. It used to sit on a hope chest in her bedroom, and it was where she kept her favorite needles and buttons and ribbons. She'd gotten it as a gift from her parents."

Slowly, gently, she traced the outline of the horse and buggy. "Only *her* box had a snowflake carved onto the lid." She closed her eyes, focused on the feel of the design. "It's funny, but I can still remember how her box felt under my fingertips."

"What happened to it?"

Tori turned to face the woman who'd left her countertop fortress in favor of blatant curiosity. "It was lost in a fire shortly after she passed away."

A soft clucking sound broke through the white noise of memories in Tori's mind, forcing her back to the here and now—and the unmistakable compassion that had chased aloofness from the shopkeeper's eyes.

"Oh, dear, I'm so sorry."

Tori shrugged softly. "It's okay. Seeing this one is kind of nice, even a little comforting."

"I'm glad." The woman reached out, tentatively squeezed

Tori's forearm with a finely wrinkled hand. "Memories are a wonderful way to link us with the past."

"I agree." Pulling her hand from the top of the wooden box, she extended it toward the woman. "I'm Tori Sinclair and I—"

"Tor—you mean, *Victoria* Sinclair? The new librarian?"

Startled, Tori nodded.

"Hmmmm. You've certainly been the talk of Sweet Briar these past few days." The woman stepped backward as her words slipped away in favor of a second, and more thorough, inspection of her lone customer.

Tori shifted from foot to foot in response, the fingers of her left hand inching the top of the paper sack more tightly into her grasp. "Then I guess that would explain the looks I've been getting all afternoon."

"People around here aren't used to seeing new faces, Victoria."

That made sense in a small town like Sweet Briar, yet some of the looks she'd been getting were—

"It's been *good* talk, right?"

"Mostly. But that's neither here nor there, my dear." The woman waved her hand in the air then brought it daintily to her chest. "I'm Leona. Leona Elkin."

"*Mostly?* Is there a problem, Ms. Elkin?" she asked quickly.

"*Leona*, please." The woman brushed her hands down the side of her long, flowered skirt, stopping every few inches to swipe at a nonexistent speck. "A problem with what?"

"Me."

Leona's hand moved from her skirt to her hair, smoothing back a few errant strands of salon-softened gray as she trained her eyes on Tori's. "You?"

"You said, just now, that talk regarding my arrival has been good—*mostly*."

Leona tipped her glasses downward and gazed at Tori over the upper rim, her brown eyes warm. "Don't you worry about a thing. Sour grapes are sour grapes; they're not worth fretting over."

"Sour grapes? I don't understand."

After several long moments, Leona turned on her sensible off-white pumps and gestured for Tori to follow. "Your position at the library . . . it wasn't vacant, my dear."

"I-I don't understand." She knew she sounded like a broken record but she couldn't help herself. If she'd done something wrong, she needed to know.

Reclaiming her spot behind the counter, Leona offered a soft shrug. "You're replacing Dixie Dunn, a woman who's been Sweet Briar's one and only librarian for more years than you've been alive. Retirement wasn't *her* idea."

Uh-oh.

Tori gulped. "You mean this woman . . . this Dixie Dunn . . . was fired because of *me*?"

"Yes—I mean, no." Leona pulled two oak chairs from behind the counter and slowly lowered herself onto one, her head bobbing at Tori to take the other. "To listen to Dixie tell it, she was fired *because* of you. But in reality it was time for her to go. She did things the way she'd been doing them for years. She balked at new programming, pooh-poohed any fresh ideas. The board wanted to bring in new blood. It just so happened to be yours."

"I didn't realize." Tori gave in to the lure of the chair, setting the bag of lightbulbs at her feet as her left temple began to throb. "I certainly wouldn't want someone to lose their job for me."

"She was granted—or, maybe I should say—*given* retirement. If it wasn't you, Victoria, they would have replaced her with *someone*. Unfortunately, they chose someone who isn't"—Leona bent her knees to the side and clasped her hands in her lap, reminding Tori of an

elegant tea party minus the cups, saucers, and table—
"*southern*."

"I was born in the south," Tori offered. "Tampa, to be
exact."

Leona peered at her over the top of her glasses. "Florida is not considered part of the south, dear."

"It's not?"

"Florida is a melting pot. The south is not. You're either a southern belle or you're not."

"And my not being a true southern belle is a problem?"

Leona pursed her lips together in contemplation before
answering. "It *can* be. But let's get back to that later.
Right now I want to know more about you. Other than the
part about being born in Tampa, bless your heart."

Forcing her thoughts from a wounded Dixie Dunn and
her own southern inadequacies, Tori smoothed her dress
and relaxed her shoulders. "We lived all over when I was
growing up—mostly the Midwest. I went to college in
Chicago, falling in love with both the city and a particular
someone during my years there."

The woman clapped her hands gently. "Oooohhh. A
romance in the big city. How enchanting."

"It was . . . for a few years." Tori looked around the
walls of the shop, desperate for anything that could
change the course of the conversation. While she considered herself a fairly open book most of the time, her disas-
trous relationship with Jeff was still too raw, too painful.
"That mirror right there"—she pointed to an oval piece of
glass encased in elegant silver latticework—"is beautiful.
How much is it?"

The shopkeeper's gaze traveled from Tori's face to the
wall beside the counter. "I love that piece, too. But if I kept
everything I love, I'd have no store and no home in which
to put it."

Mission accompl—

Leona trained her focus back on Tori, her smile disarming. "But I'd rather hear about the romance that soured."

Or maybe not.

Defeated, Tori considered simply sharing the whole story. Right down to the humiliation she'd endured when Jeff had been caught with his pants down—quite literally—in the coat closet of the hall where their engagement party was being held. But she opted to keep that information to herself. Realizing the love of one's life was a philanderer was hard enough; admitting it to others was something entirely different. Instead, she gave an abbreviated version that she hoped would satisfy without seeming too evasive.

"I was engaged to a man whom I loved very much." Tori glanced down at her entwined hands then back up at Leona Elkin. "Only I found out he wasn't who I thought he was."

"Tomcatting was he?"

That's one word for it.

She simply nodded, pulling her hands from the safety of one another to push a strand of hair from her face. "I couldn't stay in Chicago anymore. I'd spent years picturing my life there in a certain way. And after he"—her voice dipped momentarily as she struggled to cap her words in a suitable way—"showed his true colors, I knew reality was never going to match the fantasy I'd envisioned."

They sat in silence for a few long moments, each woman deep in thoughts the other could imagine but never know. Finally, Leona reached out and patted Tori's knee. "You made a good decision. Change is not nearly as bad as lingering in water that's become stagnant and cloudy."

She liked that description, hoped the older woman was right. But either way, remaining in Chicago was simply not an option. Not if she wanted to reclaim her life.

"I never married," Leona said as her eyes traveled to a distant place Tori suspected reached far beyond the walls of Elkin Antiques and Collectibles. The kind of place she, herself, had traveled to many times over the past few months.

"My twin sister, Margaret Louise, was always trying to get me to settle down. To stop traveling the world and have a family like she did," continued Leona in a quiet voice. "But what she never understood—until recently— is that I didn't share that same dream. I liked being on my own . . . learning . . . exploring . . . growing. I liked know- ing that if I was going to be let down in some way, it would be by my own doing and no one else's."

It was Leona's last sentence that made Tori sit up taller. The woman was right—absolutely right. If Tori's dreams were going to come to an end, she'd rather it be of her own doing.

"I think that's why I jumped at this job. Sure, I wanted to put as much distance between myself and Jeff as possi- ble . . . but, just as much, I want to reclaim the path I've always envisioned for my life." Tori stood and walked around the counter, her words growing in strength and animation. "Running my own library—it's been a dream since I was a little girl. I have so many ideas, so many plans."

"Be careful, dear, you're in a small town now. A small *southern* town, to be exact."

Leona's caution halted Tori's starry-eyed woolgather- ing in its tracks. Tori retraced her steps, stopping short of the chair she'd occupied just seconds earlier. "I don't un- derstand."

The woman gestured toward the front windows of her shop. "Sweet Briar is a small town, Victoria. Virtually everyone in this town has lived here their whole life. And it's those kinds of people—as wonderful as they are— who find comfort in stagnant waters. They like their food a certain way. They raise their children the way *they* were raised. They go by their *given* name, not a cutesy short- ened version. They"—she coughed quickly, then let her eyes dip to the camisole-like top of Tori's sundress— "*dress* a certain way."

"Is there something wrong with my dress?" Tori asked, perplexed.

"A hint of bosom is all right, dear, but not before dark."

Hint of bosom? What bosom?

Leona continued on, never missing a beat. "They judge people based on breeding and manners, not fancy degrees and one's status as a world traveler. In fact, life begins and ends in Sweet Briar, dear—what happens anywhere else is irrelevant."

Nibbling her lower lip inward, Tori pondered Leona's words. "But the library board *wanted* change, right?"

"Yes. But I'd suggest leaving some things as is—for familiarity's sake. At least for a while. Until the town of Sweet Briar gets to know you better."

The suggestion seemed fair enough.

"Thank you, Leona. I appreciate the advice more than you can know."

The woman's slow smile lit her face from within. "I know how exciting and scary it can be to start over some- where new. I've only been here a few years myself."

Tori sank back into her chair. "*You?* I just assumed, with the shop and everything, that you were a native of Sweet Briar."

"No. Margaret Louise and her husband settled here over forty years ago. And while she wasn't successful in convincing me to settle down and marry in my youth, she *was* able to talk me into retiring here so we could be closer to each other."

"So you understand then, about being an outsider, don't you?" Tori prompted, confused more than ever by the woman's initial coolness.

"In a way. But having Margaret Louise and all of her children and grandchildren here gave me a different status from the beginning. It gave me a leg up, so to speak."

A leg up?

"I can count on one hand the number of people who have moved into this town since I arrived five years ago," Leona continued. "Callie Waters, Robert Dallas, Thomas Hayes, Beatrice Tharrington, and Lester Norton. And every single one of us had a Sweet Briar connection already in place."

"Connection?"

"I had my sister. . . . Callie was born here and determined to die here. . . . Robert has Alzheimer's and came to live with his son, the police chief. . . . Thomas married our mayor. . . . Beatrice is the Johnsons' nanny. . . . and Lester is Dixie's son."

Ahhhh. Those *kinds of connections.* The kind Tori simply didn't have.

She felt her shoulders slump, knew her smile followed. Starting over didn't sound so easy anymore.

"But you'll find your place, I just know it." Leona tugged Tori's hands from her lap and held them gently in her own. "You have a happiness about you that will win everyone over. You just wait and see."

"Even without a twin sister or an important parent or spouse to pave the way?" She heard the momentary uncertainty in her own voice.

"Even without them."

"Even with the fact that my position at the library belonged to a woman who'd been there since it opened?"

Leona released Tori's left hand long enough to wave her own in the air. "Sweet Briar may be a small, close-knit town, but Dixie's ways are well documented. Just be yourself, make your changes at the library—*slowly*—and you'll be just fine."

The woman's words lingered in her thoughts, chasing

any uncertainty away. Leona was right. Tori had won people over all her life by simply being kind and helpful. There was no reason to think the residents of this small southern town would be any different. She was here to bring life to a library that had been operating in a decades-old rut. She wasn't here to bring harm to life in Sweet Briar.

"Now, in answer to your earlier question, consider it a gift."

Tori's gaze followed the path Leona's had taken, coming to rest on the mirror she'd admired while searching for a distraction to a conversation that had been nothing short of special. "I don't underst—"

Rising to her feet, Leona closed the gap between her chair and the wall in six quick steps. "I want you to have this mirror. Consider it a housewarming gift from someone who understands the need for change."

"I can't accept that." Tori stood, blinking furiously against the hint of moisture behind her eyes.

"You can, and you will. I insist." The woman reached up, yanking the mirror from the wall and carrying it to the counter. "And if there's one thing you don't do in Sweet Briar, it's argue with your elders."

"Leona, thank you. So much. For this"—she ran her hand along the silver latticework trim that surrounded the mirror—"and for making me feel welcome. I guess I needed it more than I realized."

"Well, I know I didn't do a very good job of making you feel welcome when you first walked in, and I apologize for that. You'd think with as much traveling as I've done in my life I'd be more open to strangers. But I guess five years of small-town living has rubbed off on me." Leona wrapped the mirror carefully in bubble wrap and then handed it to Tori. "Now, whenever you're feeling a little low or out of place, look at yourself in this and remember who you are."

"I will." With the mirror tucked under her right arm, and the sack of lightbulbs back in her left hand, Tori made her way toward the shop's front door, the mahogany sewing box claiming her attention once again. "Do you sew, Leona?"

The shop owner stopped dead in her tracks, a quick laugh escaping her lips. "Not if I can help it."

"Oh." Tori's gaze swung back to the box, the tug at her heartstrings overpowering. Maybe she didn't have a living, breathing connection to Sweet Briar, but Sweet Briar certainly held a poignant one for her. "I'll be back for that box once I get my first paycheck."

"I look forward to it, dear." Leona stepped around her and opened the door. "Now don't you pay any more mind to looks you get from people in this town. Let them gossip all they want—it gives a purpose besides quaintness to all those picket fences everywhere. Besides, it's not like you've killed anyone—the talk will die out."

Chapter 2

Startled, Tori looked up from the satin-corded pillow she was working on and glanced at the clock propped against the wall, the postdinner hour and the fact that she didn't know anyone making the knock at her door more than a little unexpected.

Back in Chicago, she'd loved when friends had stopped by her apartment unannounced. She'd throw open the door and share the contents of her refrigerator without a second thought to the hour. But that was *before* the breakup. *After it*, she'd learned to ignore knocks until they finally stopped, leaving her to the solo pity-party she'd grown to prefer.

But not anymore. Sweet Briar was her fresh start— even if she had to take it slow.

Removing the pin from between her clamped lips, Tori rose from the small wicker stool in the tiny alcove off her living room and covered the distance to the front door in mere seconds. The gathering dusk outside made it difficult to see much through the sidelight window that ran down the right side of the door, but she could tell her visitor was a woman thanks to the straw hat she wore.

Leona?

The thought was no sooner in her mind than it was out. Leona might have been the only person Tori had met so far, but she hadn't told the woman where she lived. Not that she remembered, anyway. Then again, as Leona had pointed out many times that morning, Sweet Briar was a small town. Surely everyone knew which cottage the new librarian had purchased. . . .

She unlocked the door and pulled, her gaze coming to rest on the tall, dark-haired woman standing on her front step with a covered plate in her hand.

"Victoria?"

"Yes?" She extended her hand in response to the woman's, felt it disappear inside the strong, capable grasp.

"I'm Georgina Hayes from a few blocks over and I wanted to stop by and welcome you to Sweet Briar." The woman pointed at the light fixture to the left of where she stood. "You really ought to get a bulb in there soon. It's not safe for you or your guests to have a porch light that doesn't work."

Confused, Tori popped her head out the door and stared at the bulbless light she'd replaced not two hours earlier. "I don't know what happened, I put one in this after—"

"Let's not worry about that now." Georgina Hayes's eyes left Tori's face long enough to shoot a precursory glance around the partially unpacked interior before returning to their starting spot and crinkling at the edges. "I'm here to welcome you, not lecture you. So let me start over. Welcome to Sweet Briar—we're tickled you're here."

"I'm glad to *be* here." She stepped backward and gestured the woman inside, her thoughts vacillating between the unexpected gesture and the missing lightbulb. "Please excuse the mess. I spent most of the morning unpacking boxes until I needed a break. I escaped down to the town square for a few hours and then simply couldn't find the energy to continue where I'd left off."

Georgina Hayes handed the plate to Tori and pulled off her hat, her demeanor not the slightest bit ruffled by the flattened hair underneath. "That's what tomorrows are for, Victoria."

"*Tori*, please."

"Excuse me?" Georgina furrowed her brows, a glimpse of something resembling distaste hovering in her eyes.

"I prefer to go by Tori."

"You might want to change your mind on that." Stepping farther into the tiny cottage, the woman stopped and looked around, her gaze missing nothing as she commented on her surroundings. "You know, when Douglas Harrison built these cottages, I just knew they'd be darling inside with the right touch. You've barely unpacked a third of your boxes and I can already tell it will be absolutely delightful once it's all gussied up."

"Thank you." Tori glanced at the foil-covered plate in her hand and felt her stomach respond. Chocolate was near.

"Open it up. Let's have some." Georgina waved her hand at the plate then crossed the living room to the bold plaid chair Tori had picked up at a thrift store on her way into Sweet Briar the day before. Ordinarily, green and blue with a touch of red didn't catch her eye, but together they'd conjured up a bit of the Scottish heritage she'd been given by her dad's side of the family. And like the sewing box in Leona's window, it had appealed to her need for a little nostalgic familiarity.

Tori forced her focus back to the treat in her hands, embarrassment washing over her as she mentally reviewed the contents of her unpacked kitchen. "I just realized I haven't gotten to the dishes yet."

The woman plopped into the chair and shrugged. "Who needs plates. We both have hands, right? Besides, brownies were never made for plates."

Brownies?!?

"Come, sit. Let's get acquainted."

"Okay." Tori crossed the room and perched on the edge of the love seat she'd brought from her apartment in Chicago. Slowly, she peeled the cover from the top of the plate, careful not to get any stray crumbs on the cushions.

Brownies, indeed.

Tori's stomach grumbled. Georgina laughed.

"My stomach would be doing the exact same thing right about now if I had been able to fit the last brownie from the pan onto that plate." The woman's green eyes sparkled as she patted the slight bulge beneath her mint green summer shirt. "But I wasn't."

Tori laughed. Maybe Leona was both right *and* wrong. Right that people would grow to accept her—wrong on how long it would take. Helping herself to a brownie, she set the plate down on the small end table that separated the angled love seat and chair. "I probably wouldn't be so hungry if I hadn't pinned my way through dinner."

The woman looked a question at her.

"I'm sorry. I tend to think everyone is a sewer." Tori took a bite of brownie, savoring its rich, chocolaty taste. "I thrive on multitasking. Today it was unpacking, exploring, and working on a pillow for that chair." She pointed at the chair where Georgina was seated.

"You sew?"

Tori nodded as she took another bite, fighting the urge to let her eyes roll back in her head. She hadn't realized just how hungry she was.

"Can I see what you're working on?" Georgina's head popped upward like a periscope as she canvassed their surroundings.

"I haven't gotten far. I stayed up last night cutting the

bias strips and pinning them together. I managed to stitch the cording to the strips before my eyes started crossing from lack of sleep." Tori stood and walked into the alcove that would soon be her first-ever sewing room. Lifting the dark green satin pillow into her arms, she returned to her spot on the love seat and held her work out to her guest. "I wanted to soften the chair somewhat and felt an accessory pillow would do the trick."

Georgina took the pillow from Tori's hands and turned it over in her own. "Oh Victoria, your work is beautiful. How long have you been sewing?"

"Since I was six. My great-grandmother taught me."

With her bottom lip jutted outward, the woman nodded, her attention still focused on the pillow. "I like the twist you're adding to the corded trim—that's going to take some time to get just right."

Tori shrugged softly. "I know, but it'll be worth it." She leaned over and touched her hand to the top half of the pillow. "When I'm done with the blue trim, I'm going to add a matching ribbon in a *V* pattern right here . . . with a red tassel that hangs down from the point of the *V*."

She was just about to retrieve the embroidered ribbon she'd found for the middle of the tassel when she realized Georgina was studying her intently. Suddenly uncomfortable, Tori opted to remain on the love seat instead.

"I'm sorry. I guess I got off on a tangent just then. I've always been a little bit of a sewing nut."

"Then you're a nut among many here in Sweet Briar. In fact, if you'd be interested, perhaps you'd like to come to our sewing circle tomorrow night?" The woman looked down at the pillow in her lap once again, her hands running slowly across the satiny fabric. "It's a rather exclusive group—all members must be descendants of the original founders of the Sweet Briar Ladies Society or unanimously voted in by the group."

"Well, then I couldn't possib—"

"In order to get voted *in*, they must first have a chance to meet you." Georgina handed Tori's work back, then placed her hands on the thighs of her off-white cotton slacks. "And you'll attend as my guest."

"I'm not sure I—"

"Nonsense. You'll come. It's the least I can do for our town's new librarian." She pointed at the plate of brownies. "Those were part of my *unofficial* visit. The invite to the sewing circle can be part of my *official* visit if that would make you more comfortable."

"Official visit?" Tori asked in confusion.

"Yes. In addition to being part of my very own unofficial little welcoming committee, I'm also the mayor of Sweet Briar."

Ohhhh.

"I don't really look the part right now, do I?" Georgina looked down at her shirt and brushed at a piece of the brownie she'd conceded to eating. "But after raising four children and losing my first husband to cancer, I had much too much time on my hands. Sewing and visiting with friends can only fill so much of my day. So I ran for mayor."

"Wow. That's quite an undertaking." Tori shifted in her seat in order to avoid the temptation of a second treat.

"It really wasn't that much of a stretch for me. In fact, leading this town is more or less in my blood. My father and his father before him—and his before him—had been mayor of Sweet Briar at one time, too." Georgina looked around the room again, her eyes roaming across the pictures Tori had propped against walls in preparation for their eventual hanging. "Of course I didn't expect to marry again, but love can find you in the strangest of places."

Let's hope not.

"I met Thomas a year ago and we were married six months later. He's charming and funny and wonderful.

But he travels so much with his business that I need my work with the town to keep me from getting too lonely." Tori watched as Georgina's gaze fell on the clock along the eastern wall, her mouth slacking open momentarily only to recover in quick and apologetic fashion. "Oh I had no idea it had gotten so late. I hadn't intended to take up so much of your evening."

"No, please. I've enjoyed it." And Tori meant it. So far the women of Sweet Briar were nothing short of wonderful.

"Aren't you sweet for saying so." Georgina rose to her feet, plucking her hat from the coatrack along the wall where the entryway met the living room. "Tomorrow night's meeting is at Debbie Calhoun's home. Fifteen Tulip Lane. Debbie has a few extra sewing machines for those who need them, but if you have a portable one that's best. Less time wasted waiting for a machine. Oh, and everyone brings a treat to share—something homemade, never store-bought. And we start at seven—*sharp*."

Tori smiled. She'd always wanted to be part of a sewing circle, but had set the idea aside in favor of spending every spare moment with Jeff. Attending tomorrow night's meeting would be one more way she'd be reclaiming her own dreams and making Sweet Briar her new home.

"I'll be there."

"Perfect." Georgina Hayes pulled the door open and stepped onto the porch, turning to look at Tori one last time as she pointed upward and to the left. "Now don't forget, *Victoria*—we like our homes to be lit at night. It reinforces our desire for Sweet Briar to be seen as a *safe* place to live."

Chapter 3

Tori didn't need the numbered mailbox to tell her which was the correct house. The women walking up the porch steps with sewing boxes and covered plates told her all she needed to know.

Debbie Calhoun's home was a true southern beauty, with a pale yellow two-story exterior, wraparound front porch with white wicker rocking chairs and hanging flower baskets, and large mossy trees that shaded the expansive yard on either side. In fact, it was the kind of home Tori herself dreamed of living in one day.

Carefully, she removed the pitcher of homemade lemonade she'd wedged into the floor of the backseat and shut the door, her sewing box and pillow tucked securely into the large bag on her left shoulder. A quick check of her reflection in the driver's side window removed any lingering worry about the effects of her exhausting day in the library's catchall room and the unexpected flat tire that had capped it all off.

From the moment she'd seen the makeshift storage

area that morning, Tori had known it would be the perfect children's area—equipped with comfy reading corners and a small homemade stage for acting out favorite stories. She just needed to convince the board that her vision not only had merit but solid reasoning behind it as well.

A task that would be a lot easier if she could simply *show* them. And show them she would.

But not tonight. Tonight was about making new friends, learning more about Sweet Briar, and surrounding herself with people who enjoyed sewing as much as she did.

By the time she crossed the street and headed up the Calhouns' sidewalk, the women had moved inside, their laughter escaping through the screen door and bringing a smile to Tori's lips. Her great-grandmother had always said the best medicine for any ailment a woman had was time with true friends. Time spent in good-natured gossip, occasional male-bashing, and shared tears. But most of all, she said time with other women was for laughing from deep within your soul. Something Tori hadn't done in a very long time.

When she reached the top step, Tori rapped softly on the trim of the screen door, hoping that someone would hear her despite the boisterous laughter and pockets of conversation that threatened to drown out everything in its midst.

"Come in!"

Quietly, she pulled the screen door open and stepped inside, her presence causing eight sets of eyes to turn in her direction and eight active mouths to cease any and all movement.

She gulped.

"I—uh." Tori shifted the pitcher of lemonade to her other arm as she worked to find real words—intelligent words. "I-I'm Tori. Tori Sinclair. Georgina Hayes invited me?" She knew her voice sounded uncertain and weak, but feeling as if one was in a fishbowl made it tough to portray anything else.

"Oh, yes. Georgina told me you were fixin' to come tonight." A woman in her mid- to late thirties, with dirty-blonde hair pulled into a ponytail, left the group of women huddled in the entryway to the living room and approached Tori, a smile brightening her face as she neared. "I'm Debbie Calhoun. Welcome."

Calhoun. Calhoun.

"Oh—your home, it's absolutely beautiful. Like something you might see on the cover of *Southern Living* magazine." Tori held the pitcher outward. "I brought some homemade lemonade. I hope you like it."

"Lemonade? Hmmmm. Well—isn't that sweet of you. I can't recall the last time—or anytime, I reckon—someone's brought lemonade. How very quaint. I'll set it on the dining room table alongside the desserts and I'm sure it will be delicious." Debbie took the pitcher from Tori's hands and gestured toward the rest of the crowd still standing in the same spot, their collective gaze fixed on the newcomer. "We're just waiting on Georgina and Dixie—they should be along directly."

"Dixie isn't coming," said a woman with perfectly coiffed white hair and a small, turned-up nose.

"How come, Rose?" Debbie asked.

Several of the women exchanged looks before the one Debbie had referred to as Rose finally answered. "She said she wanted to attend Cynthia's dance recital in Walbash but I think that was just"—she swung her attention squarely onto Tori—"*an excuse*, bless her heart."

Uh-oh.

"Excuse? Whatever for?"

Georgina's arrival prevented the woman from answering Debbie's question but it didn't take much to figure it out anyway. A dance recital hadn't kept Dixie Dunn from attending the weekly sewing circle.

Tori had.

The momentary lull in conversation caused by Tori's arrival ended the moment Sweet Briar's mayor swept into the room, an embroidery-topped sewing box in one hand, a cake box in the other. "I'm here. I'm here. I'm sorry I'm late, but Thomas actually made it home in time for supper this evening and I wanted to make sure he had his favorites." The woman who'd sat in Tori's tiny living room just the night before seemed larger than life as she set her box on a table and removed her straw hat. "Oh, Victoria, I'm so tickled you came. Did you have any trouble finding the place?"

"Not at all. But please, call me Tor—"

"I didn't think you would." Georgina retrieved her box from the table and gestured for Tori to follow her into the dining room. "And if you had, all you'd have to say is 'the Calhoun home.' Everyone knows where it is. Having a celebrity under one's roof tends to do that."

"Celebrity?" Tori questioned as she took in the top of the dining room table, the white lace cloth covered with apple pies, peach and cherry cobblers, cutout cookies, assorted cakes, and powdered sugar–topped brownies.

Debbie nodded as she added Tori's pitcher to the lineup, positioning it beside a silver ice bucket on the right side of the table. "Colby—that's my husband—is an author."

Tori's ears perked.

"An author? How exciting! What did he write?"

Rose, who'd entered the room behind them, snorted in disgust. "You're a *librarian* and you've never heard of Colby Calhoun?"

"Now, Rose. Colby is well known *here* . . . but Victoria isn't from here. And he hasn't written anything since before Jackson was born." Debbie straightened a stack of napkins then led the way down a hallway and onto a screened-in porch where the rest of the women had retreated to after Georgina's arrival. "Watch your step, Victoria. The power cords for the machines can be quite the tripping hazard as many of us know, right ladies?"

Heads nodded around the room as Tori stopped beside Debbie, the hostess's eyebrows suddenly furrowing. "Now, what was I saying? Oh . . . yes . . . Jackson is our youngest son. Colby wrote for years before and after our wedding, but he's resting his brilliance and watching the children these days so I can pursue my pet project."

"Don't listen to her, Victoria. Debbie's pet project is a smashing success." Leona patted the empty cushion beside her and smiled. "I'm so glad to see you here. I had no idea."

All eyes, including Georgina's, left Tori's face to scour Leona's.

"You know this one?" Rose asked as she lowered her frail body into a high-backed chair in the far corner, a gooseneck lamp bathing the spot in light.

"I most certainly do. Victoria and I had a wonderful time getting acquainted in the shop yesterday, didn't we, Victoria?"

"*Tori*. And yes, we did." Tori sat on the love seat beside her friend and pulled her pillow and sewing box from her bag.

"Oh, Victoria . . . that's lovely." Debbie crossed the screened porch to Tori's side and leaned in for a closer look. "The twist to your cord is perfect."

"Thank you." Her face warmed with the compliment. "I have a long way to go, though."

"It's just lovely," Debbie repeated. "Do you need a sewing machine tonight?"

Tori shook her head softly. "Not tonight. I'm trying to do as much by hand as possible. For this project anyway."

"How long have you been sewing?" Rose asked.

Tori considered her answer. Somehow she'd gotten off on the wrong foot with this elderly woman—an obvious friend and supporter of Dixie Dunn. And while she suspected loyalty ran deep among a group of sewing buddies, she also knew she needed to present the facts as she knew them. The first one being, she wasn't evil.

But it was Georgina who answered the woman. "Victoria has been sewing since she was a child. She learned under her great-grandmother's tutelage." Georgina claimed a rocking chair near the center of the porch. "Isn't that right, Victoria?"

"Yes. But please, just call me Tori."

A question regarding thread companies from a young girl perched at a picnic table took the spotlight off Tori momentarily and she exhaled deeply.

"How's it going?" Leona whispered in her ear.

"I wasn't sure there for a moment, but I'll be okay."

"I hear Georgina stopped by your place last night and invited you to our circle?" Leona picked a piece of lint off Tori's arm.

"She did. She even brought me a plate of brownies."

Leona carefully placed the offending speck on a cloth napkin and folded it just so. "Did you send her a thank-you note yet?"

"Not—not yet."

"Lesson number one, dear—it's never too soon to write a thank-you note in the south. *Never*."

"Okay, I'll—"

"Lesson number two—your name is *Victoria*. You're trying to blend in, remember?"

"But Tori is my na—" The disapproving look on Leona's face cut her protest short.

Al-righty then.

"Did you bring a treat to share?"

Finally she'd scored a hit.

Tori nodded. "I brought some homemade lemonade."

"*Lemonade*, dear?" Leona *tsked* softly under her breath. "Lesson number three—and this is an important one— southerners drink *tea*. Sweet tea."

"No lemonade?"

Leona scrunched her nose slightly and shook her head. *Huh.*

"And a drink—regardless of whether you grew the lemon tree yourself—isn't homemade enough. You need to *bake* something, dear. Preferably from an old family recipe that's been handed down."

"I have some of those, I thin—"

Leona reached out and patted her hand. "Recipes from Tampa don't count. Not in Sweet Briar, anyway."

She couldn't be serious.

Or could she?

But even if she was, at least Tori had sewing in common with—

She turned an accusatory eye on her new friend. "I thought you said you didn't sew."

"I don't."

"Then why are you here?"

Almost as if on cue, a woman bearing a striking resemblance to Leona breezed into the room, her arrival and its impact unmistakable.

Leona simply pointed at the woman and mumbled, "Same reason I'm living in Sweet Briar." Then, in a louder voice for everyone to hear, "Margaret Louise, I want you to meet the new librarian, *Victoria* Sinclair."

"Victoria Sinclair—now there's a mouthful. Ever think about goin' by Tori?" Leona's twin grabbed hold of Tori's hand and pumped it up and down, her smile as wide as two football fields. "Now imagine if you had a middle name inserted in there like I do—wow!"

"She likes to talk," Leona mumbled under her breath only to be drowned out by the sound of her sister's animated voice. "Has since we were children. Only she does it with a southern accent now."

"My son, Jake, said one of the guys from his garage changed your tire today . . . said you must have run across something mighty sharp to get a slash like that," Margaret Louise continued. "Did you run across any tongues on the way to work?" The woman burst into a momentary fit of laughter, stopping only to poke Debbie with a playful elbow. "Ha! Did you get it? *Sharp tongues*?"

It didn't take long to realize that twin sisters could be as different as night and day. Where Leona was quiet and easygoing, Margaret Louise was loud and boisterous. Where Leona's laugh was quiet and dainty, Margaret Louise's was hearty and room-filling. But as different as they were, Tori couldn't help but take a shine to this woman as well—the kind of person who could cause others to experience that soul-reaching laugh her great-grandmother had claimed was priceless.

As the night wore on, Tori realized she hadn't laughed so hard in a long time. Everyone there—including Rose—was a character in their own right. She soon learned that Debbie was the owner of Debbie's Bakery in the town square and that Margaret Louise baked many of the delectable desserts that were sold in the shop. She discovered that Beatrice Tharrington, the young girl who'd asked about different threads, was a nanny for a family in town, her soft British accent a nice change of pace in a room of southerners. She learned a few fascinating facts about the civil war era coin collection Georgina and her husband were painstakingly piecing together. And finally, she learned that Rose Winters was a retired kindergarten teacher from Sweet Briar Elementary who'd had Debbie in her class decades earlier. And while it was obvious on more than one occasion that the woman was close to Dixie Dunn, Tori also didn't miss the softening in Rose's demeanor as they sewed away the time.

Conversation was lively as each member—except Leona—worked on their latest sewing project. Rose was making a skirt for her daughter, Margaret Louise a blanket for her next grandbaby due in February, and Beatrice was stitching a vest for her mother in England. Debbie was making an embroidered sign for her shop, and Georgina was hemming a pair of Thomas's slacks.

"Did you hear Tiffany Ann is comin' back?" Margaret Louise asked, only to be sidetracked by a needle poke. "Good heavens, you'd think by now I'd know to bring a thimble."

"I didn't know that. But it makes sense. I saw her father in the market last week and he said they were fixin' to drive a fair piece to her graduation this past weekend." Rose stopped working on the scalloped border at the base of the skirt and looked up. "I wonder if that means she'll be helping with the floats for the Fourth of July parade."

Leona set her antiques catalogue on her lap. "Tiffany Ann Gilbert's hair is the color of spun gold, Victoria, like something out of a fairy tale you'd find in your library. Her face is flawless, her lips perfectly plump and pouty. And—"

"And she could make a *preacher* curse," Margaret Louise interjected.

"A preacher curse?" Tori whispered to Leona.

"It means she's pigheaded, dear. She believes in doing everything her way. While she's polite, it's apparent she believes she can do things better." Leona waited for the pockets of conversation to die out before continuing her description in a voice just loud enough for everyone to hear. "Tiffany Ann also happens to be the Sweetheart of Sweet Briar. And I mean that quite literally—as in pageant, literally."

Tori looked up from her cord twisting. "So she rode on the floats each year?"

Margaret Louise laughed. "She did that, too . . . but she also *designed* them. All of them. She not only had a flair for makin' herself shine, but she had a flair for makin' everything around her shine, too."

"She got a hankering to be an interior designer and

went a country mile to some fancy college. And let me tell you, that girl is going to make a pretty penny. You just wait and see." Debbie set her embroidery hoop on the side table beside her chair and rubbed her eyes.

"I could use her in the children's room," Tori said as she bent over her work once again.

"Children's room?" Leona asked.

Tori shrugged at her sheepishly. "I know it might be a bit ambitious right off the bat but I think we need it."

Leona's eyebrow cocked in her direction, the woman's voice dropping so as to be heard by Tori and Tori only. "I thought you were going to take it slow."

"I was—I mean, I am," she whispered back. "I just think this one idea will be good for the kids."

"There's no space for a children's room at the library," Rose interjected from across the room. "Though it would be wonderful."

Tori widened her eyes at Leona then turned her focus onto Rose. "I agree. And I think I can pull it off by using the old storage room in the back of the library. I spent most of the day in there, and it's wasted space."

"What would you do with it?" Rose asked.

"I'd love to paint scenes from famous stories on the walls, scatter beanbag chairs around the room, and—" She stopped, afraid she'd said too much.

"Go on," Rose prodded.

Setting her pillow to the side, Tori looked around the room at each member of the sewing circle. "I'd like to construct a small stage and add a chest of dress-up clothes so the children could act out their favorite stories."

Silence fell over the room as looks were exchanged and throats were cleared. And just when Tori thought someone was going to respond, that particular person's mouth would close.

It was Margaret Louise who finally broke the silence, her breathless voice peppered with excited laughs. "Lulu would love that. She loves the *idea* of books, loves to listen to stories and imagine being in them. But it's the *reading* she finds so difficult. Maybe something like that would be the trick."

Leona supplied the identity to go with the name. "Lulu is Margaret Louise's granddaughter. Shy little thing."

"I think your idea is marvelous," Debbie said, her smile one of encouragement and admiration. "Maybe you really should ask Tiffany Ann for help."

Tori shrugged a smile. "Maybe. But this room is so vivid in my mind, so rooted in my heart . . . I think I want to design it on my own." She set down her pillow and looked around, her voice breathless. "Can't you just imagine reading away the hours in a room with a medieval castle or tall prairie grasses painted on the walls?"

Slowly, one by one, each member of the sewing circle conceded it was a good idea. Even Rose.

"These costumes—do you have them already?"

Tori shook her head. "No. But I can make them. It might take a few months until I have enough to partially fill a chest, but it'll take a while to get the room up and running if I can get it all emptied out."

"We could sew them," Georgina bellowed. "We've been known to take on a group project or two over the years."

"Like those Christmas stockings we made in '93," offered Margaret Louise. "Do you remember all the hollerin' we did over the trim work on those? I thought Rose and Dixie were goin' to come to blows a few times."

"And the curtains for town hall." Debbie waved her hand in Georgina's direction. "When she took office, she was all tore up about the curtains they had on the office windows. And I mean *all tore up*."

Margaret Louise snorted. "We got so sick of all her fussin' we made some new ones."

Georgina made a face. "I wasn't that bad."

"Yes you were," the members said in unison, bringing a flush to the mayor's face and a new round of laughter to the room.

"What I think they're saying is they'd like to help with the costumes," Leona said, beaming.

"I don't know what to say," Tori stammered.

"*Okay* will suffice," Rose said. "We'll just need you to come up with a list of character costumes between now and next Monday, is all."

"Next Monday?"

Georgina grinned. "Next Monday. We meet every Monday, Victoria."

"But I thought I had to be voted in." Tori looked from the mayor to each of the other members, her gaze coming to rest on Leona.

"We'll get to that." Rose slowly rolled the skirt into a ball and stuffed it into a satchel beside her chair. "We've got to make sure *everyone* is on board first before we vote and we're shy two members tonight."

"I'm not sure when Melissa will be back. She's still down in Pine Grove carin' for her mama." Margaret Louise folded her blanket and tucked it under her arm. "Jake and I are looking after the six until she gets back. But I'm sure as anythin' she'd be tickled to have Victoria in the group . . . someone closer to her own age."

"I'm only thirty-six, Margaret Louise," Debbie protested. "What's Melissa? Thirty? Thirty-one?"

"And I'm only twenty-eight," Beatrice offered shyly.

"True enough. But the rest of us are old."

"Speak for yourself, twin. I'm not old," Leona said, her finger pointing authoritatively at her sister. "I was born after you."

"By ten seconds," Margaret Louise retorted.

"There's still one more vote we need," Rose interjected through the chorus of halfhearted protests and laughter.

"One more?" Tori asked.

The looks the women exchanged in response told her all she needed to know about the one potential holdout.

Dixie Dunn.

So much for a unanimous vote.

Seeming to sense the flash of doubt that rippled through the room, Leona reached over and squeezed Tori's hand, her voice audible to no one but her. "Give Dixie time, dear. There's always a few bumps in the road on the way to anything worthwhile—Dixie just happens to be *your* bump."

Chapter 4

Exhausted, Tori exhaled a strand of hair from in front of her eyes and leaned against the fifth box of dilapidated books she'd opened so far that morning. Never, in all her years as an assistant librarian in Chicago, had she seen so many worthless books. Sure, people tended to donate the bound copies they didn't care about, but to drop off books with ketchup stains and missing pages?

"Miss Sinclair?"

"Tori. *Please*." She pushed off the box and wound her way past six more like it to reach her assistant, Nina Morgan, a petite woman with dark skin, even darker eyes, and a shy smile. "How's it going out there?"

Since Monday, Tori had spent the bulk of each day culling through the library's storage room, determined to have it cleared by the time the board met for its monthly meeting next Wednesday night. That gave her the rest of today and the first three days of next week.

A feat of mammoth proportions.

"It's been fine, Miss Sinclair, until two minutes ago."

"What happened two minutes ago?" She wondered if Nina could hear her panting, certain the woman noticed the tiny beads of sweat she felt on her forehead.

"Mr. Wentworth and his class are here. For their lesson on pioneers."

"Mr. Who?" Tori swiped at her forehead with the back of her hand then took a sip from the water bottle she'd propped by the door when she started.

"Mr. Wentworth. He's the third grade teacher at the elementary school."

Her assistant's words finally broke through the mind-numbing exhaustion of the past few hours. "And he's *here*? With his class?"

"Yes, Miss Sinclair. All sixteen of them."

Sixteen?

"He said he made an appointment to bring them every Friday for the next month. It's part of their library unit."

"An appointment?"

"Yes, Miss Sinclair. Only I didn't know because—"

"The appointment book disappeared," Tori finished as she lowered her face into her hands in lieu of the panic that threatened to take hold and render her incapable of intelligent thought. "What did you say they're studying?"

"Pioneers. Like Laura Ingalls time frame."

Laura Ingalls. She could *do* Laura Ingalls.

She pulled her head up, dropped her hands to her side. "Where are they now?"

"In the reading circle, waiting. For you."

Tori resisted the urge to laugh at the mention of the ten by ten piece of carpet near the back of the library that had been dubbed "the reading circle" by her predecessor. Instead, she mentally ran through the supplies she'd hauled in from her car earlier in the week.

"Okay, Nina, here's what we're going to do." Reaching into her purse, Tori extracted a twenty-dollar bill and handed it to her assistant. "I need you to go next door to the market and pick up as much whipping cream as you can buy for twenty dollars."

"Whipping cream, Miss Sinclair?"

"Yes, Nina. I'm going to grab some of those empty baby food jars I put in the office the other day for future craft time." Tori ran a moist hand down the front of her dusty rose blouse. "Laura made butter, so *we're* going to make butter."

The hint of a sparkle flashed behind Nina's eyes as she closed her hand over the crisp bill and backed her way out of the storage room doorway. "You are brilliant, Miss Sinclair."

"Let's get through the afternoon before you say I'm brilliant." Tori touched Nina's forearm and gave it a gentle squeeze. "Now get go—wait. Not yet." Digging into her purse once again, Tori pulled out a five and held it out to the woman. "And some loaves of bread."

"For the butter?"

"For the butter."

As her assistant disappeared out the back door, Tori felt her stomach begin to churn. Shaking jars of whipping cream would kill time—but not all of it.

Oh how she wished the children's room was ready. Then the children could act out pioneer life—

"That's it," she mumbled as she strode into her office long enough to retrieve the box of empty baby food jars from the closet behind her desk. They could make butter, talk about the differences between now and then, and then she could ask them for their thoughts on her room. Thoughts and ideas she could present to the board . . .

Pleased with her resilience, Tori headed into the main section of the library. "Hello, children. I'm Miss Sinclair."

"Hel-lo Miss Sinclair," the children dutifully repeated in unison.

She set the box of glass jars on the floor beside her feet and leaned down, her hands gently gripping her thighs.

"I'm sorry I wasn't here to greet you when you walked in, but I was in the back getting a special surprise ready for you."

Her eyes traveled across each and every little face before coming to rest on the one belonging to their handsome and obviously amused teacher. But before she could give too much thought to the man, Nina ran in, out of breath, the whipping cream and bread hidden inside a brown paper sack.

"Here you go, Miss Sinclair. We got lucky, they had four whole containers of whipping cream."

"In the back getting ready, huh?"

Uh-oh.

With an apologetic shrug in their teacher's direction, Tori clapped her hands together and smiled at the students. "You've been reading about Laura Ingalls, is that right?"

Heads nodded.

"Does anyone remember where Laura's food came from?"

A little girl with strawberry blonde hair raised her hand tentatively into the air.

"Yes, sweetheart?"

"Her Pa grew the corn and the wheat. The chickens gave the eggs and the cows made the milk."

"Excellent." Tori looked around the room, pointed to another little girl who seemed as if she wanted to add something yet hadn't raised her hand. "Can you think of anything else?"

The little girl shook her head fiercely, despite the knowledge that shone in her eyes.

"Go ahead, Lulu, it's okay." The child's teacher walked around the back of the circle and lowered himself to the carpet directly beside the girl.

"They made their own butter, too," the girl whispered.

Tori clapped her hands once again. "Very, very good,

Lulu. That's exactly what they did. Does anyone remember *how* they did it?"

The children looked at one another, their faces blank.

Once again, Lulu's eyes shone.

"Lulu? Do you remember?" Tori prompted gently.

The child whispered once again. "A churn."

"You're exactly right, Lulu. Thank you." Tori smiled at the shy little girl before addressing the class as a whole once again. "It took a long time to make butter when Laura was alive. A very long time."

"My mom just goes to the market and buys it in a box," offered a freckle-faced redhead in the front.

"I bet most people do," Tori replied. "But today, we're going to make some butter just like Laura did."

"Whoa, cool," several voices said in unison as other students looked at one another with broad smiles on their faces.

"Only instead of taking turns with one churn, you're each going to get to make your very own lump of butter in one of these jars." Tori lifted one of the containers into the air and twisted the lid open. "I'm going to give each of you a jar and then Miss Morgan is going to come around and put some whipping cream into each jar."

"What do we do then?" asked the little boy in the front.

"We shake it."

Tori grinned. "That's right, Lulu, we shake it . . . and shake it . . . and shake it." She handed a jar to each child, stopping to open each and every lid. "And when you think you're all done shaking, you shake some more."

Once the students were ready to shake, Tori moved off to the side to watch them in action. Excitement turned to momentary boredom only to be replaced by excitement once again as the whipping cream began to solidify.

"Nice save, Miss Sinclair."

Tori's mouth went dry.

"I'm Milo Wentworth."

She felt his warm hand close over hers. "I'm Tori—I mean, Victoria."

"*Tori*, huh? That's pretty."

She stared at the handsome teacher, resisted the urge to ask if he was feeling ill.

"I'm sorry we barged in on you today, Tori."

"You didn't."

He leaned his mouth closer to her ear. "Nina's not good at feigning surprise."

She knew her face had to be bright red. "I'm sorry. The appointment book got misplaced somehow. It won't happen again."

He straightened up as a student approached. "Mr. Wentworth, look at my cream. It's not so runny anymore."

"I see that, Bobby. Keep shaking." As the child returned to his gaggle of friends, the man trained his focus back on Tori. "Please. No apologies. Starting a new job is always overwhelming. A lost appointment book only makes it worse. But you were amazing just now."

Amazing.

"I'll be ready for you next Friday, I promise."

He laughed, a wonderful sound that resonated from deep inside his chest. "I can't wait to see what you call ready."

"What will you be studying next week?" she asked, her face as warm as ever as her eyes studied him for the very first time. Milo Wentworth was tall—the top of his head a full eight inches or so above her own five foot five. His hair, a burnished brown, was cut short on the sides but left longish, and somewhat unruly, at the top—

"I'd like to tie that into an article we'll be reading in Kids Quest about ancient architecture."

His brown eyes were softened by flecks of amber—

"The problem is bringing it down to their level so as not to put them to sleep."

He was talking. And she was missing the bulk of what he was saying.

Focus, Tori. Ancient architecture. Ancient architecture . . .

"Egyptian pyramids?"

"How'd you guess?" He ran a hand through his hair as dimples began to form beside his mouth. "You gonna have them build their own?"

"Maybe." Realizing she was coming dangerously close to flirting, Tori decided to engage the dark-haired girl who was staring into her jar with big brown eyes. "You did it, Lulu. You made butter just like Laura did."

The smile she got in response warmed her all over.

"Now go on over to Miss Morgan and you can try it out on a piece of bread."

She watched as the little girl fairly skipped her way over to the bread line, her delight in her butter-making ability as tangible as the baby blue dress she wore. "She's precious."

"Lulu? Yeah, she's a great kid. She loves books. Loves stories. But you saw—speaking in front of people is difficult for her. And unfortunately, reading aloud is even harder for her." Milo raised his hands up in frustration. "I've tried everything I can think of to help her, but nothing works."

"She talked when you sat next to her," Tori said as her gaze traveled, once again, to the little girl who exuded a joy that was nothing short of contagious.

"But with fifteen other students I can't sit next to her all the time."

Without realizing what she was doing Tori placed a hand on Milo's forearm. "Let me think on it this week. See if I can come up with any ideas to help her."

"I'd appreciate that, Tori." The slight rasp to the man's voice startled her and she let her hand drop to her side.

What was she thinking? Was she that desperate to hear her name said correctly?

"I—uh—it looks like everyone's finished, so I'd like to ask them a few questions before you leave. I'm working on a little project I think they can help with." Tori strode across the room to the spot where the children were eating. "So how'd your butter taste?"

"Awesome!"

"Yummy!"

"Weird."

You win some, you lose some.

"Now, before you leave, I need a little help from all of you. Can you do that?"

"Yes," they said in unison.

She pulled a piece of paper and a pencil off the top of a nearby table and sat down. "If you could pretend to be a character from a storybook, who would you want to be?"

"Davy Crockett," said the redhead.

"Robin Hood," said another little boy.

"Cam Jansen," offered a stocky girl with curly brown hair.

"Ooooh, Cam Jansen—a modern day Nancy Drew. She's fun, isn't she?" Tori asked. "How about some more ideas?"

She jotted down each and every name the children shared until they ran out of ideas. "Thank you so much for all your help."

"Why did you need that stuff?" the redhead asked.

"Because I'm going to make a dress-up trunk so children who come to the library can pretend to be some of their favorite storybook characters."

"Cool!"

Tori smiled. "I'm glad you think so. Now I think it's time for Mr. Wentworth to get you back to school for lunch. So go home, tell your parents what you made today and why . . . and then I'll see you here again next Friday."

In a flash, sixteen eight-year-olds were on their feet and falling into line.

"What do we say to Miss Sinclair, boys and girls?" Milo asked.

"Thank you, Miss Sinclair!"

"You're very welcome." She watched as the class began filing out the door then looked down as she felt a tug on her leg.

Lulu.

"Laura Ingalls."

Tori squatted down to eye level with the little girl. "What about Laura, sweetheart?"

"I want to dress up like *her*."

Ahhhh.

Softly, she tapped the child on the center of the nose. "I'll make you a deal. I'll put her on the very top of my costume-making list if you'll read with me for a few minutes next week."

The little girl's body began to sway back and forth ever so gently.

"Just you and me. No one else." Tori nudged Lulu's chin upward until their eyes met. "Can you try? For me?"

The child's nod was barely discernable, but it was there.

"Good."

Tori straightened up as the child spun in a circle and fell in place at the back of the line, her black hair bobbing as she followed her classmates past their teacher and out the door.

For a long moment Milo Wentworth simply stood holding the door open, his eyes locked on Tori's as his students waited patiently on the sidewalk. Finally he waved, his mouth forming a single word as he turned away.

A single word that looked a lot like *amazing*.

Chapter 5

If it was possible, Georgina Hayes's home was even bigger than Debbie Calhoun's. But what Debbie's may have lacked in size, it more than made up for in warmth and coziness.

Tori stepped onto the freshly waxed wooden entryway flooring and waited as the housekeeper closed the door. "Miss Georgina is in the study with a few of the other women."

Hoisting her bag higher onto her shoulder, she turned and smiled at the unassuming woman with the trademark bun and aproned dress who'd rescued the plate of chocolate chip cookies from Tori's hand the second she'd entered the home. "Where would I find the study?"

The woman's face reddened. "Oh I'm sorry. I just assumed you knew. I'll—"

"It's okay. Really. Just point me in the right direction and I'll get myself settled while you greet the next guest."

"Victoria! I thought that was you." Leona came around

a paneled corner, her face beaming as she waved off the housekeeper. "How are things going?"

"Great." Tori bestowed a quick hug on the antiques shopkeeper then patted the pocket of her pants. "I brought a list of the character costumes like Rose requested."

Leona's soft brown eyes clouded momentarily, her voice dropping a few decibels. "You might want to hold off on that. See how the aura is first."

"Why? What's wrong?"

"She came this time."

"Who?"

Leona's pointed look was all the answer she needed.

Dixie Dunn.

She felt her shoulders slump, her stomach churn.

"Now don't you worry, dear. You'll win her over just as you've won everyone else over. You just need to take it—"

"A little slow, I know." Tori opened her bag and peered inside. "At least I still have some work to do on the tassel."

"Good." Leona's arm slipped inside Tori's and gently tugged. "Now let's be social, shall we?"

As they walked together down a long, chandelier-lit hallway, Tori couldn't help but feel the excitement mounting inside. Sure, she was apprehensive about her first meeting with the infamous and deeply wounded Dixie Dunn, but even more than that she was simply glad to be with the group of close-knit women who had made her feel so welcome the week before.

The days since their last sewing circle had been filled with odd and frustrating mishaps from which she'd emerged—so far—fairly unscathed. But still, how many more flat tires was she expected to endure? And how many times could the boxes of old books she worked all day to remove seem to multiply tenfold overnight?

"Why don't you two just slow down a country minute and let a slightly plump twin sister catch up."

Leona extricated her arm from Tori's as they turned. "Margaret Louise, we didn't hear you."

"Ha! I haven't heard that many times in my life." The woman planted a kiss on her sister's cheek then pushed a covered plate at Tori. "This is for you. For what you've done."

Tori looked a question at Leona before meeting Margaret Louise's eyes. "What did I do?"

"Come with me—I want everyone to hear." Margaret Louise wrapped a chubby hand around Tori's upper arm and fairly dragged her the rest of the way to the study. They'd barely stepped a toe into the room where the sewing circle was being held when Leona's twin bellowed their arrival. "Hello everyone, we're here."

Greetings ensued, followed by the claiming of chairs and appropriate lighting. Once they were all settled, Margaret Louise got straight to the reason for her hallway gratitude.

"Do you know what Victoria's done in the span of just a few days?"

All eyes turned on the new librarian. Including those belonging to an unfamiliar woman in her seventies.

Dixie Dunn.

Tori swallowed and shifted uncomfortably in the leather armchair she'd selected. "Margaret Louise, I—"

"On Saturday, I had Jake's kids. He went down to Pine Grove to visit Melissa so I hosted Baking with Nana Day."

"She's Nana," Leona said from her own leather-bound chair.

"So there we were, rolling out our cookie dough, when I realized one of them was missin'."

Tori looked a question at Leona.

"One of the grandkids. Jake's given her six."

Tori nodded and caught back up with the one-way conversation pouring from Margaret Louise's mouth.

"I leave the lot of them playin' with flour and go off in search of that knee-baby of mine."

Knee-baby?

As if she'd read her mind, Leona leaned to the side and whispered in Tori's ear, "That means the second youngest child in a southern household. Which will have to change when Melissa has number seven."

Good grief, she was going to need a dictionary of southern expressions before the next meeting.

"So off I go. In search of Lulu," Margaret Louise continued.

Lulu?

Tori's mouth dropped open.

"Do you know what she was doing when I found her?" Margaret Louise looked around the room for an answer to a question she didn't intend anyone to answer. "She was reading. Out loud. To her stuffed animals."

Leona's hands clapped in the air, a smile spreading across her face like wildfire. "Oh, Margaret Louise, how wonderful!"

"What does Victoria have to do with that?" Rose asked from her perch next to Dixie.

"I'll tell you." Margaret Louise took a rapid inhale/exhale and then began a tale which included Lulu's trip to the library on Friday. As she relayed everything she'd learned from her pint-sized granddaughter and the child's teacher, Tori felt her face grow warm with pride.

"How wonderful, Victoria." Georgina nodded her head softly, a genuine smile playing across her lips. "That's exactly the kind of community outreach the board is looking for—outstanding."

A snort from the far side of the room brought an end to the jovial mood.

"The board also understands the importance of preparedness."

Tori stared at the woman. What was she saying?

"Dixie, now is not the time," Debbie said softly.

"Of course it's the time. If Margaret Louise is going to paint a picture of our new librarian, it's only fair she gives the *whole* one."

Too stunned to speak, Tori simply waited.

"She was unprepared for Lulu's class visit. *Unprepared . . .* as in caught completely off guard despite the fact Mr. Wentworth had a long-standing appointment."

All eyes turned on Tori once again, questioning.

"The appointment book Nina keeps at the front desk has gone missing." She looked down at her hands as the explanation slipped from her mouth, weak and pathetic. The plate Margaret Louise had handed her still sat in her lap, covered.

"Missing?" Dixie prodded. "How can an appointment book that has been all but nailed to that table for forty years go missing?"

How indeed.

Margaret Louise's strapping and good-natured voice took charge once again.

"Missin' or not, Victoria landed on her feet quite well from what I hear. Do you know those children made homemade butter just as Laura Ingalls did? Lulu was so excited about it, she insisted we make our own for the cookie recipe." Margaret Louise looked around the room before bringing her focus squarely onto the town's former librarian. "As we made it—and I must say all that shakin' may have helped shed a pound or two—Lulu talked about the differences between how we get food now and how they got it then."

"Oh, Victoria, my Jackson would have loved that. He's not even in kindergarten yet and all he talks about is getting to be in Mr. Wentworth's class because of all the neat trips they take." Debbie threaded her embroidery needle with a turquoise blue floss as her face flushed a pale pink. "Suzanna had him last year and he's such a doll."

A collective sigh emerged from the lips of nearly every woman in the room—not the least of which was from Tori herself.

"It's a shame he's not found another love." Rose cleared her throat and lifted a shaking glass of sweet tea to her lips. "I guess Celia was his one and only."

"Celia?" Tori asked, her curiosity piqued.

"His wife. She died of an aneurysm not six months after they married."

She gasped. "How horrible."

"That was almost ten years ago." Rose set her glass down and dabbed at her lips with a cloth napkin.

"I can't do sad tonight. I just can't." Debbie reached into her purse and extracted a wallet-sized photograph from inside. "I brought this to show y'all. It's Jackson's fourth-year birthday portrait . . . isn't it precious?"

As *oohs* and *ahhhs* circulated throughout the room along with Jackson's picture, Tori couldn't help but steal a few glances in Dixie Dunn's direction. Leona Elkin had warned of sour grapes on the part of the former librarian, but sour grapes didn't do it justice. Dixie Dunn was furious. She could hear it in the thinly disguised barbs that seemed to go unnoticed by everyone else. She could see it in the glares Dixie shot in Tori's direction throughout the night. She could feel it in the anger that seemed to emanate from the woman's body.

"Speaking of Milo Wentworth, did anyone see Tiffany Ann Gilbert over the weekend?" Rose asked as she peered up from the zipper she was hand sewing into her daughter's skirt. "I'm telling you that pampered education she's been getting has done that child no good."

Heads nodded.

"She arrived back in town the morning after our last circle and she's been coming into the bakery for a coffee every morning since then. Though, come to think of it,

she never made it in this morning. One minute I saw her
peeking in the front window, staring at my customers, and
the next she was gone—I guess maybe she had somewhere to go and was scared off by the midmorning line."
Debbie retrieved her son's picture from the last set of
hands and placed it lovingly back inside her purse. "Anyway, on Friday she was all dressed up in a cute—and very
formfitting—little suit. Said she had an important appointment in Ridge Cove."

"What kind of appointment could Tiffany Ann possibly
have had in Ridge Cove of all places?" Rose asked, her lip
curling upward.

"What's wrong with Ridge Cove?" Tori whispered to
Leona.

"It's as backwoods as they come, dear."

"Oh. Okay, thanks." She returned to the conversation,
ready to follow the volley once again.

"I don't know for sure. She just said if things went
well, she'd be one step closer to reaching her career
goals." Debbie set her purse back on the ground and settled into her chair. "So I didn't see anything wrong. If
anything, she seemed very happy. And hopeful."

Georgina shook her head. "I saw her just yesterday at
church. She was mighty jumpy and acting more than a
little bizarre. Thomas thinks"—she lowered her head and
peeked out at everyone through lowered lashes—"she
may be into . . . *drugs*."

A collective gasp emerged from the group as machines
shut off and needles stopped midstitch.

"That's just nonsense," Margaret Louise bellowed.

"Don't be so quick to discount it, Margaret Louise. I
knew a young man once who was into drugs. When he
was on them his behavior changed drastically." Leona
shook her head as she spoke. "So sad. I hope her family
gets her help sooner rather than later."

Tori looked around at the women. "What does this Tiffany Ann girl have to do with Mr. Wentworth? I thought one of you said she was dating some boy she'd met in high school."

"She was for a while. But Cooper Riley is in love with only two things. His cars and Tiffany Ann."

"I'm confused. Is that a bad thing?"

"For Tiffany Ann it is. She has aspirations. None of which mesh with those of a small-town mechanic." Rose knotted her thread with expert hands then looked up at Tori. "Problem is, it's been mighty near eighteen months since she broke it off with him. Yet to hear him talk, they're not only still together but heading for the altar. Blasted fool."

"Some say he's a little obsessed," Margaret Louise chimed in from her spot in the corner.

"Thomas just said the other night that he finds young Riley's infatuation for Tiffany Ann alarming. There he was, buttering his roll during our first supper together in ages, and out it came. I guess I just always found it to be rather sweet." Georgina sighed and looked around the room. "Now how did we get on the subject of Cooper?"

"We were talking about Milo, which segued into Tiffany Ann." Debbie plucked a spool of turquoise-colored thread from her sewing box and held it against the sign she was making. "Perfect. Just perfect. Anyway, as to your question, Victoria . . . Tiffany Ann has had a crush on Milo since she was—"

"Good evening, ladies."

All eyes turned in the direction of the doorway, and a tall, balding man with blue eyes looked back.

"Oh Thomas. I want you to meet Victoria, the new librarian." Georgina's smile lit her face as she gestured in Tori's direction. "She bought one of Douglas Harrison's cottages."

"I remember you telling me that." The mayor's husband crossed the room, his strong hand clasping Tori's tightly. "Welcome to Sweet Briar, Victoria. How do you like it here so far?"

She felt Dixie studying her as she contemplated her answer. "I love it. It's very different from Chicago, but in a good way." And it was true. She had her dream job and a chance to start over.

"I'm glad. Life is about seeing an opportunity and making the most out of it." Thomas turned to his wife and winked. "So, what are you ladies discussing? Or is it better I don't ask?"

"I was just telling everyone about Tiffany's behavior at church yesterday."

Thomas shook his head slowly, disappointment springing into his stance as he looked around at his wife's friends. "It's quite obvious that young woman has gotten into some undesirable things in college. I feel bad for her parents. First they deal with her stories, then her stubbornness, then her desire to attend a fancy and expensive school. It's a shame."

Tori turned to Leona, her voice too low for anyone but her friend to hear. "Stories?"

"In addition to being beautiful, talented, and more than a little stubborn, Tiffany Ann has been known to tell a few tall tales. Nothing too harmful, but lies nonetheless. Personally, I think she just craves attention." Leona looked up from her magazine and leaned her head closer to Tori's. "And although it's earned her a reputation for being untrustworthy with the adults in this town, her beauty and town pride have kept them from writing her off completely. Everyone just wants to see her succeed. For her parents' sake if nothing else."

"Oh." She sat up straight, focused her attention on the talk with Thomas once again.

"Thomas has been wonderful since Robert's been away . . . keeping his eye on things around town at night when he's not traveling himself," Georgina boasted.

"Robert?" she asked Leona from the side of her mouth.

"The police chief, dear. You really must learn these thin—"

"Anyway, ladies, it's been nice chatting with you but I'm going to head upstairs. I've been wanting to polish our coins for the past week and haven't had the time."

"You polish silver?" Debbie asked.

"He polishes his *coin collection*, Debbie. Trust me, he drops his boxers on the ground just like every other man."

Thomas laughed. "Okay. I'm out of here. I know when I'm in the minority. Good night everyone. Have fun. Oh, and Victoria"—he cast his midnight blue eyes in her direction—"it was nice to finally meet you. Georgina has had nothing but good things to say."

She felt her face warm as the man waved and walked out of the room, her cheeks surely as red as Rose's thread at the compliment.

"So where were we—*again*?" Debbie asked, her laughter bouncing off the walls with its soft but pleasing sound.

"The *other* charmer in town," Margaret Louise said as she winked knowingly at the mayor. "Milo Wentworth."

"Oh, yes." Debbie unwrapped a long piece of thread from the spool. "Anyway, Tiffany Ann has had a crush on Milo since she was twelve years old and her parents asked him to tutor her. He tutored her for less than a year but it was enough for Tiffany Ann to fall head over heels. Why, she'd bring him things to all their meetings . . . drawings, apples, whatever she could find."

"She was so taken by him she plumb refused—*refused*—to speak to his wife. Flat-out ignored her," Margaret Louise offered. "And it's a well-known fact she was the only one at Celia's funeral who didn't cry."

"But what about this Cooper boy?" Tori asked.

"He was just someone to bide her time with until she was of age, dear," Leona whispered.

"And Lord help the person who talks about finding a woman for Milo Wentworth," Debbie said, picking up the conversation once again. "MaryAnn Ward made that mistake once and Tiffany Ann went crazy. And when Beatrice here first moved to town she let her know Milo was hers."

Tori stared at the quiet girl bent over a sewing machine. "She did?"

Beatrice looked up and nodded. "Once she heard I have someone back home, she was fine. A delight, really."

"But this girl is what? Twenty-one? Twenty-two?" Tori asked.

Debbie nodded. "It doesn't bother her in the slightest that he's thirteen years older. Never has. Never will."

"And boy does she get that man flustered with her flirtations," Margaret Louise said between hearty laughs. "Do you remember at last summer's fair when *she* offered to pay *him* at her own kissing booth? He sputtered and stammered like Jed Tucker's beat-up old jalopy. And then quit."

"I think women in general fluster Milo. Though, from what I hear, he seemed at ease with you, Victoria. Some even said he seemed rather *comfortable* with your flirtations," Georgina commented.

Tori felt her mouth gape open as every set of eyes in the room trained on hers.

"How did . . . I mean, I didn't . . . I wasn't—"

"But as beautiful as Tiffany Ann is," Georgina continued, "the last thing Milo Wentworth needs to mend a broken heart is a twenty-two-year-old woman on drugs."

Still stunned by Georgina's words, Tori shook her head, forced herself to keep the conversation from lapsing backward. "Just because this Tiffany Ann person is a little jumpy at church one day everyone thinks she's on drugs?

Isn't this the same girl who designed floats and won pageants?"

"Yes, but she wouldn't be the first apple to go bad," Georgina countered. "Looks *can* be quite deceiving at times, Victoria."

"Yes, they most certainly can," Dixie said through clenched teeth. "The key is not falling *prey* to the pretty package."

Chapter 6

She stood in the center of the room, staring at the box that hadn't been there the night before. A box every bit as big as the thirty or so she'd systematically culled through over the course of the past week and a half.

"Where did *that* come from?"

"I don't know, Miss Sinclair." Nina Morgan slowly turned in her spot, her eyes wide with excitement. "I never realized how big this room was, never realized it even had windows."

"That's because the boxes reached to the ceiling and filled everything in between," Tori said over her shoulder as she flipped open the lid of the box and sighed.

More books. More ripped and moldy books.

"You've done a lot of work in here."

Indeed.

She reached inside the box and pulled out a torn and tattered copy of *Macbeth* and a water-damaged copy of *Julius Caesar*. "No one stopped by the desk with a box of books?"

"No, Miss Sinclair. But that's not to say someone didn't come in the back door." Nina shifted from foot to foot, her hands clenching and unclenching at her sides. "Ms. Dunn stopped by though. She wasn't pleased with your drinking policy."

"Why didn't you call me? I'd have spoken to her." Tori turned the book over in her hands, surveying its damage by time and neglect. "I'd have explained to her that libraries all over the country are opening cafes inside their branches. The least we can do is allow grown-ups to drink a cup of coffee while they read."

"She was in rare form, and that's saying a lot. I thought it best just to tell her you were busy." Nina shook her head softly then pointed at the largest wall on the east side of the room. "That's going to be perfect for those murals you've been talking about."

Dropping the book back into the box, Tori turned around. "I was thinking Nottingham Forest would look great right there." She ran her hand along the wall to the left of one of the windows. "I want the trees to be so big that they feel real."

"The children are going to love it." Nina bridged the gap between them with sheepish steps. "I have a few old beanbag chairs from when I was a child. They're bright colors—reds and blues—but they're still in good shape. Maybe you could use those."

She squeezed her assistant's hand. "Nina, that would be perfect!" Looking around the room she continued speaking, her mouth trying desperately to keep up with the images flitting through her mind. "The best way I'm going to be able to convince the board tonight to let me do this is to show them a project that's not going to cost a lot of money. Donated beanbag chairs help tremendously. So will the fact that I've had experience painting murals and am willing to donate the time and the paint to get it done."

"I'll help, too," Nina offered. "I'm not the best painter, but my daddy always said I was a great taper."

"Good. You're hired."

"And I see those kinds of trunks you're talking about for the costumes at the flea markets around Sweet Briar all the time."

"Are they expensive?"

Nina shrugged. "Not really. I've seen some for as little as five dollars, a few for closer to twenty-five."

The board could do twenty-five . . .

"And your sewing circle is going to make the costumes, right?"

That, she wasn't so sure about anymore. Monday's sewing circle had come and gone with not so much as a question about Tori's project. At the time, she'd understood, even grudgingly agreed considering Dixie's presence and everyone's sensitivity to her feelings. But wasn't it time for the woman to accept reality? Shouldn't she love the library enough to want to help make it better?

"The costumes will get made." Tori motioned to the box once again. "I wanted the room to be empty when the board members came for the meeting tonight. So they could see the potential and visualize my plans. But now I've got to go through this surprise addition—separating the ones we can sell in the fall from the ones that need to go straight to the dump—"

"Nina? Are you coming?" A man with dark skin and even darker eyes stood in the doorway, his broad shoulders and chest contained beneath the football jersey he wore. "Your workday ended five minutes ago."

Five minutes ago?

"Miss Sinclair, this is my husband, Duwayne."

"Oh, Duwayne, it's so nice to finally meet you." She stepped out from behind the box. "Your wife is an amazing asset to this library." Tori extended her hand to the man, a gesture that went unacknowledged as Nina's husband took hold of his wife's arm protectively.

"My wife is the heart and soul of this library—has been for the past few years."

Surprised by the tension in the man's voice and stance, Tori rushed to smooth feathers she hadn't been aware of rumpling. "I can see why. The patrons love her."

"Tell that to the board." Duwayne looked around the room, his gaze fixing on the final box in the center of the room before dismissing it in favor of his watch. "It's time to go, Nina."

Nina shifted from foot to foot, her mouth turned downward. "I will be right with you, Duwayne. I need a moment with Miss Sinclair."

Tori sensed the man was about to protest, but was grateful when he didn't. Although she knew it was ridiculous, she couldn't help but feel as if she'd done something to irritate her assistant's husband.

When he left, Nina rushed to apologize, her words hesitant and shy. "I'm sorry about that . . . Duwayne is a good man. I-I guess he listened to my unhappiness with Ms. Dunn more than I realized. He just wants me to be happy and he wanted something for me I simply wasn't ready to have . . . I see that now."

"It's nice to have someone believe in you like that, isn't it?" Tori reached out and patted Nina's arm. "Anyway, he's right. It's after five."

"But your meeting," she offered.

Tori glanced at the box and then back at Nina. "The meeting doesn't start until eight. That gives me three hours to get through these books and get cleaned up before the show starts. That's plenty of time."

"I'm sorry—I'd stay if I could." Nina looked down at the floor, her body moving slightly.

"Don't you worry about it. You get going." Tori waved her assistant toward the door, a smile plastered on her

face. "We're closed now so there shouldn't be any inter-
ruptions to slow me do—"

The branch phone in her office began to ring.

"I'll get that for you, Miss Sinclair." Nina backed toward the door.

"No, you go on home. I'll get it." Tori followed
the woman into the hallway then turned in the opposite
direction—Nina toward the back parking lot and she
toward her office. She caught the phone on the fifth ring.

"Sweet Briar Library, how may I help you?"

"Hi, dear, it's Leona."

A wave of appreciation washed over her and she loosened her grip on the phone. "Leona, it's nice to hear a
friendly voice."

"Friendly voice? Is something wrong?"

She plopped into her office chair and stretched her legs
outward. "Nothing specific, other than the fact the gods
are conspiring against me."

Leona's soft laugh filled her ear. "How so, dear?"

Tori spun her chair a hairbreadth to the right and
looked out her lone office window at the town of Sweet
Briar—a white picket fence community that had grown
deserted in honor of the dinner hour. "They've comman-
deered my appointment book, let the air out of all four of
my tires, and developed an affection for watching me replace missing lightbulbs on my front porch. And just
when I think they're done . . . they deliver boxes."

"Deliver boxes?"

"Well, maybe *deliver* isn't quite the right word. They
essentially *appear* out of thin air."

Leona laughed. "Sounds like you could use dinner
out."

The clock on her desk confirmed dinner was not an
option.

"As tempting as that sounds, Leona, I have to decline.
The board meeting is tonight."

"Oh, I forgot. Are you going to tell them about your idea? For the children's room?"

"I am. The room is all cleared out—or will be by the time the meeting starts. I'm just going to have to hope that my ability to help people visualize is in tip-top shape."

"You'll be fine, dear. If the reaction from everyone at the sewing circle is any indication, you'll get your room."

"I hope so." Tori leaned her head against the seatback and closed her eyes. "I was disappointed no one asked about the costumes Monday night. I'd really hoped we could have divvied them up."

"I know, dear. But we need to give Dixie time. She'll come around."

"If the glares and comments I got the other night are any indication, I don't see that happening."

"Victoria, she can't stay mad for long."

"I hope you're right."

"I am. Now finish your room and show the board why they hired Victoria Sinclair. We'll do dinner another night."

"That would be lovely, Leona. I look forward to it." She was just about to hang up when a question formed in her thoughts. One that had been gnawing at her subconscious since Monday night.

"Leona?"

"Yes."

"Do you remember the conversation the other night? The one about that teacher at the elementary school?"

"His name is Milo, dear."

"It surprised me."

"What did?"

"Georgina's summation of something that wasn't anything more than a brief exchange between a new librarian and a teacher."

"It was essentially what I'd heard as well."

Tori pulled the phone tighter to her ear. "What you'd heard? From whom?"

"I can't recall. But it's making the rounds."

Making the rounds? As in gossip?

"I don't understand."

"Victoria, dear, you're in the south now. You're new. You're an outsider. It's only natural they're looking out for one of their own."

Looking out for Milo? From her? They couldn't be serious. . . .

"Leona, we greeted one another. We spoke briefly about Lulu's shyness and fear of reading. And we said good-bye at the end. That's it."

"Whatever you say, dear. You could certainly find a lot worse than that man—he is quite the looker. Just know Tiffany Ann won't take kindly to competition for his affections."

"I'm not looking." Tori dropped her head into her hand, massaged her left temple with the tips of her fingers.

"That's a good tactic. You don't want to appear too easy."

Good grief.

"Anyway, I really must let you get back to your work," Leona said. "Good luck tonight."

"Th-thanks." She replaced the phone in its cradle, stared at it for several long moments before heading back to the storage room and away from thoughts of Milo and the Sweet Briar rumor mill.

With finely tuned efficiency she assembled two piles on the floor—a sale pile and a garbage pile. Once the piles were complete and the box was broken down, she tackled the sale pile.

The books that were deemed to be in reasonable enough shape were stored in the library's basement. According to Nina, the books were then sold at an outdoor event in the town square each fall with proceeds benefiting the library. And if some of the proceeds from last year's sale could be used for new shelving in the children's room, it would show the annual book sale patrons where their money was going.

A win-win for everyone.

Unless she blew her pitch to the board . . .

After stowing away the sale books, Tori forced her tired legs back up the basement steps for the final time. If her calculations were correct, the remaining books wouldn't require more than three—*maybe four*—trips to the Dumpster before she could head home for a much-needed shower.

Quickly she grabbed the first pile and headed out the back door, the early evening sun making it difficult to see much of anything. Squinting against the glare, she glanced over at her car, relieved to see all four tires in tip-top shape.

No delays there. . . .

She swung her gaze back toward the Dumpster and was grateful to see the trash collectors had replaced her step stool after their rounds earlier in the afternoon. Carefully she stepped onto the first step and then the second, the pile of books making her balance a bit awkward.

Pulling her arm backward, Tori winced at the soreness in her muscles, a tribute to the countless Dumpster trips she'd made over the past ten days. But she was almost done. Finally.

With a toss, she released the books from her arms, all but one making their aim. The other—Shakespeare's *Julius Caesar*—slipped to the ground.

Mumbling to herself, she stepped off the ladder and reached down, her hand closing over the tattered book. She took three giant steps backward and threw with all her might, the muted thud that followed proof she'd overshot her target.

"Good one, Tori." She made her way around the side of the Dumpster, sidestepping an overturned coffee-to-go cup from Debbie's Bakery. "At least I'm not the only one with rotten ai—"

A single wedge-heeled sandal peeked out from the backside of the Dumpster. New shoes with turquoise straps and matching toenail polish . . .

Curious, Tori peered around the corner, nausea racking her body as her gaze fell on the lifeless girl slumped against the metal container. A girl with hair the color of spun gold and a copy of *Julius Caesar* in her lap.

Chapter 7

If there was one thing she wasn't prepared to handle that morning, it was Dixie Dunn. Not after witnessing a crime scene investigation up close and personal. And certainly not after being the one who made the gruesome discovery.

Tori glanced out the window of her tiny office, her head throbbing, her gaze barely registering the cluster of people standing on the sidewalk staring in her direction.

"Ms. Dunn is bound and determined to talk to you. I've tried every which way to get her to talk to me instead, but gracious plenty she's close to having a hissy. I think it would be best if—"

"Step aside, Nina." Dixie Dunn threw an elbow into the assistant's side and shoved her way into Tori's private office, her eyes blazing, her hand waving a hardbound book in the air. "You're not here more 'n two weeks and you already don't got the sense that God gave you, child. And to think they thought *I* was the one who should go."

"Miss Sinclair, I'm sorry. I tried to—"

"It's okay, Nina, I'll take it from here." Tori rose from her chair to offer the young woman a reassuring pat on the arm. "Can you cover things out in the library while I have a moment with Ms. Dunn?"

"Yes, ma'am—I mean, Miss Sinclair." Nina's eyes, round and worried, met Tori's as her hands nervously clenched and unclenched the sides of her ankle-length summer skirt. Dropping her voice to a near whisper, she peered over her boss's shoulder before reengaging eye contact. "Be careful."

Inhaling deeply, Tori closed the door and turned toward her uninvited guest, determined to keep her cool at all costs. "Ms. Dunn, what can I do for you?"

The five foot three cotton-topped woman slammed her book down on Tori's desk. "You can tell me why taxpayers should have to buy another copy of what *was* a pristine book."

Confused, Tori reached for the book, turned it over in her hands.

Sweet Briar City Structure and Laws.

Was this a trick question?

"I'm not sure what you're talking about, Ms. Dunn. We're not asking anyone to *buy* another copy."

"You best be."

She opened the front cover, thumbed through the relatively thin volume. "I don't see a prob—"

"Page five," Dixie spat.

O-kay.

Tori set the book down, turned the pages one by one until she reached page f—

"You see? I just can't abide by this drinking rule."

Sure enough, page four and five were stuck together. Gently, and with practiced hands, Tori separated the two pages to find a faded light brown circular stain.

Coffee.

"Ms. Dunn, it's going to happen. Fortunately, most

people *are* responsible enough to refrain from placing a cup directly on a book. As for the policy itself, libraries all across the country are inviting patrons to bring a cup of coffee inside with them. Some are even opening small cafes inside the building. It's a way to make the library seem more relaxed, more accessible." Tori ran her hand across the faintly marked page and slid it—open—to the corner of her desk. "I'll let it dry out and it should be fine."

"Drying it isn't going to make a cotton-pickin' difference."

Realizing there was more at work behind the elderly woman's anger than a faint coffee stain, Tori crossed her tiny office and opened the door, stepping aside to allow the former librarian to pass. "I really must get back to work, Ms. Dunn."

The elderly woman's eyes narrowed to near slits as she inventoried Tori's body from head to toe, taking in her soft gray slacks and matching fitted jacket. "After the board sees that book . . . realizes what happened here last night . . . you'd best be looking for another job."

"The board is aware of last night's tragedy. As for the book, I'll be more than happy to replace it with a new copy. At my own expense." Tori motioned the woman into the hallway, stepping out of the way as her stout body barreled by. "Thank you for stopping in and voicing your concern."

"You ain't seen nothing yet." Dixie Dunn stopped in her tracks and spun around, hooked a bony finger in Tori's direction. "This has always been *my* library, and it's only a matter of time before it's mine once again."

She reached into the small paper sack and extracted the sandwich she'd prepared that morning. The ham and cheese she'd hoped would sound better by the time lunch came around, didn't. Neither did the apple or chips she'd tossed in along with it.

It was official. Constant flashbacks of Tiffany Ann's lifeless body was an appetite suppressant.

Shoving the sandwich back into the bag, Tori leaned against the white cinder block exterior of the Sweet Briar Public Library and briefly closed her eyes. The moment she'd discovered the girl behind the Dumpster everything had blurred—the screams she'd cried, the panicked phone call she'd made, the hustle and bustle that had followed after nearly an hour of waiting.

Alone.

With a dead body.

When Investigator Daniel McGuire from Tom's Creek had finally arrived, she was numb, unable to say much more than how she came upon the victim. Though, in retrospect, what more could she have said? It was the first time she'd laid eyes on the young woman.

Convincing the investigator of that had been the difficult part. No matter how many times she said it, he couldn't seem to wrap his mind around the fact that she knew things about the victim yet hadn't actually met her. Then again, he'd probably never experienced the kind of gossip that took place in a sewing circle.

"He'll figure it out." The words drifted from her mouth with the same soft summer breeze that ruffled her hair. It wasn't until the hushed voices at the base of the maple tree ceased, that she realized she'd spoken aloud.

Greatttt.

Not that talking to herself changed much of anything. The circle of women had been looking at her since the moment she'd sat down on the library steps. As if she was some sort of new zoo animal. An inhabitant Dixie Dunn wanted removed—the sooner the better.

"People around here aren't used to seeing new faces, Victoria."

Leona's words filtered through her mind as she raised her face to the noonday sun and closed her eyes once again. In many ways she *was* the new zoo animal. From a big city zoo, no less.

"You'll find your place, I just know it. You have a happiness about you that will win everyone over. You just wait and see."

Oh, how she hoped Leona was right.

On impulse, Tori rose from her spot on the steps and headed in the direction of the women. Perhaps they were simply curious about who she was yet too shy to introduce themselves.

Or maybe not.

The second her destination became obvious, the women scattered like fireflies on a warm summer's night, seemingly desperate to avoid her at all costs.

"Miss Sinclair?"

Distracted, Tori turned back toward the library, saw her assistant standing at the door.

"Yes, Nina?" She knew her voice sounded flat, but she was exhausted. And maybe even a little homesick.

"Mr. Wentworth from the school is on the phone. He confirmed his class visit tomorrow morning and then asked to speak directly with you." Nina's gaze skirted across the tree-covered grounds of the library, her attention alternating between Tori and the few remaining women who'd simply moved their cluster to a patch of shade across the street. "Would you prefer I take a message?"

Tori peeked at her watch and shrugged. She wasn't going to eat anyway. So what difference did it make?

"I'll take it, thank you." She marched up the steps, grabbed her paper sack from its perch against the wall, and followed Nina into the library. In the absence of patrons, she opted to answer the teacher's call from the main library extension.

"Mr. Wentworth, I'm sorry to have kept you waiting. What can I do for you?" She exhaled slowly as she waited for the man's reply, her head pounding once again.

"*Milo*, please. Nina confirmed the third grade's visit to the library tomorrow. The kids are really looking forward to it. But . . ." His voice trailed off for a moment only to return on a slightly quieter note. "I wanted to make sure you were okay."

"Okay?" She massaged her temple with the fingers of her free hand. "I don't understand."

"Last night. Behind the library. You were the one who found Tiffany Ann Gilbert's body, weren't you?"

A deafening silence filled her ear as her stomach began to churn at the memory.

"Yes." She tightened her grip on the phone as she sank onto the stool behind the information counter. "I can't get the image out of my mind."

"Tori, I'm so sorry. It must have been awful for you." A momentary silence morphed into a parade of hurried, yet hesitant, words. "Look, I know you're new here. And that you don't really know anyone. But if you need to, um, talk or anything . . . you . . . could, um, give me a call. If you want."

Under normal circumstances, Milo Wentworth's shy gesture would have piqued her curiosity. Today, though, it barely registered.

"I appreciate that but—"

"Oh. I'm sorry. That was mighty presumptuous of me. I'm sure you have lots of people you can talk to."

The disappointment in the man's voice broke through her pity-party. "No. It's not that. I-I'm just tired, I guess. I didn't sleep much last night."

An audible breath released in her ear. "I figured as much. I figured, too, that your idea for the children's room never got presented to the board."

"In light of the circumstances, the meeting was canceled." It was funny how something that had claimed her attention for the past week had become so unimportant in the matter of mere seconds. "We rescheduled though, for next week."

"I'm sure you'll get it. It's a tremendous idea. Something the kids will just adore."

"I hope you're right." She looked around the empty library, tried not to let her thoughts travel to the parking lot. But it was no use. "I'm sorry about Tiffany Ann. I know you knew her."

"I tutored her when she was twelve, made casual conversation whenever our paths met in subsequent years . . . but beyond that, I didn't know her that well."

A tap on her shoulder made her turn.

"Miss Sinclair," her assistant whispered, "you have another call on line two. Miss Leona Elkin."

Leona.

In the span of less than two weeks, Tori had come to treasure her time with Leona, a woman who was both wise in her thoughts and generous with her wisdom. Two qualities she desperately needed at the moment.

"Tori? You still there?"

"Wha—oh, I'm sorry, Milo. I have another call." Not wanting to appear rude after he'd been so nice, she forced her voice to sound as upbeat as possible. "We look forward to seeing the children tomorrow."

"Oh. Yeah. Sure. Tomorrow then." The man cleared his throat quickly. "Um, well, take care of yourself, Tori."

"Thank you." She waited for the click in her ear before rising to her feet. "I'll take Ms. Elkin's call in my office."

"Yes, Miss Sinclair." Nina glanced down at the floor and then back up at Tori, her voice a mere whisper despite the empty room. "Ms. Dunn was sure all-fired mad. I hate to see her trying to dirty-up your name the way she is. I've worked with her and I've worked with you, and you're mighty special, Miss Sinclair."

Tori swallowed over the unexpected lump in her throat. "Thank you, Nina. That means a lot."

"And I'm not the only one who thinks that. There's no fooling children. They see what's inside a person better 'n adults, and they *adore* you."

Blinking against the hint of moisture in her eyes, Tori squeezed her assistant's hand. "If you don't quit I'm going to be sniffing my way through this phone call. But thank you."

"You're welcome, Miss Sinclair."

She headed down the small hallway off the back of the main room, the same one that led to the storage room and an exterior door to the parking lot. The staff-only exit had been a godsend when hauling worthless books to the Dumpster the past week. Though, with as many trips as she made yesterday alone, none of them had been in time to save Tiffany Ann Gilbert. Whatever had happened to the girl had happened quickly.

And quietly.

With no one the wiser.

Had Tiffany Ann had some sort of medical condition? Or had she—as the sewing circle had alluded—battled a drug problem that won out in the end?

Whatever it was, it was a shame. Twenty-two was simply too young to die.

Shaking her head free of the suffocating sadness, Tori reached for the phone on her desk. "Leona? Are you still there?"

"Hello, Victoria. How are you holding up?"

"You've heard?"

"News travels through Sweet Briar quickly, dear."

She leaned back in her chair, rested her head against the seat back. "It was awful, Leona. Absolutely awful. There she was, against the backside of the Dumpster, looking . . . looking just as perfect and pretty as everyone said. But she was *dead*, Leona!" She inhaled deeply, willed herself to calm down. "And then, when I tried to call the police, some operator told me the chief was on vacation."

"That's right, dear. Police Chief Dallas is on his annual fishing trip up north. When that happens, any problems that arise are passed on to one of the surrounding departments."

"That's what Investigator McGuire said last night."

A slow intake of air in her ear surprised her. "Ooooh. That Daniel is quite a man, isn't he?"

"Daniel?"

"Daniel McGuire. The investigator. He came into my shop this morning to ask a few questions. Twenty minutes with that man and I found myself wondering if Margaret Louise had been right about me needing to find someone. Then again, I've always been partial to a man in uniform."

She sat up. "Did he buy something?"

"Dear?"

"At your shop." Tori glanced out the window, noticed the new cluster of people staring in her direction. "Did he buy something at your shop?"

"No. He was there on official business."

"Official business?" She tried to ignore the pointing and the talking that accompanied the looks—

"Why, Tiffany's murder, of course."

Her head snapped up. "Murder?"

Leona's voice increased an octave. "Good heavens, Victoria, of course it was murder. What else could it be?"

"An overdose . . ."

"An overdose? Where would you get th—oh . . . the talk last week? At the sewing circle?"

Tori swiveled her chair away from the window. "Yes. Georgina suspected Tiffany Ann was involved with drugs."

"She said *Thomas* suspected that. But he wasn't in Sweet Briar when Tiffany Ann was growing up."

"Neither were you, Leona," she pointed out, her voice hesitant.

"Margaret Louise was. And she pooh-poohed it instantly."

"Yes she did. But even *you* said it was possible."

"Did I?" The woman's voice grew quiet as she seemed to reflect on Tori's words. "I don't recall. But either way, dear, I suspect there's much more to Tiffany Ann's death. If there wasn't, why would Daniel have been asking so many questions?"

Why indeed.

Her eyes fell on the stack of proposals she'd prepared for the board, a new thin binder playing host to each member's copy. The many ideas she envisioned for the children's room were listed in bulleted fashion on the first two pages with sketches rounding out her presentation.

As hard as it was, she needed to focus her attention back on the library. Tiffany Ann was gone. There was nothing she could do to change that. The how and why were up to the police to unravel.

Still, she was curious. "What kind of questions?" she asked as she plucked a number two pencil from the wooden holder on her desk and slid it back and forth between her fingers.

"Well, strangely enough, he asked a lot of questions about *you*, dear."

She felt her mouth go dry.

"Me?"

"Yes, dear. You."

Feeling the room begin to spin, she closed her eyes tightly. "Why would he be asking questions about me?"

"You're new in town."

"So?"

"This is the first murder Sweet Briar's ever had."

She swallowed back the bile that threatened to gag her where she sat. "And therefore *I* must be *a murderer*? Is that what he thinks?" She knew her voice sounded shrill, near hysterical even, but she couldn't stop. This had to be some sort of joke.

"That's what a lot of people are going to think, Victoria."

Swiveling back toward the window, Tori stared out at the pockets of people standing around—virtually everyone either pointing or staring at her. They weren't curious about the new librarian. They didn't care about the changes she would bring to the library. And they couldn't care less whether she was from Chicago or Beijing. They were there for one reason and one reason only . . .

To catch a glimpse of Tiffany Ann's murderer.

"But *you* don't think that . . . right, Leona?"

An awkward silence filled her ear as she waited, desperately, for the answer she needed to hear.

"Leona?" she repeated.

"Victoria, Daniel is a *trained* investigator."

She blinked against the tears that accompanied her friend's unexpected skepticism, willed them to fortify the tenacity she knew she possessed. Investigator McGuire didn't know her. The residents of Sweet Briar didn't know her. And, apparently, neither did Leona Elkin.

But she knew who she was. And she knew who she wasn't.

Turning her back to the townspeople, Tori popped the pencil back into the wooden holder and tightened her grip on the phone. "Then perhaps he needs to investigate based on *facts*, Leona. Not on a person's birthplace."

Chapter 8

Try as she might, she simply couldn't concentrate on her pillow. Not on the threading, not on the stitching, not on the pleasure she usually derived from a project so near completion.

In fact, for the first time since her great-grandmother had placed a needle in her six-year-old hand, sewing didn't provide a comfort or a distraction. Though being a suspect in a possible murder investigation *was* a bit harder to gloss over than a grueling day at work or a pie recipe gone wrong.

Still, she could only justify knocking her head against the wall for so long before facing facts.

Setting the pillow on the end table beside the love seat, Tori looked around her cottage. In just two short weeks, she'd managed to unpack all but one box, finding a spot for each and every household item that had made the move from Chicago. Pictures were hung on the walls and even a few shelves had been arranged and rearranged to her satisfaction. But none of that seemed important anymore.

When push came to shove, it didn't matter where her great-grandmother's picture was placed or which lamp was best suited for her new sewing room. It didn't matter if her bedspread was a perfect match for the wall color she'd chosen or whether the antique clock her parents had given her was better suited for the kitchen or the entryway. The only thing that mattered in a new home was whether you felt welcome and wanted—neither of which she felt when it came to Sweet Briar, South Carolina.

In just two weeks she'd gone from feeling like all eyes were on her every move to a brief sense of belonging. And then, just as she was starting to relax—WHAM!

Only *this* time the looks had nothing to do with being the outsider from up north and everything to do with the murder of Tiffany Ann Gilbert. A crime which—according to Leona Elkin—*she* was suspected of committing.

If the notion weren't so upsetting she'd find it rather funny. As would anyone who'd ever known her—including her high school biology teacher who routinely won free lunch from other faculty members for knowing which bathroom stall she'd be hiding in on animal dissection days.

How could these people seriously think she'd hurt another human being? Especially someone she'd never even met? What could possibly be her motive? Some insidious desire to take over the town of Sweet Briar, one person at a time? A deep-seated need to rebel against the confines of acceptable southern belle behavior? A calculated move to eliminate all potential competition for the eligible bachelors in town—

She gripped the armrest of the love seat.

"This can't be about Milo Wentworth," she whispered as reality dawned in her mind.

Was *that* why she was considered a potential suspect? Because of Tiffany Ann's infamous attraction to the elementary school teacher and her own rumored flirtations with the man?

"No. No, it *can't* be."

Surely the residents of Sweet Briar couldn't be that *out* of touch with reality. . . .

Or could they?

Besides, if that was the motive, wouldn't *she* have been the one slumped against the Dumpster?

"Okay, okay. *Enough*." Tori pushed off the love seat and headed in the direction of the one unpacked box that remained: a refrigerator-sized carton that contained a wide range of supplies she hoped to use in her job at Sweet Briar Public Library.

Unpacking the various plastic containers would keep her mind engaged, her energy channeled. The woolgathering she was engaging in simply wasn't cutting it anymore.

Milo Wentworth's class was due at the library at ten the next morning. And while she'd set aside numerous picture books that would showcase Egyptian pyramids, she'd learned enough in her early library years to know kids retained more when actively engaged.

Which, in the case of third graders, meant a little hands-on time with Popsicle sticks and glue.

Both of which she had ample supplies of in the lone unopened box that sat against the wall in the small entry foyer. Or, rather, the lone box she didn't remember opening despite the telltale broken seal.

Reaching into the box, she extracted the first two plastic containers she could reach most easily. The first held colored pom-poms; the second contained a large assortment of crayons and colored pencils.

Strike on—

A firm knock on the door pulled her attention from the search and deposited it squarely on the butterflies that took flight in her stomach at the sound. Despite their last conversation, she couldn't help but hope Leona Elkin had come to her senses.

And to Tori's front door—with a much-needed apology in tow.

The woman's comments, or lack thereof, had hurt Tori more than she'd been willing to admit to herself. It had tugged at her heart since the moment they'd hung up.

Surely the woman had come to her senses. Or been helped there by Margaret Louise . . .

Setting the crayon bin on the floor, Tori bridged the gap between the packing box and the front door, smoothing the lines from her khaki cargo pants as she walked. "I was so hoping you'd come b—" The words drifted away as she yanked open the door and came face-to-face with her visitor.

Police Investigator Daniel McGuire . . . in full uniform.

She swallowed.

"Good evening, Miss Sinclair, how are you this evening?"

"Uhhhh, I-I'm fine." She knew her voice sounded forced, nervous even. But it was virtually impossible to feign otherwise.

This man—this police officer—considered her a *suspect*. In a *murder investigation*.

"I was hoping to have a few moments of your time." The man tugged his hat more firmly into place as his eyes surveyed the foyer before coming to rest on her face. "That is unless you're too busy *packing*, Miss Sinclair."

"I'm not packing." She turned, her gaze sweeping across the cardboard box that had claimed her attention just moments earlier. A box that was obviously in the officer's line of vision. She hurried to explain. "I'm not packing, Investigator. I'm *un*packing. Or trying to, anyway."

The second the words left her mouth, she regretted them. This man wasn't standing at her door in an effort to be sociable. Or to welcome her to Sweet Briar.

Squaring her shoulders with every semblance of courage she could muster, Tori met the officer's intimidating gaze head-on. "Is there something I can help you with, Investigator McGuire?"

"Why Miss Sinclair, I believe you can." He gestured toward the door, his eyes never leaving hers. "May I?"

"You want to come in?"

"Is that a problem?" His gaze traveled over her head once again, roamed around the portion of the cottage he could see from his vantage point. When he'd completed his visual inventory he simply looked at her and waited.

She swallowed again. "No. I—uh—of course it's not. Please. Please come in."

As she stepped aside to grant the officer entrance, she couldn't help but recall all those mystery novels and detective shows she'd seen over the years. The ones where suspects retained counsel *before* talking to police.

But she hadn't done anything that warranted a paid watchdog. She hadn't stolen anything. She hadn't offered or accepted any bribes. And she most certainly hadn't murdered anyone.

So, really, what harm could come from talking to the man?

"Nice place you have here," he commented as he strode past the box and into the living area, the late afternoon sun filtering through the back window and reflecting off his gun belt as he removed his hat and placed it on the armrest of the love seat. "Must be a big change for a city girl like yourself."

She shrugged. "In some ways, I suppose. Having my own place rather than an apartment has been nice."

Daniel McGuire's steel gray eyes flickered across the

pictures on the wall to the knickknacks and flowering plants scattered on bookcase shelves and assorted table-tops. "Bet the people are different here."

"A little more closed-minded perhaps but that's all I've noticed so far." The words were barely out of her mouth before she realized her mistake. The burly uni-formed shoulders tensed immediately, the probing gaze now searching her face.

"Closed-minded?"

Feeling her hands begin to tremble she returned to the box she'd been unpacking when the man arrived. "Do you mind if I continue what I was doing as we talk? I've got a classroom of children due at the library tomorrow morn-ing and I'm trying to locate a few supplies."

The man nodded, his gaze never leaving her face.

Al-righty then.

"You always wanted to be a librarian, Miss Sinclair?"

"Always." Reaching into the box she extracted two more plastic containers. One with colored pipe cleaners, the other filled to the top with a rainbow of colored sequins.

"You never considered anything else? No science or maybe chemistry?"

"Science or chemistry—uh, no. I tend to favor the right side of my brain."

"The right side?"

Tori stopped her search long enough to shrug. "You know . . . the creative side. The side that doesn't need black-and-white answers." She turned back to the box and retrieved two more containers.

Hmmmm. Would buttons make pyramids?

"Have you ever been *curious* about a subject like chemistry? Ever wished you'd gone that route?"

Where on earth were those darn Popsicle sticks?

"I'm sorry, Investigator. You asked if I ever wished I'd gone that route? No. Not at all. I love what I do." She peeked over the edge of the box once again, the next layer of covered supply bins just out of reach. "As for being curious about a particular subject . . . that's one of the many reasons I wanted to be a librarian. You can find the answer to just about any question simply by knowing which book to open. Chemistry included."

She stood on tiptoe, leaned over the side, her reach just as futile. "I guess I better find a step stool." Glancing up at the officer, she motioned toward the kitchen with her head. "Would you like a glass of water or lemonade?"

"No."

"Then I'll be right back. My stool is in the pantry." Tori started across the living room in the direction of the kitchen, the intensity of the officer's eyes nearly burning a hole in her back.

What did he want? And why all the questions about her career choice?

"No. It's not."

She turned. "Excuse me?"

The man dropped his arms from his chest and pointed toward the box. "Your step stool is right there."

"I didn't—" She stopped, swallowed again. "That's odd. I don't remember getting it out."

"You seem mighty nervous, Miss Sinclair. Is there something wrong? Something you'd like to get off your chest?" Hooking his thumbs inside the loops of his belt, the officer spread his stance ever wider.

"Nervous? I'm not nervous. I just don't know how the stool got there."

"I imagine you put it there, Miss Sinclair."

Ooooh. An investigator and *a rocket scientist. Could she get any luckier?*

Tori returned to the task at hand, scooting the small stool to the right roughly eight inches before stepping up and reaching into the box once again. Empty milk cartons, glue bottles, and X-acto knives filled the next three or four containers she removed.

Strike two.

"Tell me why you think folks around here are closed-minded."

Choosing her words carefully, she tried to explain the frustration she felt as a newcomer. "In a city like Chicago, people come and go all the time. Tourists, businesspeople, whomever. It's just part of life there. And everyone takes it in stride." As the contents of the main box grew harder to reach, Tori stepped off the stool and set the carton on its side, a motion that caused the remaining six plastic boxes to slide forward. "But here . . . in Sweet Briar . . . virtually everyone here is a native. Someone from out of town instantly stands out. The first week I was here I felt like I was in a fishbowl all the time. Not because I necessarily look different than anyone else or because I was causing a commotion to make myself stand out. But simply because I was an unknown."

"That must be hard."

It was amazing how four seemingly innocuous words could make such a difference in a person's mood, but they could. And they did. Knowing that her words had touched a sense of compassion in Daniel McGuire helped steady her hands and slow her heart rate.

"It can be." She opened each bin one at a time. The first held googly eyes, the next—toothpicks. A deep container housed various colored bottles of tempura paint and two-dozen clean sponge brushes. The final plastic storage box held rainbow-colored packets of yarn and small pre-cut squares of thin cardboard.

Strike three.

"I bet that kind of scrutiny could make a person lash out."

"I suppose. It can certainly get under your skin after a while. . . ."

Uh-oh.

Pulling her gaze from the inside of the now-empty cardboard packing box, she fixed it on the man still standing in the middle of her cottage, arms crossed. Only now the sheep's clothing was gone and the wolf was staring her straight in the face.

"Investigator McGuire, I get the sense you didn't stop by to welcome me to town or find out how I'm fitting in . . . so why don't you get to the point." She gestured toward the various bins she'd piled haphazardly on the floor. "As you can see, I've got work to do."

And like that the niceties were gone.

"Tell me again how you knew Tiffany Ann Gilbert."

She shook her head, resisted the urge to grab the man by his salt-and-pepper flattop. "As I told you last night, when you *finally* arrived on the scene, I never met Tiffany Ann. In fact, I'd never even seen her until I found her behind the Dumpster."

The man slowly removed his left hand from atop his right tricep and ran it across his freshly shaven chin. "Then how—may I ask—did you know who it was?"

The question was fair. Made perfect sense, even . . .

When it was asked the night before.

"Didn't I answer that last night? Several times in fact?" She knew her tone was clipped, bordering on snippy, but he was seriously trying her patience.

"Then I'm asking again."

She exhaled loudly and deliberately. "I'm in a sewing circle, and during the course of our first two meetings, Tiffany Ann has been a topic of discussion. The description I was given matched the woman I found. The hair color, the sense of style, her age. It simply fit. End of story. And, as it turned out, I was right."

The man's steel gray eyes narrowed to near slits as he studied her, a move she suspected was designed to make her nervous.

It didn't.

"During those same meetings did you learn anything else about the victim?"

Tori shrugged. "She was the town sweetheart or prin-
cess or some such nonsense and she had an interest in
fashion—wait, no. Interior design."

"You see the titles the victim won as nonsense, Miss
Sinclair?"

She shifted uncomfortably. "I didn't mean nonsense.
Not really. It's just not the kind of thing I have any in—"

"Or did you see those titles as more of a threat?"

Her mouth gaped open. "A *threat*? Of what?"

"Not a threat *of*, Miss Sinclair. A threat *to*."

She stared at the man, waited for him to offer an explanation for his bizarre words.

"A threat to your standing with a particular teacher?"
he baited.

The ludicrous notion that had popped in her head less
than thirty minutes earlier wasn't so ludicrous at all. In
fact, if she was reading the situation correctly, her brief
meeting with Milo Wentworth at the library on Friday was
now a motive for a murder.

Her motive.

"Okay. I've had enough. If you want to have a discussion, I'd be happy to talk with you. But this"—she flipped
her index finger back and forth between them—"is not a
discussion. It's an interrogation."

She spun on her feet and headed toward the entryway,
meeting the officer's gaze as she stopped at the door.
"Unless you're prepared to charge me right now, I have to
ask you to leave."

For a moment the officer simply stood in the same exact spot he'd held since she'd allowed him inside, his jaw
squared, his arms folded once again. But if his posture
and accompanying glare were designed to intimidate, they
didn't work. A fact he seemed to sense as he finally
grabbed his hat and joined her at the door.

Leaning over, the man brought his mouth mere inches

from Tori's ear. "In case you think small-town cops are closed-minded . . . know this, Miss Sinclair. I always find my man. Always."

She met his icy stare with one of her own, a move that not only surprised but emboldened her as well. Pulling the door open, she stepped aside, waited as the man lumbered onto her front porch. "For Tiffany Ann's sake, I certainly hope that's true."

She wasn't sure how long she'd been sitting in the exact same spot staring out at the quiet, tree-lined street in front of her cottage. And she wasn't sure when, exactly, her leg had finally stopped bouncing. But if she had to guess, a good hour had passed since Daniel McGuire had climbed into his Tom's Creek dome-topped car and headed south.

The nightly changing of the guard between day and dusk was well underway and yet she stayed put. In the exact same rocking chair she'd slid into as her unexpected visitor had disappeared from sight.

She knew she should be looking for the Popsicle sticks or, at the very least, working on the last section of trim on her pillow. . . . But she wasn't. The sticks were obviously MIA due to a memory crash on her part and the disappearing front porch bulb made it nearly impossible to see anything in the impending nightfall.

So she sat.

And rocked.

And contemplated her genius decision to accept the position of a woman who'd been forced from her job and mentally chastised herself for leaving the one place she felt at home. Or *had* prior to Jeff's betrayal, anyway.

"Are you going to sit there from can-see to can't-see or are you waitin' all the way to the crack of dawn?"

Margaret Louise.

She started to jump up from her chair but stopped herself midmotion. The people of Sweet Briar—not the least of which was this woman's sister—thought she was a murderer.

Without waiting for a reply or an invitation, the heavyset woman with the dark gray mop of hair who seemed to sport a face-splitting smile twenty-four/seven stepped onto Tori's porch, followed by five children ranging in age from twelve all the way down to three.

"If you're goin' to live in Sweet Briar, Victoria, you'll need more 'n one chair on your front porch." Margaret Louise motioned to the oldest of the children. "Jake, you go inside and bring me out a chair. The rest of you"—she looked around at the remaining four—"go see what kind of trouble you can get into in the backyard."

The woman followed the older boy's path into the house with her eyes and then lowered her voice so only Tori could hear. "That one is the spittin' image of his daddy. Right down to the name. Which means my boy is going to have his hands full." A satisfied smile crept across her face. "I suspect I'll be getting some long overdue thank-you presents when that day comes."

Tori simply smiled in return. Any hesitation she'd felt when Margaret Louise had appeared began to evaporate as the woman's actions and conversation continued to flow with ease.

Young Jake stepped back onto the porch, the small step stool in his hands. "Will this do, Mee-Maw?"

Mee-Maw?

"It will, son, if you're hankerin' to get me up off the floor. Good heavens Jake, that's a fool thing to bring out as a chair."

The boy's face turned red as he tried to shield his eyes from Tori.

Jumping up, she took the step stool from his hands and placed it on the floor. "I actually sit on this all the time, so it's perfect." She gestured to her now-empty chair. "Margaret Louise, please sit."

"You hadn't ought to have done that but—okay." Margaret Louise marched over to the white rocking chair and plopped down. "Now, Jake Junior, you go play with the others until it's time to go. But don't you be egging them on, you hear?"

The boy dropped his head downward. "Yes, Mee-Maw."

"Now get."

A smile that nearly matched his grandmother's sprang across his face as he rounded the corner and jumped from the porch to the walkway below, disappearing behind Tori's cottage with lightning speed.

Margaret Louise shook her head. "They're a handful—every last one of 'em. Except Lulu."

Tori felt her shoulders ease at the memory of the shy, raven-haired girl. "She is precious, absolutely precious."

Margaret Louise smiled proudly.

"Where is she this evening?" Tori asked.

"Practicin'. For you."

Startled, Tori leaned forward on the step stool. "Practicing what?"

"Readin'. When I left the house, my Jake was attemptin' to fold laundry and Lulu was reading *The Little Engine That Could* to an elephant, a tiger, a polar bear, and a monkey."

"Excuse me?"

Margaret Louise chuckled, a quiet, steady sound that started deep in her chest and brought a welcome release to the charged air that had surrounded Tori all evening. "She's practicin' in front of her stuffed animals. So she can read well for you tomorrow."

Ah. Lulu's class visit to the library.

Tori looked down at her hands. "I'm sure she'll do just fine."

"And so will you, Victoria."

Confused, Tori looked up.

"With everythin' that's goin' on right now." Margaret Louise waved her hand in the air, setting the chair to rock with a pudgy, sandal-clad foot. "No one in their right mind can accuse a woman who makes butter with a class of eight-year-olds, and inspires my Lulu to read, of something as-as cotton-pickin' awful as murder."

If there had been any doubt in her mind how closely she'd been guarding her heart from possible hurt the moment Margaret Louise appeared, it vanished with the whoosh of air that escaped her mouth.

"You don't believe I-I—" She stopped, steadied her voice, and then tried again. "You don't think I killed Tiffany Ann Gilbert?"

"Not any more 'n I believe Carter Johnson uses real eggs."

She looked a question at the woman on her porch.

Margaret Louise waved her hand in the air once again. "We'll save that for another day. Just hold off eating at Johnson's Diner until we do."

She bit back the first smile she'd felt on her face all day.

"I see that smile. And you let it out. You've got nothin' to be down in the mouth about, my friend."

"Everyone in this town thinks I murdered the town sweetheart. That makes smiling a little tough," Tori said, her voice raspy as it emerged from her mouth.

"That's not true. I think the town's split."

She sat up. "Really?"

Margaret Louise nodded, her foot moving the rocker even faster. "My son, Jake, for one."

"I don't know your son."

"But he knows Lulu."

She made a mental note to give the little girl an extra hug in the morning.

"And his wife, Melissa, doesn't think so, either."

Okay, make it two hugs.

"I passed Nina on the way out of the market earlier this evening, and she doesn't believe it either."

Tori looked at her hands once again, linked them together and twisted them around. When she spoke, her words were barely audible to her own ears. "Your sister does."

"Don't mind Leona. My twin ain't got the sense God gave her since about ten o'clock this mornin'."

"I don't understand," Tori said, dropping her hands to her side.

"I've been after her for years to find a man. Does she listen? Of course not. Then suddenly, a man walks in her shop—the kind that thinks the sun comes up just to hear him crow—and she loses her mind. Literally."

Tori couldn't help it. She had to smile.

"That's better." Margaret Louise leveled her foot against the ground and brought the rocker to a stop. "Leona will come to her senses. You just wait 'n see. In the meantime, we need to do some figurin'."

Tori stood. "Figuring?"

"You didn't kill Tiffany Ann. But someone did. The sooner we figure out who, the sooner I can sample some new pie recipes." Margaret Louise rose to her feet.

"Pie recipes? I don't understand."

"Once the real killer is caught, Sweet Briar will be lined up right here on this porch looking for your forgiveness." Leveling the index and middle fingers of her right hand in her mouth, Margaret Louise blew a whistle loud enough to be heard three streets over. In an instant five sets of feet clambered up the porch steps. "And around here, Victoria, gratitude and apologies are expressed with pie."

"I'd be happy with a box of Popsicle stick—"

She clamped her mouth shut as an official-looking white car turned down her street, the occasional street-lamp reflecting across its telltale rack of overhead lights. Would it ever stop? Would she ever be truly welcome in this town?

"I wouldn't count on those pie recipes anytime soon," she mumbled as she slumped back onto her stool and gestured toward the police car as it drew closer. "Investigator McGuire is determined to brand me a killer."

Margaret Louise followed the path of Tori's hand, pitching her head forward as she squinted at the car. "That's not McGuire. He's driving around town in a Tom's Creek car. That's one of ours and"—she jogged her head to the left and back to the right as the car passed, her eyes narrowing even more—"if I'm right, that was just Georgina's husband."

"I'm glad. I've seen enough of Daniel McGuire to last a lifetime." Tori reached down, lifted a ladybug off the porch floor, and held it out for the children to see. "Did you guys have fun out back?"

"Yes, ma'am, we threw my sister's bouncy ball back and forth and . . . uh-oh." Jake Junior hurtled down the stairs, followed by his siblings. "We'll be right back. Sally left her ball in the backyard."

As she watched Margaret Louise's grandchildren run around her cottage she felt her shoulders begin to relax. Sure, Daniel McGuire was still nipping at her heels but at least he wasn't checking up on her less than an hour after he left.

"You mentioned Popsicle sticks." Margaret Louise stepped back as the children returned, their breathing heavy from the extra run. After several gulps of air she shooed them back down the stairs, falling into step behind them. "Whatever do you need Popsicle sticks for?"

Tori leaned over the railing, offered a wave and a smile

to each of the children before focusing on the woman who'd given her the first ray of hope she'd felt all day. "Tomorrow's version of butter-making with Lulu's class."

"I see. Though how I can see anythin' without a porch light is beyond me." Margaret Louise stopped at the spot where Tori's front walk joined the street. "Put the sticks out of your mind—you'll have them in your hand first thing in the mornin'. In the meantime, make sure your eyes are wide and your ears are open. We've got ourselves a criminal to catch."

Chapter 9

Margaret Louise was right. The key to getting Investigator Daniel McGuire and the rest of Sweet Briar off her back was to hand them Tiffany Ann Gilbert's murderer on a silver platter. Problem was, Tori didn't know much about the girl besides the obvious—she'd been drop-dead gorgeous and had an undeniable knack for fashion.

Bearing down on the pen she'd been playing with for the past fifteen minutes, Tori made her first entry on the sheet of paper she'd titled Suspects.

A jealous friend . . . someone who resented her beauty . . . or maybe wanted her boyfriend.

It was a start. A lame one, but a start nonetheless. Then again, it was the last five words on the list that made her a viable suspect in the eyes of Sweet Briar residents.

She crossed them off her sheet.

But even as she did so, she knew it was a possibility.

Soap operas created monthlong story arcs out of an emotion like jealousy. Nighttime crime shows were littered with the corpses of people who'd been on the receiving end of jealousy's wrath

It happened. On TV and off.

Unfortunately for her, everyone in Sweet Briar was missing one crucial piece in the Who-Killed-Tiffany Ann puzzle.

Tiffany Ann Gilbert had a *crush* on Milo Wentworth. A simple puppy dog crush. Nothing more. Tori wasn't a threat to that in any way, shape, or form. Other than a brief encounter at the library a week ago, she didn't even know Milo Wentworth. And she'd never laid eyes on Tiffany Ann until—

She closed her eyes, inhaled deeply, then opened them once again.

She had to stay calm. It was the only way to stay on her toes.

"Miss Sinclair?"

"Yes, Nina?" Tori looked up from the sheet of paper on her desk and smiled at the petite woman standing just outside her office.

"Mr. Davis just dropped this off for you." Nina took a tentative step inside the room then stopped. "If it makes more sense for me to keep it up front, I can do that."

Tori looked from the white box in her assistant's hand to the expression of uncertainty on her face. "I don't know a Mr. Davis."

"He was real nice. Asked me to make sure you got these right away." Nina set the box on Tori's desk and opened the lid to reveal its contents. "Looks like we've got more 'n enough, don't you think?"

She sucked in a breath. "Mr. Davis—*Jake* Davis . . . of course," she said, her voice dipping with a burst of unexpected emotion. Margaret Louise had come through for her—just as she'd promised. "Is he still here?"

Nina shook her head. "He just asked me to make sure you got them."

She pulled the box closer, reached in, and fingered the top layer of one-inch sticks that would soon be the tools with which sixteen eight-year-olds would delve into the past. "We need to make sure to get some pictures today. We can use them in photo collages I'd like to see on some of the walls throughout the building, and we can send a few copies to Mr. Davis as a thank-you."

"I take it you didn't find your sticks?" Nina asked.

Tori tossed her hands into the air. "I found virtually every other craft supply known to mankind except them." She pushed her chair back from the desk and stood. "Casualty of a scattered mind, I guess."

"Scattered? You?" Nina laughed—a soft, happy sound that lit the tiny office despite the cloud-filled sky outside. "You're the least scattered person I've ever met. You're *always* on the ball."

"Not the past few days." Tori slipped her pathetic attempt at detective work into a folder on her desk. "I can't seem to focus on anything."

"That's understandable, Miss Sinclair. And it's most unfair." Nina's eyes, round and solemn, chased away any remnants of the smile that had graced her face just seconds earlier. "I don't understand how anyone could think you'd kil—I mean, that you would mur—I mean—"

"It's okay, Nina. Just knowing you don't believe it helps more than you can know." She left the safety of her desk and embraced the woman who—along with Margaret Louise—was her most loyal supporter. "We need to go about our day as if nothing is wrong. A library is supposed to be a place of peace. And I think we both need that right now, don't you?"

"Yes, Miss Sinclair." Nina turned toward the door, Tori on her heels. "Mr. Wentworth and the children should be arriving any minute now."

Tori glanced down at her wristwatch then backtracked to her desk for the box of sticks. "You have the glue, right?"

"Yes. I set out all the bottles on the table over by the reading area—"

"Hello? Is anyone here?"

Milo Wentworth.

"Perfect, Nina. Thank you." She fell in step with her assistant as they made their way up the narrow hallway and into the library. "Mr. Wentworth . . . children . . . we're so glad to see all of you again. How is everyone?"

A chorus of *good*s echoed against the wall despite the students' efforts to use their best library voices.

"It looks like we're missing a few students today." She mentally counted each student, stopping when she hit nine. "Is there a stomach bug going around?"

Milo Wentworth shifted from foot to foot, his eyes searching her face as he spoke. "Possibly. It's hard to tell just yet—"

"Jeffrey isn't sick. His mama is bringing him to school as soon as we're back from here." A sandy-haired boy leaned back on his hands and wiggled around. "And Jonathan was in school for spelling and writing but his dad came and got him when we lined up. Guess he don't like the li-berry too much."

"I saw Caroline last night. We blew bubbles together and chased some fireflies. She's not sick neither." A little girl with the name tag Hanna filled her cheeks with air then pushed it out with her finger. "But she loves the library. She likes books more 'n toys!"

A collective gasp distracted the children as Tori met their teacher's eyes.

"Milo? What's going on?"

With a clap of his hands he stepped forward, breaking eye contact with Tori in deliberate fashion. "Okay, boys and girls, we need to give Miss Sinclair our undivided attention. I know she's got lots of fun prepared for us today."

"We'll talk later," she hissed under her breath as she took the man's cue, her stomach twisting at the unspoken reality.

The missing students hadn't been *allowed* to come.

Because of her.

Blinking quickly against the tears that threatened to make their debut, Tori took her place in front of the students. "I understand you've been studying pyramids in history, is that right?"

"Yes!" shouted the children.

"Who can tell me where we would find pyramids."

The sandy-haired boy raised his hand.

"Yes?"

"In the sand."

"O-kay. Very good. But does anyone know what country?" Tori looked around at the faces of the children assembled in front of her, spotted Lulu's long dark hair off to the side, the child's face tilted downward. "Lulu? Can you help us?"

Startled, the child looked up, her large, dark eyes meeting Tori's. Margaret Louise's granddaughter simply nibbled her bottom lip inward and shook her head.

"Are you sure?"

The child dropped her head, shaking it even harder.

Milo Wentworth lowered himself to the ground beside the little girl, his hand finding her shoulder and offering a gentle squeeze of encouragement. "You know this answer, Lulu. And I think Miss Sinclair could use your help."

Lulu slowly raised her face once again. "Egypt," she whispered.

"Excellent, Lulu. Yes, pyramids are found in Egypt. Very nice." Tori winked a smile at the child and then moved on with the lesson, anxious to undo any cloud that might be hanging over the field trip whether the children were aware of its presence or not. "Did you know that scholars today believe it took twenty thousand men more than twenty years to build the Great Pyramid?"

A collective *wow* rose up among the students.

"Pyramids were made of stone, which means they're solid. No walls or pillars were needed to support them like you'd find in your home or"—she motioned around the room—"this library.

"While it is still a mystery how these structures were built, we do know that the pyramid's large square base kept it stabilized."

"What's *stabilized* mean?" the sandy-haired boy asked.

"*Stabilized* means it didn't move or sway. It just stayed put." Tori retrieved a picture book from the table at her side and opened the cover, turning the book for the children to see. "Do you see this picture? Do you see how the pyramid seems to be pointing at the sky?"

Heads nodded while a few hands wandered.

"Does anyone know why it may have had that shape?" Tori looked around the room as she continued to slowly turn the pages of the book, each picture showing a different pyramid. "The belief is that the pyramid was built to symbolize the sacred mountain—a way for people to reach—"

"Heaven." Lulu's voice, quiet but sure, permeated the silence in the room. "That's what Mee-Maw told me."

"Your Mee-Maw is a very smart lady, Lulu. That's exactly right." Tori turned the page, peeking over the edge of the book to smile at the little girl who seemed as shocked as her teacher that she'd spoken without prompting.

"Now, because the pyramids were built of stone at a time when there weren't big trucks to move them from place to place, it is a mystery as to how they were constructed."

"Cool!" The four little boys in the class shot their hands into the air and high-fived each other.

"I like mysteries," said one of the boys. "I like trying to

figure stuff out—'specially the kind nobody else can figure out."

"Are you available for consultant work?"

"What's *con-sul-tant* mean?" the boy asked.

Oops.

Ignoring the look of blatant curiosity Milo Wentworth shot in her direction, Tori simply smiled and shook her head. "Don't mind me. I had a silly moment. But I will say that you're all going to get a chance at trying to figure out the mystery of how a pyramid is built."

"Really?" asked the group of boys.

"Really." Tori set the book down and motioned to Nina for the box of Popsicle sticks. "We're not going to be able to answer the question as to how they moved the stone . . . but we are going to try and figure out how a pyramid is built."

Taking the box of sticks from Nina's outstretched hand, she opened the lid and removed a stick. "We have glue and scissors on the tables to my left. If you find it hard to cut the sticks, let either Mrs. Morgan or me know and we'll be happy to help." She removed several handfuls of sticks and scattered them around the tables. "I'd also like everyone to take a moment and thank Lulu for making this activity possible."

"Thank you, Lulu!"

The little girl looked up, surprise evident in her dark eyes as her fellow classmates made a beeline for the tables.

Tori picked up a stick and waved it at Lulu. "I misplaced the sticks I had for this project. But Marg—I mean, your Mee-Maw—asked your father to bring me some this morning. And he did." She reached behind her back and pulled out a chair for Margaret Louise's grand knee-baby, tapping her tiny upturned nose as she scurried past. "Do as much as you can on your pyramid and then," she lowered her voice, "we'll read."

"Okay," the little girl whispered, a mixture of pride and anxiety rippling across her face. "I've been practicing."

As the nine eager third graders set to work on solving the mystery of the Egyptian pyramids, Tori inched her way over to their teacher.

"You're very good with them," he said as she closed the gap between them.

"That's what librarians are supposed to do."

"If that's the case, then you're an overachiever."

Tori stifled a small laugh. "That's not the first time I've heard that."

"I'm not surprised." Milo Wentworth pushed up off the ground, his face contorting in momentary discomfort. "You think I'd avoid the Indian-style position after a while, wouldn't you? The old body simply isn't as limber as it once was."

"I think the nursing home is still a few years off, Mr. Wentworth." Tori gestured toward the students who were verbally sharing their construction triumphs and challenges with one another. "So what's the real reason nearly half your students didn't show?"

"I, uh"—the elementary school teacher shifted from foot to foot in dramatic fashion—"should it take this long to regain feeling in your legs?"

"No." Tori folded her arms across her chest and lifted her chin. "Don't change the subject."

"Okay, look, I imagine Jonathan had a doctor's appointment. Jeffrey probably did, too. Sometimes parents put off physicals until the kids are back in school. It's disruptive to their learning but it is what it is." He looked at his class, his desire for a hand to raise almost as tangible as the navy blue button-down shirt he wore atop a pair of khaki slacks. "I think Brian might need a hand."

"Nina has two." She stepped forward, blocking the man's path. "I'm the reason they didn't come, aren't I?"

Milo's face reddened. "Tori, I-I don't know what to say."

"You don't need to say anything." Swallowing over the lump that sprang into her throat, Tori blinked away the threat of tears. It wasn't that she was surprised—not really. It was more the pain that accompanied the confirmation.

Sweet Briar hated her.

"I didn't harm that woman." The words, tentative in nature at first, grew more forceful as she grit her teeth and repeated the mantra. "I didn't harm that woman, Milo. You have to believe me."

The man reached out, his surprisingly muscular lower arm making a brief appearance as his shirt sleeve fell back. His hand, warm and caring, sent shivers through her body. "I never considered otherwise, Tori. And I suspect"—he nodded his head at the children—"their parents didn't either."

His hand left her arm and traveled to her chin, tilted it upward until her eyes opened. "The parents all knew we were coming to the library today. And they all know you're the librarian."

She slowly nodded, waited for the man's words to chip away some of the hurt.

"Some people have a brain in their head, Tori. And that's all they really need to know these suspicions are ludicrous." He dropped his voice even lower. "A woman who dreams of putting together a place for children to re-create their favorite stories isn't the kind of person who would drug someone. It just doesn't fit."

Her head snapped up. "Drug?"

"Yeah. I heard it at the bakery this morning. Apparently it showed up on the preliminary lab work."

She felt her shoulders slump with relief. "Then it wasn't murder?"

Milo's eyebrows formed an upside-down *V*. "Of course it was. Tiffany Ann was anything but a drug addict. Besides—traces of whatever it was were found in some drink they found near the body."

"Drink?" In an instant she was behind the Dumpster once again, her mind inventorying everything she could remember about the body. "There wasn't a—"

The coffee cup.

"Oh." She dropped her head into her hand, kneaded the skin above her eyes. It made sense now. Investigator McGuire's questions about chemistry and science weren't designed to lighten the mood or foster a little small talk. No siree. They were a net. A great big net.

And she'd jumped right in without so much as a moment's hesitation.

"I'm such an idiot," she mumbled.

"Excuse me?"

"Nothing." She popped her head up, glancing over at the children. There wasn't a thing she could do about the comments she'd made in her home the night before. As incriminating as they may have sounded, they'd been stated with the utmost innocence. Because she *was* innocent. A fact she would prove one way or the other.

"Is it okay if I take Lulu into my office and read with her for a few minutes?" She glanced back at Milo. "I promised her we'd read together and I want to make good on my word."

He cocked his head to the side as he studied her closely. "Are you sure you're up for that? We can postpone until next week."

"No. This is every bit as important. To me." She nodded to her assistant. "Nina, can you hold down the fort with Mr. Wentworth? I only need about ten minutes."

"Of course, Miss Sinclair." The woman looked over the head of the sandy-haired boy. "We're doing fine."

Satisfied, Tori knelt beside Lulu. "Are you ready, sweetheart?"

The little girl looked up from her work in progress as a shy smile inched her mouth upwards. "I think so."

"Then let's go." She slipped her hand around the child's

smaller one and led the way to her office. "Are you having fun, Lulu?"

After an awkward beat of silence the child nodded. "You make learning fun. All the kids think so. Even the ones who couldn't come today."

"I'm glad." And she was. She just wished people would believe in her innocence. They rounded the corner from the hallway into her office and made a beeline for two small rattan chairs she'd grouped in the corner. "Does this look like a good place to read, Lulu?"

"Yes, ma'am." The child settled into the chair with the soft yellow cushion and waited—eyes wide—for Tori to claim the lavender one. "I forgot to bring a book."

"I have one for you." Reaching into the tote bag she'd set next to the chair when she arrived that morning, Tori pulled out a well-worn copy of the first Little House picture book she'd found. The easy-to-read stories were based on one small memory from the larger independent reader volumes. "Do you know who this is?"

Lulu's eyes searched the cover as her mouth stretched into a wide grin. "Laura?"

Tori nodded. "That's right."

"I didn't know she had books *I* could read. I just thought she had the stories Mee-Maw reads at bedtime."

Pulling the empty chair even closer to Lulu's, Tori sat down. "I didn't either. And then one day, when I was visiting a tiny little bookstore in Chicago, I found them. There's lots of them just like this one. Within a week I had a copy of each in the library where I worked . . . and bought duplicates for my own collection."

"Wow." Lulu slowly opened the cover. "This is about her birthday."

Tori clapped her hands softly. "You're right. Great reading. Now, read me the whole story."

Scooting farther into the chair, Lulu began to read. Her shy, quiet voice was nearly impossible to hear as she stumbled through each and every word on the first two pages. When she reached the end of the second page, Tori stopped her with a gentle hand.

"That was very good, Lulu." She leaned forward, made eye contact with the child behind the pages of the raised book. "Who likes Laura's stories best . . . your monkey or your elephant?"

"Ellie does."

"Which one is Ellie?"

"My elephant. She likes to play Laura with me. 'Cept when we play, Ellie is Laura's dog, Jack."

"How about we pretend Ellie is sitting on my lap, listening to you read. She can hardly wait to hear the kind of presents Laura gets on her birthday. . . ."

Sure enough, the child's words became more relaxed as she continued on, her voice more sure with each passing word. At the end of each page she stopped to look at the pictures that accompanied it, pointing out different things to the pretend elephant.

Before either of them knew it, the book was finished. Lulu's eyes danced across the front cover as the smile returned to her face.

"Did you enjoy that, Lulu?" she asked.

"Oh, yes!"

"You're a very good reader."

The smile disappeared. "No, I'm not. Jeffrey says I'm slow. And Annabelle says no one can hear me."

Tori lifted the book from the child's hand and placed it in a small grocery bag she'd packed inside the tote bag. "I don't think you're slow—I think you read just right. And Ellie and I heard you just fine."

Lulu looked up from the book. "Really?" she whispered.

"Really." She handed the bag to Lulu and stood. "Now how about I let you borrow this for the week. You can take it home and read it to all of Ellie's friends."

The child gasped. "Mee-Maw, too?"

"Mee-Maw, too."

Jumping down from the chair, Lulu grabbed hold of Tori's waist. "I love you, Miss Sinclair."

Choking back an unexpected sob, Tori simply rubbed the child's back. Somehow, despite the facts she knew to be true, she'd let the way Sweet Briar saw her affect the way she saw herself.

But no more.

Inhaling courage and determination, Tori gently extricated herself from the child's arms. "Shall we get you back to your class?"

Lulu nodded, the heartfelt emotion she'd shared through her hug evident in her sparkling eyes. She looked down at the bag she'd grabbed and then back up at Tori. "I'll bring this back next week. I promise."

"I know you will. And maybe you could read me another one then?"

"Oh, yes!"

Hand in hand the pair returned to the library, the smile on Lulu's face a match for the one Tori felt on her own. Suddenly the hurdles in front of her didn't seem so insurmountable any longer. The truth would come out. It had to.

"Well, I think that went well, don't you?" Tori popped the last of the Egyptian pyramid books onto the shelf and turned to face Nina. "The kids did a great job on their pyramids, and they were talking a mile a minute on the way out the door."

"They sure love you." Nina rounded up the last of the leftover Popsicle sticks and placed them into the box. "Do you see the way all the glue bottles are back in the basket and the scissors stacked beside it? That was the kids' idea—with no prompting. They did it to please you."

"I think they're just good kids." Tori strode across the room and reached for the stack of books on the information desk. She turned the top one over and studied the spine.

"I imagine you're right. But they organized the supplies for you. I heard them." Nina placed the basket of glue and pile of scissors behind the counter and grabbed a second pile of books. "And I don't think they're the only ones in that class who are taken by you."

"You mean, Lulu? She is such a precious little girl, Nina. You should have heard how hard she worked to read that book to me." Tori placed the reference book on the proper shelf then moved on to the next book in the stack. "I think she's capable of being an amazing reader. Her love for books will see to that."

"I wasn't referring to Lulu, Miss Sinclair."

"Huh?" Tori placed the next four books in their proper place with barely a thought, her feel for a library akin to a plane's autopilot feature. In fact, ever since she was about Lulu's age, she'd never felt more at home anywhere than she did in a library. Within moments of being in a new branch she had the layout memorized—cookbooks, reference, mysteries, romances, international culture, children's . . .

She glanced down at the final book in her hand, a wave of anger threatening to chase away the hard-earned peace she'd found over the past hour.

Sweet Briar City Structure and Laws.

"I was talking about their teacher—*Mr. Wentworth.*"

She heard her assistant's voice, even suspected she should be paying attention. But all she could think about was Dixie Dunn.

Tori turned to page five, the pages turning with ease.

"I can hardly believe the ruckus that woman caused all because of a stain you can barely see now." She held the book into the air for Nina to see. "To hear her talk you'd think a coffee stain in a book was worthy of the gas cham—"

Coffee.

Tori gulped. "I can't believe I just said that."

"Said what?" Nina asked.

"About the coffee."

Nina moved between shelves, replacing books that had been left on tables by various patrons throughout the morning. "Yeah, I heard what Mr. Wentworth told you earlier. About that poor girl and the coffee."

Confident the stain wasn't a hindrance to the book, Tori closed the cover and shelved it in the local section. "It's heartbreaking. For her family. Her friends. The town. I can only hope she didn't suffer."

"I know. I've been thinking about it ever since." Nina shelved the last of her books and met Tori at the information desk. "I just wish . . . I don't know."

"Wish what?"

Nina shrugged, her voice hesitant. "I don't know. I guess . . . I guess I just wish I could have taken that cup of coffee away from her."

"I think everyone does," Tori said, her hand closing over her assistant's and offering a gentle squeeze. "It's what sets decent people apart from the kind who could do something like that."

Chapter 10

She couldn't help but feel as if she should be standing behind one of the booths charging a fee for the right to stare. There was certainly a booth for everything else—barbecue, roasted ears of corn, pies, and fried dough sprinkled with powdered sugar. So why couldn't there be one that provided fairgoers with an up close look at the scarlet librarian? At least then the humiliation she felt would be for a good cause.

"Miss Sinclair?"

Disengaging herself from the mental pity-party that was in full swing inside her head, Tori tightened her grip on the tiny hand clasped inside her own. "What is it, Lulu?"

"Heritage Day is my favorite day of the year . . . 'cept maybe Christmas." The little girl's long dark hair swayed in the evening breeze as they followed Margaret Louise and Lulu's siblings across the Sweet Briar town square. "Mee-Maw always gives us each five whole dollars to spend on whatever we want."

"Do you know what you'll buy before you come?" Tori inhaled deeply, savored the tangy smell of barbecue sauce that wafted across the grounds. "Because if my grandma gave me five whole dollars, I think I'd get some barbecue chicken."

Lulu giggled. "They don't have chicken, silly. Just pork."

"No chicken?"

"No. But it's still good." The little girl stopped and pointed to the west side of the square, the night sky dotted with bright colored lights that turned and spun and flickered on and off. "That-that's what I like to do. More 'n anything. 'Cept read."

The midway.

Tori squatted beside Lulu, releasing her hand and wrapping it around the child's shoulders instead. "You're a ride girl, huh?"

"Uh-huh. I like the merry-go-round best of all." Lulu hopped from foot to foot as she grew more and more animated. "But sometimes . . . sometimes they have a boat ride. My brother, Tommy, says it's for babies because it just goes round and round in a circle but"—the child looked left to right before meeting Tori's gaze with an undeniable sparkle—"I like it anyway. 'Cause the boats look like canoes and I feel like . . . I feel like—"

And then she stopped, kicked at the ground with her pink and purple sneaker, and blew a stray strand of hair from in front of her eyes.

"I bet I know. Because I'd feel exactly the same way."

Lulu looked at her with hopeful eyes. "You do?"

Tori nodded. "Riding in a canoe makes you feel like Pocahontas, doesn't it?"

A smile that rivaled the lights of the midway sprang across Lulu's face. "You *do* understand. You do!"

"You bet I do—"

"That woman should be locked up, not roaming around Heritage Day freely."

"Isn't that one of Margaret Louise's grandchildren? I can't imagine letting a woman like that within a mile of one of my babies."

The conversation disappeared into thin air as quickly as it had appeared, but the words remained, the scope of their meaning bringing an ache to her heart. What *was* she doing here? How could she not have foreseen this happening when Margaret Louise and all six children appeared at her door just before dinner?

Not that it would have mattered. Margaret Louise was not a woman who took no for an answer.

Lulu reached out, pushed an errant strand of hair behind Tori's ear. "I like being with you, Miss Sinclair. So does Mee-Maw."

Blinking against the burning sensation in her eyes, Tori squeezed the child closer. "I like being with you and your Mee-Maw, too."

"There you two are. We walked near a country mile before Jake Junior noticed you two had done and gone." Margaret Louise pulled a paper fan from one of her grandchildren's hands and waved it near her cheeks. "I'm fixin' to pass out if I don't get me some ice-cold tea."

Tori let Lulu go and stood. "Margaret Louise, can I speak to you for a moment?"

"You're speaking to me now, aren't you?"

She looked down at Lulu and smiled, then motioned the child's grandmother to the side. "I was hoping to have a word with you . . . *alone*."

"Well, why didn't you say so?" Margaret Louise gripped Jake Junior's shoulder and held it firmly. "You keep track of everyone. I'll be but a minute."

The women sidestepped passersby as they found a spot removed enough from the children's range of hearing. "Is everythin' okay, Victoria?"

"No, Margaret Louise, it's not." Tori gestured to the faces that walked by, the majority of which stopped to stare at her. "I don't belong here. These people don't want me in their town, let alone at their fair. And I don't want people second-guessing your decision to have me around the children."

She knew her voice was growing shrill despite her efforts to keep from being overheard. But it was hard to keep emotion from her words when her heart was breaking in two.

Margaret Louise raised a finger in Tori's direction as her eyes darted momentarily in the direction of her grandchildren. "Now you listen up. The people in this town, bless their hearts, have been hurtin' for something to talk about for a long time. I mean, you can only get so much mileage out of Jeb Taylor's drinkin' or Harriet Johnson's clumsiness. A murder is somethin' this town ain't never seen."

"I get that but"—she looked around at the faces once again, felt the hatred in the eyes that glanced back—"I'm not used to being a pariah."

"And you won't be for long. I'm bound and determined to figure out who killed Tiffany Ann, but you have to be willing to dirty-up a little in the meantime." Margaret Louise clamped her mouth shut and shook her head firmly over Tori's shoulder. "That Jake Junior he's gonna be the death of me, you wait and see. Anyway, as for people thinking I'm putting my grandbabies in danger by having you around—let 'em talk. I know a gem when I see it. And so does Lulu."

Lulu.

Tori looked over her shoulder and smiled at the little girl who'd stolen her heart. No matter how low things got, Lulu had a way of making her feel okay. Like maybe there was hope.

"Can I get some tea now?" Margaret Louise pulled the fan from her face long enough to offer a brief burst of air in Tori's direction.

She laughed. "Get yourself some tea. But . . . can I . . ."

"Yes." Margaret Louise took three steps forward and then stopped. "You can take Lulu on her rides."

She felt her mouth drop open. "How did you know?"

"I know my Lulu." Margaret Louise marched across the flattened path of grass that separated them from her grandchildren, barely missing a step as she herded five of them in the direction of the food and drink booths. "We'll meet you at the merry-go-round in thirty minutes."

Tori stopped beside Lulu and reached for the child's hand once again. "You hear that, Lulu? We've got thirty minutes. Let's go see if the canoes are here again this year."

The only answer she received was a tug on her arm and the bobbing of a head as Lulu skipped along, the bright lights of the rides calling to them like a beacon in a storm.

"Have you ever seen such bright lights, Miss Sinclair?"

"Chicago is all lit up at night. But those are just white lights, they aren't colorful like these ones."

"White . . . like porch lights?"

Tori laughed. "Kinda. Though I can't really say since my porch light keeps disappearing."

The little girl stopped skipping long enough to stare, wide-eyed, at her companion. "Disappearing?"

"That or someone is playing a trick to try and drive me crazy." She swung her hand with Lulu's, her eyes scanning the midway crowd—a group of people who seemed far more intent on having fun than on the gossip surrounding the librarian in their midst.

"Maybe it's a *mystery*. Like the pyramids." Lulu squealed as they rounded the corner between the merry-go-round and the bumper cars. "There they are! They have it! They have it!"

Sure enough, a circle of six canoes anchored to metal rods floated around a pool that had been set up near the far corner of the midway. Each canoe was painted a different color, the burnt red claiming Lulu's attention. "That's the one I want to ride. It looks just like Pocahontas's canoe, doesn't it?"

"It sure does, Lulu." The strong voice cut through their conversation and made them both turn.

Milo Wentworth.

Tall and handsome in a faded pair of jeans, scuff-toed boots, and a white button-down shirt, Lulu's teacher dipped his head. "Good evening, ladies."

"Hi, Mr. Wentworth." Lulu stopped skipping and stood—perfectly still—at Tori's side.

"It's nice to see you, Milo."

"Ditto." The man gestured toward the boat ride. "I was hoping they'd let me ride, but the sign says I'm too big."

Lulu giggled and hid her face behind Tori's leg.

"I thought about complaining but figured I shouldn't." He winked at Tori then peeked around her leg at his shy student. "I'd sure like to watch you ride it though."

Tori looked over her shoulder at the little girl. "I would, too, Lulu. What do you say?"

Dropping her hand from Tori's grip, Lulu reached inside her pocket, her eyes large and serious as she extracted five crisp dollar bills and looked at the sign nailed to a post beside the ride.

50 Cents.

"How many times could you ride the canoes if you wanted to spend all your money right now?" Milo Wentworth asked, his gaze trained on Lulu's.

As one hand grasped the money, Lulu's other began counting, finger by finger, bent knuckle by bent knuckle. "Ten whole times!" she shouted.

"Very good." Milo nodded his pleasure at Tori. "My star math pupil."

"I see that. That was very good, Lulu." She bent down beside the child. "Is that really how you want to spend all your money?"

Lulu nibbled her lower lip inward, glanced back and forth between the money in her hand and the canoes making their way around the pool's center platform. "No. Maybe just a dollar. Or—two."

"Ready, Lulu?"

The child's face was all the answer Tori needed as she guided her toward the nonexistent line. As the boats came to a stop and children disembarked, Lulu began to jump in place. "I can get the red one! I can get the red one!"

"Then off you go, Pocahontas. Give my regards to John Smith." Milo's antics brought a smile to Lulu's face as she skipped in the direction of her preferred canoe.

"She is just precious, isn't she?" Tori whispered.

"She is most definitely that." Milo leaned against the railing that encircled the pool and waved at his student as the canoes slowly began to move. "And you're a natural with her, you really are."

Tori shrugged. "She makes it easy. Though, I have to confess, whenever I've dreamed of having a child of my own—the one I picture is almost a carbon copy of Lulu."

She waved at the child as she went by, grinned at the realization that Lulu Davis was a million miles away, paddling through the river, careful to avoid any dangers that might be lurking. She envied her that—the ability to escape the real world and disappear into a different one.

What she wouldn't give to be able to do that right now. . . .

"You'd like to have children one day?"

Realizing the man beside her was talking, she willed her mind back to the here and now. "Of course. Doesn't everyone?"

"No. My late wife didn't. Though I didn't know that when we were first married."

Unsure of how to respond to this unexpected piece of private information, she simply waited, leaving the conversation in his hands.

"It wasn't something she knew when we married. But rather something she discovered about herself afterward. I tried to tell myself it was okay, that I was around children all day long. But . . . since her death"—he lifted his hand in a wave once again, dropping it back down to the railing as he, too, seemed to realize Lulu was no longer in Sweet Briar—"I've come to realize having children is something I want."

"I'm sorry about your wife." It was all she could think to say.

"Thank you. But it was a long time ago. Sure, the hurt still remains. But I've come to accept it and to look forward to the rest of my life."

Without thinking, Tori reached her hand to the side and gently squeezed his arm. "I'm glad. Everyone needs to live life to its fullest. And I can't imagine you *not* being a dad one day. I've seen you with your students. I suspect you'd be lost without them."

"I would be." He pushed off the railing as Lulu's boat came to a stop, reclaiming his spot as the little girl handed the ride operator two more quarters. "How about you? Are you, um, I mean, er, are you see—"

"Seeing someone?" She blushed as the words left her mouth, prayed they were the ones he was struggling to say.

He nodded, his cheeks sporting a slightly reddish hue.

"No." She flashed a thumbs-up at Lulu as the ride began again, the familiar lump making its way into her throat at the mere thought of Jeff. "I'm not seeing anyone. I want to focus on my job, be the best librarian I can be. Though now . . . with everything that's going on . . . I'm not sure if I'm going to lose my shot."

"You're not going to lose anything. The police will figure out what happened."

Tori stared, unseeingly, at the water as it rippled along the sides of each canoe. "That's going to be hard to do when they're only looking in one direction."

"One direction?" Milo pushed off the railing and turned to the side, leaned his hip along the wooden two-by-four.

"Yeah. *Mine*."

Before he had a chance to comment, Lulu was by their side, her tales of Indian chiefs and smoke rings filling the night air. "And I pretended I had a papoose on my back while I paddled."

Tori forced a smile to her lips as she rubbed the youngster's back. "I'm so glad you had fun, sweetie." She looked around at the other rides, pointed at a few. "Is there anything else you'd like to ride?"

The child shook her head.

"Hungry?" Milo asked.

Again, Lulu shook her head.

"You still have four whole dollars," Tori reminded.

"I know." She looked up at Tori then shifted her focus to her teacher. "Mr. Wentworth, would you walk over there with me?" Lulu pointed toward a souvenir stand on the other side of the canoe ride.

"I'm game, are you game, Miss Sinclair?"

"You're not here with anyone?" Tori asked.

He shook his head.

Lulu tugged on her teacher's arm. "I don't want Miss Sinclair to come with us."

Tori felt her heart drop.

The child rushed to explain. "It's a surprise."

A smile crept into Milo Wentworth's eyes. "I like surprises."

Solemnly, Lulu looked up at Tori. "We'll be right back. Don't go anywhere. Okay?"

"Okay." She bent quickly, planted a kiss on the top of Lulu's head, and then stepped back against the railing. "I'll be right here. I promise."

Seemingly satisfied, Lulu slipped her hand inside her teacher's and fairly pulled him across the lawn to a small white and blue checkerboard tent, disappearing with him behind the flaps of the makeshift shop.

"Seems things are working well between you and the elementary school teacher, Miss Sinclair."

Her head snapped up at the sound of her name, her stomach churning at the sight of the man who'd spoken it.

Investigator Daniel McGuire. In regular everyday clothes.

"I guess the threat Tiffany Ann Gilbert posed to your relationship is gone now."

"Excuse me—" She bit the words from her mouth, anxious to avoid a repeat of the glares and gossip she'd left on the other side of the fairgrounds. Steadying her voice, she looked around at the still-uninterested fairgoers before meeting the officer's gaze. "There is no relationship, Mr. McGuire."

"*Investigator* McGuire. And that's not what I was told." Stepping his legs apart, the officer folded his arms across his chest. "In fact, I have it on good authority your attraction started almost immediately upon your arrival in Sweet Briar. When Mr. Wentworth first came to the library with his students."

She opened her mouth to protest then closed it again. Who was filling his head with this stuff? Nina—no, she was in Tori's corner. Who else knew?

And then she remembered. Everyone knew. Georgina had teased her about Milo's flirtation at the sewing circle, had shared it with everyone there. Had she said something? Had Dixie Dunn?

Or had Leona?

Tori swallowed. "Assuming there was a relationship— which there isn't—why would I see Tiffany Ann as a threat?"

"Because you were *told* of her feelings for Milo Wentworth."

At the sewing circle.

Had Leona fallen for this man so quickly she'd sell Tori out?

"Then, Investigator McGuire, if you know that . . . you should also know that Milo Wentworth wasn't the slightest bit interested in Tiffany Ann Gilbert. So why on earth would I have seen her as a threat?"

Dropping his hands to his sides, he stepped forward, his voice lowering to a brusque whisper. "That's what I intend to find out."

"What do you intend to find out, Investigator?" Milo Wentworth appeared at her side, a bag-wielding Lulu in tow.

Daniel McGuire looked from Tori to Milo to Lulu and back again. *"The truth."*

"Then may I suggest you start looking?" Tori reached down, grasped Lulu's empty hand. "In the meantime, I have a fair to enjoy."

She knew the officer's eyes were watching her every move as she walked away, felt his attention perk as Milo jogged to catch up with them as they headed toward the picnic tables on the other side of the midway. But she didn't care. Investigator McGuire had his mind made up. As a result, he was incapable of seeing the truth.

It was up to her to find it and drop it in his lap with a bright red bow on top.

"Hey, wait up. What was going on back there?" Milo grabbed her arm and spun her around gently. "Are you okay?"

Before she could answer, Lulu tugged at her arm.

"I have a surprise for you, Miss Sinclair. Wanna see it?"

"Wha—oh, yeah, sure, sweetie." Squatting beside the little girl, Tori forced her mind to focus on something other than Daniel McGuire.

Slowly, Lulu reached inside the bag, her gaze bouncing between the contents and Tori's face. "I hope you like it."

The words were no sooner out of the child's mouth when a hard white object was placed in Tori's hand.

"Do you? Huh, do you?"

Tori stared down at the white porcelain spoon rest bearing the inscription Sweet Briar Heritage Day.

"I wanted to get you a bonnet—like the one Laura wore. It was yellow and had white lace on it and it was so pretty. But"—the child glanced down at her empty hand—"I didn't have enough money."

"You spent the rest of your money on-on me?" She heard the tears in her voice, felt them hovering in her eyes.

"I wanted you to have a souvenir. Something to help you remember tonight."

Margaret Louise did.

Summoning up every ounce of courage she could find, Tori rounded the corner of the Sweet Briar Ladies Society Sewing Circle booth and stopped. Bonnets and shirts, skirts and scarves, jackets and wall hangings, and a wide array of baby clothes hung from hooks and filled table upon table inside the white tent. Exquisite work created at the hands of some of Sweet Briar's most prominent citizens.

A group she wanted desperately to be a part of . . . *if* they believed in her the way Margaret Louise did. Unfortunately, the lone woman working inside the tent was one of two circle members surely counting down the days to her conviction. With glasses ready for clinking.

"Well look what the cat dragged in," Rose Winters said as she looked up from a bin of smocked dresses she was reorganizing. "I dare say, Victoria, you've looked better."

Not quite sure how to take the woman's gruffness, Tori simply nodded. "I've been better." She lifted one of the dresses from the bin and studied the smocking. "Rose, this is exquisite. Did *you* do this?"

"I most certainly did," the woman said, an undeniable lift surfacing in both her frail voice and body. "Have you ever tried?"

Carefully Tori turned the dress inside out, her gaze riveted on the detailed stitches. "No. I've wanted to—many times. I guess I'm just not confident enough in my ability yet."

Rose waved her long bony hand in the air. "Nonsense, child. I've seen your work, your great-grandmother taught you well."

Tori closed her eyes at the mention of her great-grandmother, a woman who'd taught her so much about stitches and thread and . . . life. "I'm not sure I was always the best pupil but I sure treasured her lessons." She opened her eyes and turned the dress right side out. "I remember the excitement I'd feel when I saw the sewing box in her hand. Sometimes she'd just sew for herself and I'd sit quietly by her side, watching. And sometimes she'd take my hand and lead me to her sewing room—a tiny room off the back of her home that had a chair for her and a smaller one for me. The only things in that room were the chairs, a lamp, and a big window. Yet it was magical. Our time together *in* it was magical."

She folded the dress then placed it back in the bin, aware of Rose's eyes studying her every move. "I cherish every second of that time. I still wish I could go back and have just one more rainy afternoon with her."

"She's with you. Every time you sit in a chair and sew." Rose hunched slightly at the waist, a loud cough racking her body. When she straightened, she moved on to the hooks that held baby bonnets in assorted colors. "How are you holding up?"

Still stunned by the woman's gentle encouragement, Tori simply shrugged, her mind as far from the Tiffany Ann Gilbert issue as possible.

"You may be new and you may have robbed Dixie of a job but—"

"Rose, I had no idea your friend was removed to give me a job. I was under the assumption the head librarian spot was vacant. Please know that."

Rose smoothed her hand across several pale yellow bonnets before removing a white lacy one from a top hook. "It's hard when you get to our age . . . people think we're not up to task any longer. They instantly think younger means better."

Tori's shoulders slumped.

"But after your first circle meeting"—Rose retied the bonnet's strings and repositioned it on the hook—"and hearing your ideas for the children's room, I can't help but feel as if the library might benefit from a little freshness."

Was she hearing what she thought she was hearing? Was Rose Winters putting down her weapon?

"When I was teaching, it was fairly easy to get children interested in books. But today—with all the distractions these young people have—I think they need to be helped along. I think your room might just be able to do that." Rose stepped away from the hooks and shuffled over to a set of chairs arranged behind a table. Lowering herself into the first one, she pulled the flaps of her sweater tighter against her body. "Dixie can't see that. Not yet, anyway."

"Thank you, Rose." It was all she could trust her voice to say without cracking.

The woman patted the vacant chair, waited for Tori to join her. "How are the plans coming?"

"They're not." Tori plopped into the folding chair, placed the bag with Lulu's gift beside her feet. "My meeting with the board was cancelled because of Tiffany Ann's . . . death."

As soon as the words were out of her mouth she wished desperately she could recall them. Things were going so well with the elderly woman, why push it into unpleasant territory?

A soft clucking noise emerged from Rose's mouth, her head shaking from side to side in accompaniment. "I hope they figure out what happened to her soon. It won't bring her back but it will give Sweet Briar residents a person to blame."

"Oh they have one." She heard her voice crack, nibbled her lip inward to stop it from trembling.

Damn.

"They have the *wrong* one."

Tori stared at the older woman, her heart thumping inside her chest.

What was it about compassion and scraps of support that moved her to tears so quickly these days? Oh yeah—they were few and far between.

"How do you know?" she managed to ask between steadying inhales.

"Fresh ideas may come with youth but wisdom comes with age, Victoria." Rose reached up to the bridge of her nose and repositioned her glasses a hairbreadth. "Have you started on any costumes for the children's room yet?"

"I'd planned to start this weekend . . . before everything happened. Laura Ingalls was going to be my first. But"—she looked down at her hands, linking them inside one another—"I just can't concentrate. On the costume or my pillow or much of anything."

"You need to try. Let the sewing quiet your heart and your mind."

Tori heard herself gasp, felt her lower lip drop open. "My great-grandmother used to say that very same thing."

"Then your great-grandmother was a smart woman."

A group of women entered the tent, their gasps of pleasure at the hand-sewn clothes an unwelcome distraction. Twenty minutes earlier, Tori had been certain she knew where Rose stood on the murder gossip. And now she knew better.

Margaret Louise was right.

Rising to her feet alongside Rose, Tori touched the woman's arm gently. "Thank you, Rose. For everything."

The woman looked over her shoulder as she approached her customers. "I'll see you Monday night. At my home."

Sewing Circle.

Tori squirmed. "I'm not sure that's such a good idea."

"That was not a question, young lady. It was a statement. There *is* a difference."

It was amazing what a little moral support could do to one's mood. Suddenly the curious glances and covered-mouth conversations she passed on the grounds didn't hurt the way they had when she'd arrived.

Sure, they still stung, still made her aware of the task in front of her, but knowing Margaret Louise, Lulu, Milo, and Rose were in her corner made it all more bearable.

The key now was to harness that sense of hope and use it as the flame that ignited her sleuthing efforts. She didn't kill Tiffany Ann Gilbert. But someone did, someone who stood a good chance of slipping under the radar if she didn't step up to the plate.

First, she needed a starting place. A window into who Tiffany Ann was in order to stand a chance at deducing who might want to harm her.

Her knowledge was limited, a product of nothing but hearsay. The sources of that hearsay, however, seemed to be fairly reliable, if for no other reason than they'd known the victim her whole life. That kind of background information could surely hold a few gems of information, couldn't it?

Sidestepping a line of people gathered outside a fried dough stand, Tori made her way over to the roped-off section of parking lot on the east side of the square. Hot rods and classic cars were scattered across the blacktop, hoods raised, muscled bodies in ripped-sleeve shirts standing watch.

She may never have met Tiffany Ann Gilbert, may not have known all the paths the town sweetheart crossed, but she had one thing Investigator McGuire did not— knowledge of what it was like to be a young woman with aspirations. Which meant the muscled bodies that had been so appealing in high school had a tendency to stop looking like the be-all-that-ends-all once college rolled around. And if the ladies in the circle were right, one muscled body in particular had been merely a detour to what Tiffany Ann really wanted in life.

Milo Wentworth.

"Excuse me." Tori stopped beside an early model Mustang to address its fifty-something owner. "Would you happen to know where I could find Cooper Riley?"

"Coop? Yeah, sure, he's over there. Black ragtop Mustang." The man gently pushed off his car and spun around, pointed over the roof.

"Thank you."

She made her way around hordes of giggling teenagers and through throngs of car-obsessed men, her mind playing through the questions she wanted to ask. And the manner in which to ask them. She didn't know diddly about Cooper Riley, but she knew the type. They liked to talk. About their car and their conquests.

Despite the crowded lot, Cooper Riley stood alone, his backside resting against the passenger door, his arms folded across his chest, tanned muscles nearly bursting the seams of his shirt. A thatch of sandy-colored hair that swooped across his clear blue eyes did little to disguise the far-off look he sported.

"Cooper Riley?" She stopped about three feet from the car, her gaze soaking up everything about the man's stance.

Slowly, the young man brought his focus to her face, his gaze studying her every feature before slipping slowly down her body and back again. "Who's asking?"

She stepped forward, extended her hand. "Tori Sinclair."

If he'd heard the scuttlebutt surrounding her suspected association with his former girlfriend, he didn't let on. "Tori. That's a pretty name."

"Thanks." Gesturing toward the car, she backed up, forced her attention to focus on the lines of the car. "My brother used to have a Mustang like this, only he didn't take care of his way you obviously do."

A smile spread across his face as he pushed off the car.

"It's the only thing you can do with a car like this. It's a classic. And it demands to be treated with reverence."

She resisted the urge to roll her eyes. *Reverence?* Was he serious?

"Virtually every paycheck I make gets spent on her."

Her?

Tori's ears perked up. "Your girlfriend?" she prodded.

His smile disappeared. "I don't have a girlfriend."

"But you said, 'her.'"

"My car."

"Oh." Anxious not to miss the opening she'd glimpsed for one glorious second, Tori steered the conversation back in that direction. "I bet former girlfriends have been jealous of her."

Cooper shrugged. "Nah, my girlfriend loved my car. She got off on having me pick her up on a Friday night and drive her around in a car that got almost as many looks as she did."

"Pretty, huh?" Tori forced herself to appear more interested in the car than the conversation, hoped the tactic would keep him talking.

"Tiffany Ann? She was smokin' hot. Everyone in town knew it."

"I bet that made you proud." She winced as she waited to see whether he'd take issue with her wording, but he seemed completely unfazed, his words coming on the heels of her questions in a steady flow.

"Hell, yeah. Who wouldn't be? Everyone wanted her. Even that . . . that *teacher* creep."

Milo?

"Teacher creep?" she made herself ask.

Cooper's arms dropped from his chest, his hands balling into fists at his sides. "Yeah, some loser who spends his days blowing kids' noses and mopping up vomit. I mean, how smart do you have to be to teach third grade? As long as you know who the first president was and how to add and subtract . . . you can teach third grade. Hell, *I* could walk in the door on Monday and teach third grade if I wanted to."

Not likely.

She walked around the car, still pretending to be interested in it.

"So this teacher had a thing for your girlfriend?"

"Big-time. Tiffany Ann had this kissing booth at the Summer Queen festival and he tried to act like he didn't want to kiss her, but c'mon, what guy wouldn't?" Word by word, memory by memory, Cooper Riley retreated from the parking lot to some distant place littered with emotion. A place—if she was reading his hardened jaw and clenching fists correctly—that was ruled by anger.

But surely he knew his prized ex-girlfriend was dead, didn't he? So where was the disbelief? Where was the devastating sadness?

"Is it possible he wasn't interested?"

His head snapped up. "No!"

"Oh. I just thought . . . if he didn't want to kiss her . . . that maybe it was *her*—"

"No!" he repeated, his voice louder and more insistent. Heads turned in their direction.

Uh-oh.

Desperate to continue their conversation without the prying ears and contributing mouths of others, Tori clapped her hands softly and pointed inside the car. "You have a baby shoe hanging from the rearview mirror. Is that yours?"

Shoving his hands inside his jean pockets, he shook his head, his words less harsh as he answered. "Nah, that was Tiffany Ann's. When we started dating I asked her mom for something of hers I could hang in the car. She gave me one of her shoes."

"You really loved her, didn't you?"

Once again, Cooper Riley's gaze traveled into the distance, fixed on something only he could see. "Still do. She was going to be my wife."

Tori gulped so quickly it triggered a series of coughs that refused to subside long enough to talk.

Tiffany Ann Gilbert and Cooper Riley were supposed to get married? Her sewing buddies had neglected to mention that little fact—

"It's been mighty near eighteen months since she broke it off with him. Yet to hear him talk, they're not only still together but heading for the altar. Blasted fool."

Rose's comments from the last sewing circle flashed through her mind like a lightning bolt, stopping her coughing fit in its tracks.

This guy was delusional. Completely out of touch with reality.

But just how delusional was he? She had to know.

Inhaling deeply she straightened up, looked over the top of the car at Cooper Riley. "Were you afraid this teacher creep was going to ruin your plans?"

A burst of anger rolled across his face as he met her gaze head-on. "No way. She was destined to be mine. I mean look at me"—he turned his hands inward and gestured at himself—"you think she was going to be lulled away for long by some . . . some *old* guy who can recite the Pledge of Allegiance by memory?"

She snorted.

"Besides, there was no way in hell I was going to let anyone else have her." Cooper Riley slammed a closed fist on top of his car, his continued rant barely audible through clenched teeth. "Tiffany Ann was mine. *Mine!*"

If he realized how threatening he sounded, he didn't care. In fact, he was so wrapped up in his anger he barely noticed the elderly couple who approached his car with fond memories they were all too willing to share.

Shrugging her shoulders she bid a hasty farewell, grateful for the opportunity to slip into the crowd, alone with her thoughts. Cooper Riley was one angry young man. Angry and in denial.

Anyone listening to Tiffany Ann Gilbert's ex-boyfriend would be hard-pressed not to throw up a question mark where he was concerned. As infatuated as he'd obviously been with her, Tori suspected he'd been even more infatuated with what she represented—an enviable conquest and a visible trophy.

But as disturbing as his words were, it was his next to last statement that brought a chill to her soul.

"There was no way in hell I was going to let anyone else have her."

Murdering her would certainly accomplish that goal. . . .

"There you are! Why'd you disappear like that?"

She looked up, surprised to see Milo jogging through the rapidly decreasing crowd in her direction.

"I, uh—" She stopped, swallowed, started again. "I figured those were parents of your students and I knew I'd already caused some issues regarding the field trip on Friday. I didn't want to make matters worse." She tucked her hands into her pockets, Lulu's bag dangling from her wrist. "Besides, I needed to see Lulu and her grandmother off. They'd been so nice to invite me along tonight."

He hesitated a moment then briefly touched her back, guiding her toward the food booths in the center of the town square. "Are you glad you came?"

"I am." And she meant it. In less than four hours she'd felt her confidence soar. She had more people in her corner than she realized and it felt good. Really good.

Even better, she couldn't help but feel as if she was onto something where Tiffany Ann's murder was concerned. Whether Cooper was responsible or not remained to be seen. But it was a starting place. Something she desperately needed.

"You okay?" Milo asked, his eyebrows lifting slightly.

"I'm fine. Just a little distracted."

They walked for a few moments, each lost in their own thoughts, the smell of barbecue and fair treats guiding them forward. "Hungry?" he asked.

"No. I'm too wound up to eat."

"A good wound up or a bad wound up?"

She thought for a moment. "A good wound up."

"I'm glad." He stopped, turned toward her. "Do you like coffee?"

"I do. Very much. Why? Do they have a coffee booth?" She looked around, spotted just about every food and drink known to mankind except coffee.

He shook his head. "I was thinking more along the lines of getting a cup together another . . . um . . . time."

Surprised, she met his gaze, saw the brief color that warmed his cheeks. "Sure."

"Tomorrow night?" he asked quickly.

Why not? After her conversation with Cooper Riley she couldn't help but have a few questions for Milo Wentworth as well.

"That sounds nice. Is there a coffee shop in town?"

"Debbie's Bakery."

"Oh, right. I've been wanting to check that out. Debbie is in my sewing circle."

"Good. Then I'll pick you up and we can go there." A slow smile appeared at the corners of his mouth, crept slowly across his face.

"That's per—" She stopped. What was she doing? Word of Milo Wentworth picking her up at home was sure to fuel Investigator McGuire's fire all the more. "Actually, can we just meet there? At maybe seven?"

A momentary display of disappointment chased the teacher's smile from his face. "I'd be happy to pick you up."

She held up her hand, her answer gentle but firm. "Really. I think it would be best for everyone if I just met you there."

He opened his mouth in what appeared to be an argument and then shut it again. "Okay. Debbie's Bakery. Tomorrow evening. Seven o'clock." The smile from earlier reappeared on his face, an undeniable happiness that made her squirm ever so slightly.

"I better head home. It's been a long day." She stepped back, her hand sliding out of her pocket long enough to wave. "It was nice seeing you tonight, Milo."

"You, too, Tori. You, too." He toed a pebble off the ground, a cloud of dust chasing it into the air as she turned and headed toward the parking lot designated for fairgoers. "Oh, hey, Tori?"

She turned back. "Yes?"

"You-you don't make matters worse."

Chapter 12

For as long as she could remember, she'd always viewed a trip to the bakery as something akin to nirvana. The kind of place where one's choices were relatively painless—brownies with or without nuts, chocolate or vanilla frosted cakes, chocolate chip or macadamia nut cookies, chocolate or strawberry mousses—and the payoff was nothing short of mind-blowing.

Yet there was something about her impending meeting with Milo Wentworth that made her first visit to Debbie's Bakery a little less inviting. It wasn't that the desserts looked less scrumptious than they had in Chicago or that the shop wasn't decorated in an enticing manner. They did and it was. It was simply a matter of nerves winning out over the urge to eat chocolate—a rarity in Tori's life, and one that didn't go unnoticed.

"Can I help you, ma'am?" A young girl in her late teens skidded to a stop behind the glass case Tori was inspecting and flashed a friendly smile. "The Long Johns are buy one get one free this evening. Though the black and white cookies are extra yummy today."

"Uhhhh, I'm not sure. It all looks so good." She meant it, she really did. Tori just didn't have the heart to tell the girl the items she'd pointed out only served to make her stomach churn harder.

"Take your time. There's a lot to choose from." The girl reached behind her neck and tightened the straps of her apron. "I've never seen you in here before. Are you visiting?"

"Mmmm, something like that, I guess." She knew she was being evasive, but she didn't care. She wanted to be somewhere—even for just a little while—where people didn't look at her with either curiosity or controlled rage. She wanted to just *be*.

"Sweet Briar is a nice town. Calm. Peaceful. Or"—the girl looked toward a closed door at the far end of where she stood and lowered her voice to a near whisper—"or at least it was until four days ago."

So much for just being.

Tori leaned closer to the case, made a show of examining each and every item that graced the glass shelves inside.

"This girl, Tiffany Ann, she's one of our regulars. Or, at least, a regular when she's not in school. She shows up every morning between ten thirty and eleven like clockwork and gets a vanilla latte. It's such a habit we start making her drink before she ever even reaches the register." The girl looked toward the door once again, her voice dropping even lower. "Sometimes she takes it and sits right there"—she pointed to a stool on the other side of Tori—"and sometimes she gets it to go . . . like she did *that* day."

That day? Tori straightened up, her ears far more interested in the sudden conversation than her eyes were in anything behind the glass case.

Seemingly aware of the fact she had Tori's full attention, the girl babbled on, her eyes big and luminous in the fluorescent overhead lighting. "Tiffany Ann is a belle through and through."

"A belle?" Tori asked.

"A southern belle. All prim and proper and very into how she looks." The girl stepped back, motioned to her floured apron. "Unlike me, who doesn't look in a mirror more 'n once a day . . . as you can probably tell, huh?"

Tori smiled. "You look fine. A lot better than I would if I was baking desserts and working a register all day."

"Thanks." Scooting out from behind the counter, the clerk leaned against the corner of the glass case, stealing a peek at the door behind the counter from time to time. "Weird thing is . . . *that* day . . . Tiffany Ann wasn't all belled up."

A white linen dress with turquoise-colored sandals wasn't belled up?

She bit her lip, waited for the girl to continue.

"I mean, sure, she looked pretty . . . Tiffany Ann makes— I mean—*made* everyone around her look like a total bow-wow . . . but *that* day she seemed off. Her dress wasn't pressed within an inch of its life, a few hairs were out of place . . . you know, that sorta thing."

"Normal human things?" Tori asked, then regretted her words. Sometimes even the smallest comment could take a conversation in a different direction. And, judging by the time on the clock behind the counter, Milo was due any moment.

"*Abnormal* Tiffany Ann things." The girl rested more of her weight against the case as her occasional glances toward the door grew few and far between. "She was kinda strange . . . up and down, up and down."

"What do you mean?"

"One minute she was real jumpy, the next she seemed almost subdued. Then, just as a few new customers came into the shop, she got real jumpy again. Real impatient . . . like I couldn't get her order made fast enough. When I set it down beside the register she hurled her money at me and took off in a sprint—nearly knocked the mayor's husband off his feet. As it was, she made him drop his wallet and stuff fell out everywhere."

Tori looked again at the clock, prayed Milo would get detained along the way by an overfriendly dog or a handful of students out for a Sunday night stroll. "Any chance she was on drugs?"

The girl's mouth dropped open. "Tiffany Ann? On drugs? Uh—no. She was way too clean, way too perfect." The girl eyed her closely. "If you hadn't already told me you were new to the area, I'd have known all on my own based on that one question. Even without your funny accent."

Funny accent?

"Okay, so then what happened?" Tori prompted.

"Wiiiittthhh . . ."

"With *Tiffany Ann*. Bumping into the mayor's husband."

"Oh. Yeah. Okay. Anyway, I was so busy picking his money and credit cards up off the floor I didn't even notice she'd left her coffee behind. By the time the next customer handed it to me, Tiffany Ann was already out the door and halfway across the parking lot. Debbie went running after her." The girl shoved her hands into her apron pocket and wandered back behind the register. "Me? I wouldn't have bothered bringing it out to her. That one was just a little too pampered for her own good."

A jingle from the other side of the bakery made them both look up, the customer it ushered in bringing an added flutter to Tori's stomach.

Milo.

Waving a quick hand at the schoolteacher, she looked back at the young salesclerk. "By the way, I'm Tori."

"I'm Emma. Emma Adams." The girl's face broke out

into a mischievous smile as she looked from Tori to Milo and back again. Lowering her voice to the level it had been when she first started talking, she added, "He's way cute."

Milo?

She spun around, mentally prayed he didn't hear the salesclerk. It wasn't that it wasn't true—Milo Wentworth was most definitely a good-looking man. He was tall and lanky, his arms sporting just enough muscle to make a woman feel safe. His hair was just long enough to explore with gentle fingers. His eyes had a wonderful ability to smile before his lips did. . . .

Not that she'd noticed or anything.

The last thing she needed was a man in her life. Especially one that gave the local police some bizarre motive in the death of Tiffany Ann Gilbert.

"I'm sorry I'm late. I got waylaid by Jonathan's parents." Milo approached the counter, gave Tori's arm a brief and gentle squeeze. "Were you waiting long?"

"Not—"

The door Emma had been watching throughout their conversation opened, and out came Debbie holding a small tray of miniature pudding pies. "Emma, we're just going to set out a few of these now and—" The shop owner stopped, a slightly pink hue coloring her cheeks. "I'm sorry, I didn't realize we had customers. Victoria . . . Mr. Wentworth . . . how are you this evening?"

"Fine. How are you, Debbie?" Tori clasped her hands inside one another, unsure of how to read Debbie's reaction to seeing her.

Debbie waved her free hand in the air, her long ponytail bobbing with the sudden movement. "Busy. It's my evening with the bakery's books, which means I've been staring at numbers for the past two hours. I wouldn't be surprised if I'm cross-eyed."

Tori leaned forward, made a point of studying the bakery owner's face with all the drama she could muster. "Nope. No crossed eyes yet."

Debbie laughed, a genuine happy laugh. "Thank heaven for small favors." The woman set the tray down on a back counter and began shuttling the miniature pies between the counter and glass case. "Let me get this stuff taken care of and then I'll stop by your table and visit for a little bit. That is if"—she looked from Tori to Milo and back again—"you're staying."

"We are," Milo answered. As Debbie focused on her task, he turned his attention back on Tori. "You were saying . . . ?"

"Um, I don't remember." Tori shrugged an apology.

"About my keeping you waiting . . ."

"Oh, that's right. You didn't." She looked in Debbie's direction then winked at Emma. "I only beat you by a few seconds and it gave Emma a chance to show me some of the day's specials. She's a very good salesperson."

Emma's head dropped but not before Tori caught the pleased smile that spread across her face.

"In fact, after talking to her, I think I'm leaning toward a black and white cookie. They look pretty yummy."

Milo nodded and pulled his wallet from his back pocket. "Two black and white cookies, please."

Tori shot her hand out. "No, please. I can get mine."

"Women don't pay for dates. Not in the south they don't."

A date?

Uh-oh.

"But I—"

"Don't argue, Victoria."

Fantastic. Now Debbie was under the impression it was a date as well.

"What would you like to drink?" Milo asked as he extracted a crisp twenty-dollar bill from his wallet. "They have flavored coffees and teas."

And deadly vanilla lattes.

She scanned the menu above Emma's head. "I'd love a small hot chocolate. With just a little whipped cream if you could."

"You've got it." Emma took Milo's money, counted back his change, and then pointed to a table by the windows. "I'll bring it out to you in just a second."

Milo led the way to one of two turretlike alcoves that overlooked a tiny park on the northern edge of the town's square. The tables in this section of the bakery were round with wiry legs, the chairs cushioned and wire-backed. The comfortable chairs and private feel of the room invited patrons to linger over coffee and a piece of chocolate cake as they read the paper or to share a friend's birthday over cupcakes or to enjoy a date—

She met Milo's gaze as she sat down, swallowed over the dryness that enveloped her mouth.

"I, uh—" She dropped her hands to her lap and looked out the window, her eyes searching for something, anything, her mouth could talk about. She skimmed the park grounds in search of a familiar child to discuss or a now-familiar library patron she could reference, but there was nothing. Nothing except emptiness. . . .

"I can't believe the fair was less than twenty-four hours ago." She swept her hand through her hair before returning it to her lap. "There's not a single ride still up, or a booth that hasn't been taken down, or even a piece of litter to be seen."

"Georgina is a stickler for cleanliness and order." Milo rested his elbows on the edge of the table and leaned forward. "And, come to think of it, she's the same about safety."

"I know." Tori felt her shoulders begin to relax as she

focused on a topic she could address—one that had nothing to do with whether this was a meeting or a date. "She was after me the very first night we met about getting a bulb into my porch light."

"I could do that for you," Milo offered quickly, his eyebrows furrowed.

She pulled her hands from her lap and set them on the table. "I can do it. In fact I have . . . many, many times."

"You've only been here a few weeks, right? They shouldn't be burning out that quickly unless maybe you've got a bad fuse. I'd certainly be happy to take a look."

She shook her head softly. "I wish it were that simple. The bulbs work just fine. Until they disappear."

"I don't understand." Milo leaned back as Emma set their cookies and drinks on the table.

"Thanks, Emma. It looks great." Despite her still unsettled stomach, Tori placed a napkin on her lap and broke off a bite of cookie as the girl walked away. "I put the bulb in at night and by morning—and sometimes even sooner—it's gone."

Milo stopped drinking mid-sip. "Gone? As in no bulb?"

"No bulb. It's the strangest thing." She popped the piece of cookie into her mouth then took a quick sip of her hot chocolate, retrieving her napkin in order to wipe whipped cream off her nose. "If I let myself believe all the talk around here about me, I might actually start to think I'm losing it, too. But I know I'm not . . . so there must be another reason for the bulbs disappearing."

He set his cup down. "Teenagers?"

"Maybe. Or maybe it's just someone who hates me."

"I can't imagine that," he said, his voice softening.

She shrugged. "Before I came here, I couldn't either. But, honestly, disappearing bulbs are the least of my worries these days. Does it make me angry? Sure. Do I want to wring someone's neck every time I walk outside and another one is missing? Absolutely. But those emotions tend to fade away rather quickly when they're up against the kind that come with being the town's favorite murder suspect."

Milo reached across the table and patted her hand. "C'mon. The talk will die down."

"I hope you're right." She wrapped her hand through the handle of the ceramic bakery mug and inhaled slowly, deliberately. "The only way I want my name coming into conversations around town is in regards to feedback— positive feedback—on the children's room. Assuming it gets approved, of course."

"Tell me about it." Milo pushed his chair from the table by a few inches then leaned against the wire back, brought his right ankle to rest across his left knee.

"Tell you about what?"

"The children's room. The way you envision it looking when it's all done."

Any remaining tension or apprehension she felt was magically gone as she took him through her proposal one step at a time. She told him about the various storybook scenes she wanted to paint on the walls, the beanbag chairs that would be scattered throughout the room, the small wooden stage she intended to construct in the corner of the room.

As she spoke, she felt herself coming to life for the first time since finding Tiffany's body, felt the excitement and eagerness that had propelled her to leave Chicago and take on the Sweet Briar librarian job. She knew her hands were moving as she spoke, knew her mouth was stretched into the kind of smile she hadn't smiled in days. And it felt good. Really good.

"The room itself is perfect. Sure, I wish it could be even bigger, but it will serve its purpose just fine the way that it is. The windows aren't large but that's okay, too. What they don't provide the room in terms of natural light, a few fluorescent lights will." Tori took another bite of her cookie, savored the cakelike treat with the perfect mixture of chocolate and vanilla frosting. "The only thing it was being used for was the annual book fair storage. Problem was, more than 50 percent of the donated books were in awful condition. The ones that weren't fit just fine in the basement."

"You culled through all of the boxes yourself?" Milo dropped his foot to the ground and leaned forward. "They had to be heavy, especially if they were filled with books."

"Oh they were heavy alright. My arms are still sore even now." She squeezed her upper arm and then reached for her cookie once again. "The day of the meeting . . . the day I found Tiffany Ann . . . I did nothing that entire day other than sort through old books, tossing out the bad and keeping the good. I couldn't have done it without Nina. She kept everything running smoothly with the patrons and I just kept hauling books out of the room."

"I'm surprised there were that many." Milo smiled at the disappearing cookie on her plate and pushed his own in her direction. "Have some of mine."

Tori held up her hand. "No thank you. One was enough." But even as the words left her mouth she found her hand tentatively reaching across the table and breaking a small piece of Milo's cookie as she continued talking. "I was, too. Nina and I made quite a few jokes that day about a growing rabbit population."

Milo's brows furrowed just a little. "I don't follow."

"As soon as I'd get through a box and take its contents to either the Dumpster or the basement, another one would appear by the time I got back."

"Were they filled with lightbulbs by any chance?" he asked, with a playful lilt to his voice.

"Lightbulbs?" She looked at Milo, recalled their conversation thus far. "Ohhhh, I get it." She pushed a strand of hair behind her ear and laughed. "Now *that* would have been welcome. Though Mr. Duncan over at the hardware store probably wouldn't agree. I think I'm single-handedly keeping that man in business."

Tiny lines beside Milo's eyes deepened as he laughed. "I'm sure Morton appreciates your support." She watched as he looked down at his plate then back up at her. "So, was it as yummy as it looked?"

"I, uh"—she swallowed the last nibble of cookie—"well, truthfully? Yes, it—I mean—*they* were every bit as yummy as I thought they'd be." Tori stood and gestured toward the glass case. "But you need to try one of your own. Otherwise you'll never know what you're missing."

"I think I'm okay. Besides, watching you enjoy mine was ten times better."

"Wait and try one. Then you can decide whether that's true or not." Tori made her way over to the counter, zig-zagging around various tables and chairs. She knew Milo was watching, she could feel his eyes on her body as she moved, but she didn't mind. Just because she wasn't ready to date didn't mean she didn't get a charge out of knowing men might be interested. Especially someone as sweet as Milo Wentworth.

"Everything okay with the cookies and drinks?" Emma asked as she looked up from her place behind the counter.

"Everything was wonderful. Too wonderful in fact." Tori peered inside the glass case, noted the plate of black and white cookies that remained.

"*Too* wonderful?"

Shrugging, Tori nodded and pointed at the plate. "That's why we need one more."

Emma laughed. "Just one?"

"Okay . . . two. But why don't you put the second one in a to-go bag so I'm not tempted."

The girl reached inside the case and removed two cookies from the plate. "I don't think you have to worry about temptation. I'd kill to be as skinny as you are."

"A condition that is sure to change if I come in here again." Tori shadowed the girl over to the register, the counter and cases between them as they walked. "So how much do I owe you?"

"Three dollars even." Emma set the plated cookie on the overhang beside the register and rolled down the top of a little white bag that contained the second treat. "Here you go."

"Thanks." Tori handed a five-dollar bill to Emma as her gaze skimmed the pegboard wall behind the clerk. Ignoring her own reflection in the small rectangular mirror in the center of the board, she focused, instead, on the assorted handwritten notes from satisfied customers, each one written on real stationery. Scattered across the board were a handful of snapshots, faces she recalled from photographs around Debbie's home. But it was one just beneath the mirror that claimed her attention, the black Mustang it depicted more than a little familiar—

Was that Cooper Riley?

Emma followed Tori's line of vision, confusion etching her brow. "Is something wrong?"

Shaking her head she grasped the plate with one hand, the bag with the other. "No. Nothing's wrong. I just recognize that guy."

Emma turned, a flush rising up her neck. "Isn't he adorable?"

"You put that there?" Tori asked.

"I sure did. First thing Wednesday when I came in."

Wednesday?

"Is he—is he a friend of yours?" Tori felt her body stiffen as her thoughts traveled back to a topic she'd almost managed to forget while talking to Milo.

Emma's face lit like the proverbial Christmas tree. "He's more than that. I think." She stopped to release a nervous giggle then continued on, her voice bordering on breathless. "I think now we actually have a chance to be something."

"Now?"

The girl's smile slipped just a little as she looked toward the door that separated her from her boss. Leaning forward across the register she spoke as quietly as possible. "Now that Tiffany Ann is—well, you know. *Gone*."

Nothing like cutting to the chase.

"Well, I better get back to my table. Thanks for the cookies."

"My pleasure."

As Tori made her way back to Milo's table, she couldn't help but mentally review everything she'd learned over the past twenty-four hours. Information that was slowly beginning to form the outer edges of the picture she needed in order to find Tiffany's killer.

By all accounts among the sewing circle, Tiffany Ann Gilbert was long past her relationship with Cooper Riley. Cooper Riley, on the other hand, was still quite infatuated with Tiffany Ann—to the point of being rather out of touch with reality. And now there was Emma Adams. A girl who obviously had a thing for Tiffany's ex. A girl who—by her own words—wasn't as enamored with the town sweetheart as everyone else seemed to be.

Was Cooper Riley truly interested in Emma Adams or was Emma seeing something that didn't exist?

It was a question that would have been worth investigating if she hadn't already talked to Cooper. But she had. And no matter what Emma believed to be the case, Cooper Riley had eyes for only one woman.

Tiffany Ann Gilbert.

So did that make Emma as delusional in her view of her relationship with Cooper as Cooper was in his with Tiffany Ann?

It certainly seemed that way.

"I thought you disappeared into some giant well of cookies never to be seen again." Milo stood as she approached the table, reaching for the plate she carried with one hand and her chair with the other.

Then again, if Tiffany Ann was a nonissue that would certainly make Cooper a more viable option. . . .

"Tori?"

But Emma was sweet. Sweet people didn't poison a person's coffee to get them out of the picture.

Or did they?

Tori looked back over her shoulder, studied the girl behind the counter as she mooned over the picture that had claimed Tori's attention not two minutes earlier. All gossip-and-dessert camaraderie aside, there was no denying the fact the salesclerk certainly had the means to commit such a crime.

Not only was she aware of when Tiffany Ann came into the bakery, she also made the coffee that Tiffany Ann had been drinking prior to her death. The same coffee that was poisoned.

"Tori? You okay?"

"Huh? What?" She turned back to the table, Milo's words an unwelcome break in her train of thought. "I'm sorry, what did you say?"

"I asked if you're okay." He motioned to the chair with his head. "You're a million miles away right now, aren't you?"

She stole another peek at Emma, her stomach tightening once again.

"Another cookie?" he prompted.

"No." *I'm not sure it would stay down.* She pushed the bag to the side of the table and rested her chin atop linked hands. "Can I ask you a question? It's kind of personal."

Milo lifted his cookie to his mouth only to set it back down again, untouched. "Okay."

"Were you aware of Tiffany Ann's feelings for you?" It was a question she'd been dying to ask ever since her conversation with Cooper the night before, yet she'd hesitated for fear of putting Milo on the spot in the same way Investigator McGuire had done to her. But now, after everything she'd learned tonight, she couldn't ignore it any longer.

"Wow. Nothing like sticking me with a big one, huh?" Pushing his plate to the side, Milo leaned back once again, his feet remaining on the floor as his hands came together to rest against the back of his head. "Hmmm. Okay. Well, I knew she had a crush on me. I'd be an idiot if I didn't. The whole town of Sweet Briar knew."

She nodded, her attention fully focused on the man seated across from her, the handsome and sweet man who'd been nothing but welcoming and encouraging since the day they met.

What was she doing?

"Wait. I shouldn't have asked that. It was out of line." She waved her hands in front of her, then dropped her face into them. "Can you forgive me?"

He pulled his hands back down, placed them on the table just inches from her elbows. "There's nothing to forgive. You've had a lot of questions thrown at you where this girl was concerned and you're curious. I get that."

"You do?"

"I do." He scooted his hands forward, closing the gap between them and her elbows to give them a gentle and reassuring squeeze. "Rumor is Tiffany Ann had grown restless with her life—with the reputation she'd earned for crying wolf one too many times, with her choice in men, with her predictable life. She loved Sweet Briar but she wanted to do more than was expect—"

"I'm finally done," Debbie interrupted as she appeared beside their table, chair in hand. "The week's numbers match up, inventory is counted, and all vendor orders have been placed. All I've got left to do is bake. Which I will start around four."

Mouthing an apology to Milo, Tori turned and smiled at the bakery's owner. "Four? As in the morning?"

"That's right. I have to be ready with fresh breads and assorted breakfast pastries before we open at seven." Debbie plopped into the chair, stretching her long legs beneath the table between Milo and Tori. "It's been a long week. I haven't sewn a thing since last Monday. As God is my witness I wouldn't get a thing sewn if it wasn't for our circle meetings. It's the only time I sit in one place all week."

The woman tossed her ponytail off her shoulder and looked from Tori to Milo and back again, a curious smile tugging at the corners of her mouth. "You coming tomorrow night, Victoria?"

"I don't think so. I think it could be awkward. For everyone."

Milo looked a question at her, one Debbie made no bones about asking.

"Why on earth would it be awkward for everyone? I think you were starting to fit in quite nicely."

"I was."

"And now would be different because . . . oh, I get it." Debbie scooted her left hand around the table as she collected a few cookie crumbs and pushed them into her other hand. "Look. No one in their right mind could possibly think you had anything to do with Tiffany Ann's death."

"My sentiments exactly," Milo chimed in.

Tori tilted her head just a little as she took in Debbie and Milo with one glance. "Someone is feeding stuff to the investigator. Stuff that was discussed at the meeting. Stuff he's trying to use to build a case against me."

"What kind of stuff?" Milo asked.

Debbie brushed her hands against each other, knocking

the collected crumbs to the ground. "Victoria, you need to understand that when someone is asked a direct question, they must answer. Fortunately, I've been able to dodge many of them. And with as much scrutiny as you're facing right now, I'm certainly not going to knock on Daniel McGuire's door to volunteer things."

Volunteer things? What was she saying?

"I don't understand. What kind of information do you have that you think would hurt me further?"

Debbie motioned to Emma then made a sweeping motion. Turning back to Tori, she lowered her voice so as not to be heard by the girl with the approaching broom. "Wednesday morning Tiffany Ann left here without her coffee."

"And?" Tori prompted, her stomach beginning to churn once again.

"I ran outside and gave it to her. She was edgy . . . very preoccupied. When I handed her the to-go cup I asked her about her plans for the day as a way to help calm her down a bit." The shop owner pointed to the sitting area on the other side of the bakery. "Emma, why don't you start over there."

Tori followed the salesclerk with her eyes as she made her way to the opposite side of the shop. "Okay. But I still don't see what that has to do with me. And information you don't want to volunteer."

"She said she was on her way to the library."

Tori gripped the edges of the table as Milo stared at her.

"Did she ever make it inside?" he asked.

"No."

"Are you sure she didn't make it inside?"

She stared at Milo, a lump lodging itself in her throat and making it hard to breathe. Why didn't he believe what she said? Why would he assume she was lying?

"No."

His hands reached across the table, tugged hers down with his own. "You said yourself you were going through boxes in the storage room that entire day. Isn't it possible she made it inside and you just didn't see her?"

"I guess, I just—"

"Who was manning the library?" Debbie asked.

"Nina was," Milo supplied for a speechless Tori.

"Maybe you need to talk to her." Debbie rose to her feet, patting Tori's shoulder as she stood. "But either way, we expect to see you tomorrow night, Victoria. You need to tell us what costumes you need for the children's room."

"Oh. Okay. Thanks." Tori forced a smile to her lips as she watched the mother of two gather her stuff from behind the counter, wave to her employee, and then disappear through the swinging doors that led to her office.

"You should go, Tori. You have every right to be there." Milo's finger grazed the underside of her chin as he redirected her focus back on him. "And Debbie is right, you need to talk to Nina. See what she has to say when you see her at work tomorrow."

"If Tiffany Ann had made it into the library that day, Nina would have told me. I know she would have. . . ."

And then she remembered. Nina's words echoing through her thoughts almost as surely as if she was sitting right there at the table with her and Milo.

"I guess . . . I guess I just wish I could have taken it away from her."

Tori gripped the edge of the table once again as the room began to spin.

Nina hadn't meant the tragedy itself. She'd meant the *coffee.*

Chapter 13

Rose Winter's home was by far the most modest of the bunch with its small one-story cottagelike exterior. Unlike Debbie's and Georgina's homes, this one had just two windows facing front and a narrow porch that failed to wrap around the sides. Nonetheless, it exuded an undeniable warmth and charm that made you long to close yourself up inside its walls with a good book or a pair of strong arms.

The walkway, bordered on both sides by freshly planted yellow and white mums, conveyed a welcoming feel almost as if it was pulling you inward, begging you to come and stay for a while. The small front porch boasted a pair of rocking chairs and a small wicker table perfect for a pitcher of lemonade and a couple of glasses.

"See? I told you, Victoria, having just one chair on your front porch doesn't work. You want to fit in—you get another chair. Or *two*." Margaret Louise huffed her way up the steps behind Tori, stopping long enough to lift the aluminum foil lid that covered the librarian's dish. "Are those miniature Black Forest tortes?"

"They most certainly are." Tori pulled the foil back even further to afford her friend a better look. "My great-grandmother used to make these for special occasions. Like holiday gatherings and birthday parties."

Leona's twin sister leaned even closer, inhaling the dessert's aroma like that of a fine wine. "You didn't use a boxed cake mix."

"Me? A boxed cake mix? You can't be serious." A laugh escaped her mouth as she leaned forward and hugged the woman. "Actually, I may have given in to temptation and taken the easy route if it weren't for the fact I'm trying to make a good impression."

"Store-bought whipped cream?"

"Nope. I made that from scratch, too."

Margaret Louise pursed her lips as she replaced the foil across the plate and straightened up. "Black Forest tortes . . . from scratch? You're in, Victoria."

"If only it was that simple." She folded the edges of the foil around the plate and shifted it to her other hand, the tote bag with her pillow and sewing box dangling from her wrist. "I don't think a homemade dessert is going to make everyone forget there's a murder suspect in their midst."

"It's a start." The woman tucked her arm inside Tori's and pulled her toward the door. "People who make Black Forest tortes for their fellow sewing circle members don't poison coffee."

"What about people who make coffee?" The second the words were out she regretted them. She'd vowed to herself on the way over she wasn't going to talk about Tiffany Ann's murder. If it came up, she'd deal with it then. But if it didn't, she'd count her blessings.

Margaret Louise pulled her hand from Rose's front door. "People who make coffee? What are you talking about, Victoria?"

"Can I tell you later?" Tori waved at Rose as the elderly woman approached the door. "I want to avoid the topic of Tiffany Ann as much as possible."

"As if that'll happen, bless your heart." Margaret Louise yanked the screen door open and stepped inside, Tori blinking in her wake.

She knew the woman was right. The likelihood of making it all the way through sewing circle without the biggest news story to ever hit Sweet Briar being discussed was wishful thinking.

Still, she couldn't help but wish for it anyway as she gazed up at a sky still too light for stars.

"I'm glad to see you listened, Victoria." Rose tugged the edges of her sweater tighter against her body as she backed up to let Tori pass.

"I am, too." She handed the plate to Rose and swept her hand toward the door. "Your front walkway is absolutely beautiful. I love the yellow mums, they're so cheerful."

"Thank you, Victoria." The elderly woman set the plate down on a nearby counter and took Tori by the arm. "I want you to see something."

As she walked with the woman down a small hallway off the kitchen, Tori couldn't help but marvel at the way the ice had begun to melt between them. The woman who'd studied her with such coolness at Debbie's home was emerging as one of her biggest supporters.

"This is my special room." Rose stopped as they reached a doorway halfway down on the left. "It's where I sit and sew."

Tori gasped as she took in the small room with little more than a cushioned wicker chair, a gooseneck lamp, and a large picture window that took up the entire back wall.

"Oh, Rose. This looks just like my great-grandmother's room."

Pleased, Rose rubbed Tori's lower arm with her cold fingers. "I suspected you'd think that after you described it to me the other night."

She nibbled her lower lip inward, resisted the urge to cry as hard as she could. "It's perfect, Rose. Just perfect."

Slowly the woman moved her head as close to Tori's ear as she could. When her mouth was mere inches away, she spoke. "You are welcome to sew here anytime you want. Especially those costumes for the dress-up trunk."

She blinked against the tears that refused to be kept back, her voice shaky. "Thank you, Rose."

And then the woman was gone, her tiny frame moving slowly back down the hallway from which they came, the ever growing number of voices pulling her back to her job as hostess. Tori followed, her thoughts traveling down a hallway she hadn't literally walked in years to a place she visited every single day.

"Victoria, *there* you are." Debbie appeared beside her right shoulder as she entered the kitchen, a few conversations stopping long enough to acknowledge her presence with a look if not a greeting. "Did you talk to Nina?"

Tori shook her head, dropping her voice to a level she hoped couldn't be heard by anyone else. "Duwayne called in first thing this morning. Nina has laryngitis. She did a little too much screaming at the fair Saturday night."

"Nina? Nina Morgan?" Debbie asked, her mock surprise a near perfect mimic of Tori's earlier that day.

She laughed. "I know. Can you believe it? But she must be good at it, because her booth apparently earned over five hundred dollars for their church."

Debbie stepped back a few feet and motioned Tori to follow her to the room where the circle would meet. "Okay, but you still need to talk to her."

"I will. As soon as she's back. If she can't talk a whole lot, I'll give her some paper and a pen."

"Good idea." Debbie glanced over her shoulder as they

neared the noisiest part of Rose's home. "By the way, I saw what you brought tonight. I want the recipe."

"I think Margaret Louise has dibs."

"Dibs?"

"Dibs . . . first crack at . . ."

Debbie's eyebrows raised.

"She wants the recipe as well." Tori bit back a laugh as Debbie finally nodded in understanding.

It never ceased to amaze her how different Sweet Briar was from anywhere she'd ever lived, especially Chicago. She hadn't moved more than fifteen hundred miles yet it felt, sometimes, as if she'd crossed oceans and continents to get from one to the other.

It also made her miss Leona all over again. The woman's desire to school Tori in southern ways the first few weeks was sorely needed. And truly missed.

At least by Tori anyway. Whether Leona had even batted an eye over the situation was anyone's guess.

Still, she was unprepared for the stiffened shoulders and tightened mouths that greeted her arrival in Rose's sunroom. Somehow, amid the unexpected show of support from Rose and Debbie, she'd let her guard down, assumed the rest of the circle knew she wasn't capable of murder as well. But she'd been wrong. One only had to see the looks that passed between Georgina, Leona, and Dixie to face that fact. Beatrice simply looked downward at the vest taking shape as the machine's needle sped along, her discomfort at the situation virtually impossible to miss.

"Victoria, I'm surprised to see you here." Georgina pulled her straw hat from her head and placed it on the floor beside her feet.

Rose pushed her way into the room, her hand grazing Tori's arm as she passed. "I *told* her to come."

A hint of betrayal shot across Dixie's face as she worked her lips into a tightly closed circle.

"Come, Victoria, sit here . . . by me." Rose slowly lowered herself onto a sofa covered in a bold floral pattern. "The light over here is quite good for detail work."

"Shouldn't you be at your home, where you can be watched?" Dixie finally asked.

"Where I can be watched? By whom?" Tori froze in her spot, her mind and body suddenly plagued by an overwhelming desire to bypass Rose's invitation in favor of a tear-drenched sprint back to her own house.

"The police."

"Daniel is on top of everything in this investigation," Leona piped up, her perfectly manicured hand draped across the base of her neck, a magazine poised on her lap in lieu of the more popular sewing basket or latest project. "You should see him work, he's so thorough."

"Thorough?" Tori spat. "You think Investigator McGuire is thorough?"

Leona's hand dropped to her lap as her voice grew indignant. "I most certainly do. He's working on this investigation around the clock."

"Is that why he's had time to stroll around in front of the library every day this week? Or why I've seen him at the hardware store and the market simply hanging out, chatting up the staff and various customers about the weather and politics?" Tori tugged her tote bag up her arm, gripping it against her shoulder. "I think maybe he should spend less time wandering and more time actually investigating. Maybe then he'd actually have half a chance of solving Tiffany's murder."

By the time she was done with her rant there wasn't a closed mouth in the room. Including her own. Only hers was draped open out of shock—at herself.

Georgina shifted in her seat, her hands clenching and unclenching the pair of slacks she'd pulled from her bag. Dixie's mouth, while open, still managed to be twisted. And Leona—

"Daniel is not wandering aimlessly. There's been a rea-

son you've seen him in every place you have." Leona
yanked open the cover of her magazine then stopped to
smooth the page with a gentle hand. "That man doesn't
have an aimless bone in his body."

"That little tidbit might well qualify for what the kids
refer to as"—Margaret Louise shot the index and middle
fingers on both hands into the air and wiggled them up
and down to indicate quotation marks—"too much information."

Mouths gaped open once again.

"I mean, really, Twin, do we need to hear about the aim
of this man's various body parts?" A mischievous grin lit
Margaret Louise's face as she dug her elbow into Debbie's side. "Get it? His *aim*?"

"I get it, Margaret Louise." Debbie ducked her beet red
face into her oversized canvas bag and pulled out the sign
she'd been working on at each of the past two circles.
"How about we focus on sewing for a little while, ladies?
Leave the whodunit solving to the authorities?"

"And to a pair of Nancy Drew types like Victoria and
myself."

All eyes moved from Tori to Margaret Louise and back
again.

"Nancy Drew types?" Georgina asked.

"That's right." Margaret Louise unrolled a piece of
brown thread from a spool, the length extending farther
and farther with each turn of her hand. "Since Investigator
McGuire has failed to look for the truth, Victoria and I
will. And we'll find it."

"That's why we have police: it's their job to solve the
case," Georgina said as she held a steadying hand against
Leona's magazine-holding hand. "Civilians getting involved will only slow the process."

"Investigator McGuire getting in *his own* way only
slows the process," Tori corrected.

"I find that offensive," Leona said, her cultured voice

causing everyone to sit a little taller. "Daniel is working night and day to solve this crime."

"It's not working. The more time he wastes focusing on Victoria, the more time he gives the real killer to get away." Margaret Louise raised the dark brown spool to her mouth and bit the foot-long piece of thread loose.

"I wouldn't do that if I were you," Rose offered from across the room, her hand still patting the empty spot on the sofa beside her own. "Do I need to open my mouth to remind you of what will happen if you keep that up?"

Tori looked a question at her newfound friend, torn between the desire to cut short the conversation at hand and the urge to plead her case.

Opening her mouth wide, Rose pointed at the missing corner of her top left tooth. "You need to use scissors to cut your thread, not your teeth."

"Biting off thread did that?" Tori ventured across the room and boldly claimed her spot beside Rose.

Take that, nonbelievers. . . .

"It most certainly did. Happened at a sewing circle about six months ago." Rose scooted over a few extra inches on the couch to give Tori ample room to work on her pillow.

"My great-grandmother used to bite her thread all the time." Tori pulled the pillow from her bag, aware of the envied glances it drew. "She never broke any of her teeth."

"That's because most threads now are polyester and they weren't back when your great-grandmother was sewing," Georgina said. She rolled a leg of the slacks inside out and held a miniature tape measure to the hem, shaking her right arm from time to time. "The polyester thread will wear a groove in your tooth over time. And eventually—*snap*."

Rose nodded, her finger tapping her tooth. "I considered getting it fixed but I just don't have the money. Besides, it's not like there are any men my age left to impress."

"I thought that same thing less than a year ago and look at me now," Georgina said as she gave her arm a quick shake before rolling up her tape measure and tossing it into her sewing box. "Thomas and I couldn't be happier. Unless maybe he didn't travel for work quite so much. But you can't question success, now can you?"

Tori didn't know quite how it had happened, but somehow Rose's tooth had managed to turn an evening of sewing into exactly what it was supposed to be—time to get caught up on sewing projects while engaging in a little good-natured conversation. And she was glad.

As hurtful as it was to see Leona support the same man who seemed hell-bent on destroying her reputation, Tori was grateful for the reprieve. It gave her a chance to cool down and provided yet another opportunity to show who she was to the group's members. To prove to them, somehow, that she was as far from a murderer as anyone they could ever find.

"What does Thomas do?" Tori asked in an attempt to set aside the swords for at least one evening.

Georgina beamed as she looked up from her hemming and shook her arm once again. "He's a salesman. He sells products designed to make senior citizens' lives easier. Walkers, wheelchairs, special beds, and those kinds of things. He has a very large territory that requires a good deal of traveling to places like Pine Grove and Washington Falls, though lately he's found plenty of untapped business in Ridge Cove."

"What on earth is wrong with your arm, Georgina?" Margaret Louise bellowed. "You look like you're shaking out a rectal thermometer."

"Margaret Louise!" Leona stated between closed lips. "Must you really be so-so crude?"

"Lighten up, Twin." Margaret Louise winked at her sister before looking back at Georgina.

"I've been signing a lot of paperwork for Thomas the

last week or so. He's compiling a few petitions to lobby for the rights of seniors on the state level and he thinks it would help their fight if they had some mayoral signatures. He's hoping my name will carry clout." The woman shook her arm once again before retrieving a needle from the tiny box in her lap. "But I have to say, I'm beginning to wonder how your Colby, bless his heart, can sign hundreds of books on any given day. Thirty papers nearly did me in. Thank heavens I didn't have to read them."

Debbie shrugged over her project, her eyebrows knitted together in concentration as she worked her turquoise thread in and out through her canvas-backed sign. "I think he's so glad to be out from behind a keyboard for months on end that signing his name on a book is no big deal. But even that gets tiring after a while, too."

"How many books has your husband written?" Tori asked as she bent over the tassel she was trying to attach at the bottom of the pillow's triangular flap.

"Four. The first two were about getting his feet wet. The next two propelled him further up the ladder. The newest one he's working on—when he can find some quiet time between the kids' hectic schedules and my crazy hours at the bakery—might be *the* one. You know, the *big one*. At least that's what his agent is saying. She thinks this could be the one that gets him known nationally." Debbie looked up from her sign long enough to exhale a piece of hair away from her eyes. "That is, if he finishes it."

"He will. Colby is bound and determined to write, you know that. It's in his blood. Like baking is for you and me." Margaret Louise fussed with the lampshade beside her chair in an attempt to get as much light as possible before tackling the hole in Jake Junior's brown church slacks. "As for feeling guilty about your schedule at the bakery . . . don't. You're allowed to pursue dreams, too."

Tori peeked at Margaret Louise across the room, a smile tugging at her lips at the sight of the more-than-a-little plump woman. She'd liked Margaret Louise the very first night they met—once she'd come to realize the woman's outspoken nature meant no malice. But her fondness for the woman had increased tenfold in the two weeks since, a fact that was as much about who she was as a grandmother and a person as it was her steadfast belief in Tori's innocence and her desire to help prove it to everyone else.

She only wished the woman's twin sister had been as steadfast. Sneaking a look at Leona, Tori felt her smile disappearing. They'd gotten along so well. And then— boom—she'd been cast aside for a man who looked good in a uniform.

Women.

Why was it that the female gender was so quick to cast each other aside for the sake of a man?

"I hear you and Milo Wentworth were on a date last night," Dixie pried, her tone more than a little bitter.

Tori met Debbie's gaze across their projects. "Did you—"

The woman vigorously shook her head.

"How did you know?" But even as she posed the question, she knew. She knew without the knowing glances the former librarian exchanged with the mayor and Leona.

Investigator McGuire.

Leona was right. The officer wasn't wandering aimlessly around town. He was following her. Everywhere she went.

"He's a very nice-looking young man," Rose offered, her attempts at preventing a disagreement thinly disguised by her honest observation. "I'd go on a date with him, too."

"As Tiffany Ann would have." Georgina cut the end of her hemline with a tiny pair of scissors and continued, "Had she known, she'd have been crushed. Though Cooper Riley would have been fixin' to celebrate."

"He sure was all tore up about Tiffany Ann not coming back to him. He was so sure she would once she graduated." Debbie turned her sign over and raised it up for all to see. "I'm gonna put this in the dining area, closest to the turret on the left."

"Perfect," said Rose.

"Pretty as a picture," Margaret Louise echoed. "Hmmm. *Live. Love. Eat Baked Goods* . . . couldn't think of a better sentiment for the bakery if I tried."

"The last letter is a wee bit crooked," Dixie offered.

Tori shook her head. Any sympathy she'd had for Dixie regarding her forced retirement from the library was long gone. No one came by that kind of meanness by way of one slight. "I think it's just what that wall needs, Debbie, and it's going to look great."

"Are you sure? Should I redo the last letter?"

"No. It looks wonderful." Tori shot a defiant look in Dixie's direction before focusing on Debbie once again. "Does Cooper have much of a temper?"

"Young Cooper Riley has but two speeds. Lazy and spittin' mad." Georgina rolled up the other pant leg and held it against her tape measure. "Rose, do you remember that time at the school when Cooper's parents had to be called in because he'd tossed a classmate into the trash can for looking at him cross-eyed?"

Rose nodded as a coughlike laugh shook the couch. "I sure do. I was still teaching the kindergarten class and Cooper was in seventh—no, eighth grade. He was always getting in scraps. Mostly with anyone who dared look at his Tiffany Ann."

"They dated that long ago?" Tori asked.

"They didn't start dating until high school. But that didn't stop him from shadowing her every move for years before that," Rose explained. "Once high school rolled around she fell for the same thing all high school girls fall for—a cool car and a body that's finally begun to shed its baby fat. And he created a distraction until she was old enough to be with Milo."

"True. But Tiffany Ann was always hankering to go somewhere," Debbie interjected.

"She wanted to leave Sweet Briar?" Tori knotted the last thread into place and peered down at her completed pillow, a familiar sense of accomplishment spreading through her body.

"No. Never. Tiffany Ann loved this town. She just wanted to be one of the ones who made something of themselves rather than one of the ones who simply existed. She wanted to earn Milo's attention as a woman with goals. A little girl who'd finally grown up." Debbie stood and crossed the room to see Tori's pillow up close. "You did a great job on that. Want to make one for my house?"

"After I make all the costumes for the dress-up trunk, I'd be happy to make you one." Tori handed the pillow to Rose, watched as the elderly woman turned the finished product over and over in her frail hands.

"Beautiful work, Victoria."

"Thank you, Rose."

"Are you still planning on asking the board for permission to turn the storage room into a children's room?" Leona asked, her head bent forward so she could look at Tori over her glasses.

"Absolutely. I make my presentation on Wednesday night."

"Wednesday night?" Dixie asked quickly.

"Wednesday night," Tori repeated as she glanced at her wristwatch. "Which reminds me, I better start heading out. I've got lots to do over the next two days to make my pitch as persuasive as possible."

She pulled her tote bag onto her lap and opened it, placing her sewing tools and pillow inside. "Let me know how you like the tortes."

"I'll walk you out," Rose said as she pulled a plain

brown paper-wrapped package from underneath the couch and struggled to her feet beside Tori.

She placed a hand on the woman's sweater-clad wrist. "It's okay, Rose. I can show myself out."

"*That* wasn't a question either, Victoria," the woman mumbled beneath her breath so only Tori could hear. Though judging by the near tangible pop-up bubble above Leona's head, Rose's mumbling was unsuccessful. Only *this* time, Tori didn't need the woman's whispered coaching to learn her latest lesson on the ways of the south.

Lesson number four—sentences that sound like questions are usually, in fact, statements.

Debbie jumped up from her reclaimed spot and offered Tori a quick but supportive hug. "I'm glad you came."

"Thank you, Debbie. So am I."

And she was. For the most part. Sure, she would have preferred to have everyone in her corner where Tiffany Ann's murder was concerned, but she'd take the three she had.

"Don't forget to talk to Nina."

"I won't." She squeezed Debbie's hand and then turned to Margaret Louise. "If you're not doing anything Wednesday evening I'd sure love to have you in the audience. I think I could use the moral support."

"And I'd be all-fired-up happy to be there. I'll be sure 'n get supper on the table early that night so I don't miss a minute."

"Thank you, Margaret Louise."

"I'll be there, too," Rose offered after all the good-byes had been exchanged and they were heading toward the front door. "Your children's room is the best idea I've heard in a long time and it would be a fool thing if the board didn't agree."

"I hope you're ri—" Tori looked down at her hands as Rose pushed the brown package into them. "What's this?" she asked as her fingers sunk into the softness of the bundle. "Chocolate?"

"Chocolate, schmocolate. You can make that on your own time." Rose pulled her sweater close against her body as an early autumn breeze swept through the screen door. "Then again, from what I've seen, you could have done a better job on this—if you weren't bogged down with such nonsense."

"What is this?" she asked again, her curiosity piqued.

"You'll find out soon enough." Rose reached around Tori and pushed the screen door open. "But wait until you're on your way. I'm not a fan of gushing and I suspect you're a gusher."

Tori glanced down at the package and back up at Rose. "That wait part—that wasn't a question, was it?"

"No, Victoria, it wasn't."

"I knew that." She stepped onto the porch and stopped. "I had a really nice time tonight. Thank you, Rose."

The woman nodded in reply, her hand pulling the door inward. "Get home safely."

And then she was gone, her thin body disappearing down the very same hallway from which they'd both come. Only this time she was alone, as was Tori. But only in a physical sense.

A good forty years older, Rose was emerging as one of her closest friends in Sweet Briar. A woman who may have been quick to assume at the start yet wasn't afraid of making necessary corrections when the assumption proved wrong.

As her hostess disappeared from view Tori slowly untied the strings of the bundle, the brown paper wrapping coming loose at the same time.

"Oh, Rose," she whispered, her hands drawing the child-sized pioneer dress and matching bonnet into the glow of the porch light. "Lulu is going to love this."

Chapter 14

She was losing it. Absolutely losing it. How could someone who'd been praised for her organizational skills by every employer she'd ever had suddenly lose everything she needed? How could someone who'd had relatively good luck in her entire life suddenly have an overpowering urge to hang garlic from her neck?

"I don't get it, Nina, I've been staring at these binders every day for the past week. And now, suddenly, they're gone. Poof!" Tori pulled everything off her desk for the umpteenth time in the past hour searching for the presentation she'd spent hours putting together for the library board. "Are you sure you didn't put them somewhere when you were cleaning up in here?"

"*You* cleaned in here, Miss Sinclair. I tidied the library and set up the chairs for the meeting." Her assistant wrung her hands, her voice a poor disguise for the apprehension she felt in having to correct her boss.

"I'm sorry, Nina. It's not your fault. I can't seem to keep track of anything." She dropped into her office chair and buried her face in her hands. "What am I going to do? I'm going to look like an idiot. A complete and utter idiot."

"How's it going in here, ladies?"

Her head snapped up at the sound of Milo's voice, the overwhelming urge to beg him for a power hug more than a little surprising. "Um, I think *rotten* would sum up our answer pretty well . . . what do you say, Nina?"

Milo's eyebrows furrowed as Nina shrugged her agreement. "What's wrong?"

"Everything." Tori swiveled her chair and stood looking out the plate glass window into the gathering dusk. "I wanted them to see I'd thought this through, that I had plans to keep the cost to an absolute minimum, and that the idea went way beyond something that looks neat and pretty on the surface."

"Miss Sinclair gathered studies from libraries across the country that have done a similar thing," Nina added, defeat evident in her words as well.

"And?"

"Communities in those areas actually showed an increase in reading scores at the elementary school level."

Tori saw Milo's head shake in the reflection from the window. "And what's changed? Why can't the board see all this?"

"Because I've turned into a walking, talking black hole." Tori slowly turned from the window, her arms clasping one another across her dusty rose sweater set. "First, I nearly miss your classroom's first visit to the library. Why? Because I can't find the appointment book I've been told was virtually nailed to the information desk for forty years. Then, I can find every craft supply known to mankind except the Popsicle sticks I needed in order to make pyramids with your students."

The left corner of Milo's mouth twitched. Followed by the right side.

"What's so funny?" she asked, her hands dropping to her sides.

"You're kind of cute when you're losing it."

She rolled her eyes. "I doubt *that*."

"Listen. Whether or not you were ready for us that first day or whether you had to get wooden sticks from another source . . . it doesn't change one simple fact. My kids *love* coming here. Do you know I've been getting a jar of butter every day since? You've single-handedly stymied apple sales across Sweet Briar."

"Don't worry, I'm sure Investigator McGuire will be knocking on my door any minute now to harass me about that as well."

Milo's smile disappeared. "I'm sorry, Tori; I was just trying to lighten the mood. You seem so stressed."

The unmistakable concern in the man's eyes tugged at her heart, made her wish they could slip away to Debbie's Bakery for a break in the insanity. But they couldn't.

"I *am* stressed. I prepared a binder for each member of the board last week. In them were facts and figures I've compiled as well as plans I have for the children's room I'm proposing. But now"—she gestured toward her desk as her voice broke—"they're gone. Every single one of them."

"Gone?" He strode across the room, his head ducking to look below the desk and then popping up to scan the top. "How could they be gone?"

She threw her hands into the air, exhaling a piece of wavy brown hair from her face. "*That* is the million-dollar question. Though, quite frankly, I'm growing more and more certain that someone is deliberately trying to sabotage me. I mean, really, what other explanation is there?"

Milo looked from Tori to Nina to the clock hanging on the wall. "Unfortunately, you've only got ten minutes to figure out what you're going to do."

"*Ten* minutes—oh, Nina, what am I going to *do*?" Tori

nibbled her lower lip inward, her hands beginning to tremble at her sides. "These people are coming to my first meeting as head librarian—a woman they brought down from Chicago only to have her show up on the top of the suspect list in the town's first-ever murder investigation. This was my chance to show them I'm not crazy."

She heard the shrillness of her voice, felt Milo's concern and Nina's pity. And for once in her life she was at a complete loss on how to dig her way out of a mess she hadn't seen coming.

"This idea had nothing to do with Tiffany Ann's murder. You didn't come up with this to show them anything. You came up with this first. Because it's a tremendous idea."

Tori leaned against the desk. "It *was*."

"It still is." Milo leaned against the desk beside her, his hands curled around its edge. "You don't need a binder with bullet points and numbers to convince them you know what you're doing or that this is going to be a home run for the library."

"Of course I do," she said flatly.

"No, you don't. I didn't have a binder sitting in front of me at Debbie's the other night. I didn't have numbers and studies and projections to cull through. I just had you and your ideas and your excitement." Milo pulled his right hand from the desk, tentatively raised it to her face and brushed a wayward curl from her forehead. "Trust me, if they see what I saw . . . if they hear what I heard . . . you'll get your room."

She closed her eyes as his skin brushed against hers, felt the shiver that began at the place of contact and reverberated through her entire body. Was he right? Could she pull it off simply by talking?

"He's right, Miss Sinclair. You had me imagining the storybook scenes on the wall that first day in the storage room simply by the way you described it. And that was with all those boxes still stacked to the ceiling."

"Just get out there and tell them everything you told me Sunday night." Milo pushed off the edge of the desk and extended his hand to Tori, encircling hers and pulling her to stand. "Forget Tiffany Ann, forget these silly suspicions, forget the next box of lightbulbs you might have to buy."

She grinned. "Have to."

He looked a question at her.

"You mean the next box of lightbulbs I *have* to buy, Milo."

His mouth fell. "Are you serious?"

She rolled her eyes again, though this time it was as much with amusement as it was exasperation. "I may have hurt the apple industry but I've more than made up for it with the lightbulb folks."

"You gonna be okay?" he asked as he walked across the office and stopped just before the door.

"I am. Thank you." And she meant it. Before Milo Wentworth had arrived in her office she'd been the epitome of the desperate female. His calming voice and clear thoughts had been the only thing to talk her off the cliff.

"You had it in you the whole time, Tori. Your eyes just got a little cloudy for a minute." He nodded at Nina. "Good luck you two."

And then he was gone. A sense of determination and hope left in his wake.

"We can do this, Nina." She looked at her assistant, knew the optimistic smile she saw on the woman's face was a mirror of her own. "But I need you to do something for me."

"Anything."

She grabbed a pad of paper from the top of her desk and wrote ten children's titles on the top page before ripping it off and handing it to Nina. "Can you find these books for me and place them in a pile by the head table?"

Nina's gaze skimmed down the page, a light twinkling

in her eyes. When she reached the bottom of the list she looked up and nodded in satisfaction. "Consider it done."

And then she, too, was gone.

Buoyed by the confidence of both Milo and Nina, Tori flipped off the light switch and headed into the hall, her mind focused on the task in front of her. The children's room was a no-brainer. It simply made sense—from a standpoint of utilizing a perfectly good room and from the board's desire to bring some fresh ideas and positive change to the Sweet Briar Public Library.

She was simply backing up the very reason they hired her. And in less than a month. All she needed to do was lay out her idea in as persuasive a way as possible. The rest was out of her hands.

Knowing that made it easier to walk down the hallway and face the people who'd hired her for this position. Winston Hohlbrook, the board's president, had been high on her from the very first interview. And if Lincoln Porter and James Polk had had any initial reservations about bringing in someone from up north, those were gone by the second interview.

The one commonality between all of their feedback? They liked her enthusiasm for books and her passionate ideas for reaching the community through various literary endeavors. The children's room should simply be seen as the first concrete step in fulfilling those initial impressions.

"Good evening, everyone." Tori smiled as she walked into the branch, a hush falling over the assembled crowd as she stopped to shake a few hands before taking her place at the head table beside the board members.

As she looked out over the larger-than-expected crowd of Sweet Briar residents she felt her mouth go dry at the sight of Investigator Daniel McGuire in the front row— Leona Elkin at his side and Dixie Dunn at hers.

She swallowed over the lump that sprang into her

throat. Who was she kidding? The board hadn't gotten a
young librarian with fresh new ideas and energy to spare.
They'd gotten a murder suspect.

A quick motion to the left of the investigator brought
Milo within sight—the man who'd single-handedly rallied
her mood. A raspy cough pulled her attention even farther
to the left, to a group of women who'd come to support
her efforts. Lifting her hand in a tiny wave, she felt her
eyes grow moist as she smiled at Rose, Debbie, and Margaret Louise.

You can do this, Tori.

"I'd like to welcome everyone to the Sweet Briar
Public Library's monthly meeting." Winston Hohlbrook
stood behind his chair, his shoulders arched back as he
addressed the crowd. "I'm not quite sure when we last
saw this many people at a library meeting but I, for one,
am thrilled.

"Now I wish I could say the turnout is for me and my
ease with a crowd but as much as I hate to do it, I need to
acknowledge you're not here for me." Winston gestured to
Tori, encouraging her to stand and face the audience. "I
believe you're here on account of our brand-new librarian,
Victoria Sinclair."

A polite smattering of applause sprang up around the
room, followed by an ear-piercing whistle.

Margaret Louise.

"People are naturally drawn to a train wreck," mumbled Dixie beneath her breath.

If anyone in the room heard the former librarian, they
gave no indication.

"Victoria, would you like to take over?" Winston
pulled out his chair and lowered himself down, his genuine smile giving no indication he was fazed by the murder
talk making the rounds of Sweet Briar.

Forcing herself to disregard Dixie's slam, she clasped
her hands together and looked out over the crowd. "Yes,

thank you, Mr. Hohlbrook. Although I haven't been here three weeks yet, I can honestly say I love this library. I love the collection the board has built, I love the patrons, and"—she gestured to Milo—"I love the students who have been visiting our branch on a weekly basis."

A few heads nodded in the crowd as the board members beamed.

"You mean you love their *teacher*," Dixie quipped.

Tori felt her face warm as the woman's words echoed through the room, knew her palms were sweating as Investigator McGuire crossed his arms and narrowed his eyes in intrigue.

She didn't need to look to know the board members were growing uncomfortable with the former librarian's barbs. She didn't need Milo or anyone else to fill in the blanks as to what would happen to her idea if she didn't plow ahead anyway.

"I love the *children*, Ms. Dunn," Tori gently corrected before moving on with her plan. "But perhaps what I've enjoyed the most so far is looking around this building and seeing the amazing potential to serve Sweet Briar residents on a grander scale." She stepped out from behind the table and swept her hand across the shelves of picture books and independent readers. "In particular, the children of Sweet Briar."

Winston Hohlbrook shifted in his seat as he brought his chin to rest between his thumb and index finger.

"Most people develop their love of reading as children. Those who love to read as youngsters tend to read throughout their life. Those who don't tend to avoid books altogether."

Heads nodded.

"For some children, the simple act of reading stirs the imagination and they can lose themselves in the pages of a book. They need no prompting. Others"—she looked at Rose and Margaret Louise—"need someone to show them the excitement of books. To help make them come alive.

"And that's what I want to do with a brand-new children's room."

Tori stole a look in the board's direction, saw the shifting and posturing she'd anticipated. Focusing back on the community she continued. "A children's room that I can create without a construction crew and without spending more than about four hundred dollars, at most."

"How is that possible, Miss Sinclair?" Lincoln Porter, one of the board members, asked.

Tori clapped her hands softly as the excitement she'd been feeding off of since the moment she saw the storage room bubbled up. "Before I explain the specifics of my plan I'd like to take a little field trip. Right down that hall." She pointed to the hallway visible in the back center of the room. "I think seeing the gem that's lurking under this roof will make the rest of my ideas easier to envision."

Grabbing the stack of books Nina had gathered, Tori headed down the hallway toward her office, bypassing her door in favor of one across the hall. "C'mon everyone, there's room for all of us."

She stepped inside the former storage room, a spacious section of the building that was finally rid of the countless boxes and moldy books that had claimed the space for far too long, and waited for the others to follow. Sure enough, as each person made their way into the room, various *oohs* and *ahhs* invariably followed.

"James, did you know this room was so big?" Lincoln Porter asked his fellow board member.

"I had no idea. Did you, Winston?"

The board president studied the room, a look of genuine surprise spreading across his face. "I most certainly did not."

As the remaining visitors found a place inside the

room, Tori continued. "This room went unnoticed because of the countless storage boxes that were in here at any given time." She pointed to her assistant. "Nina and I spent hours going through each and every box. What was salvageable has been put down in the basement for the sale and what wasn't—due to neglect—was thrown away."

"This is tremendous, Miss Sinclair."

She nodded, her enthusiasm obviously spreading to the board. "The windows, although relatively small, provide a nice amount of natural light during the day and ensure that we won't break any code violations by using this as an extension of the library."

"What are your plans, Miss Sinclair?" Winston Hohlbrook prodded.

"I want to make this a children's room—the kind of place that ignites a child's love for reading by bringing books to life."

"And you think you can do that for under five hundred bucks?" James Polk asked in obvious disbelief.

"Less than *four* hundred, actually." Tori set the pile of books at her feet and opened the first one with one hand as she swept her free one across the wall behind where she stood. "Can't you just see Cinderella's castle on this wall right here? And Jack's beanstalk over here?" She spun around and walked to the wall behind the board president. "And maybe Laura Ingalls's house in the Big Woods right here?"

"Wouldn't that kind of artwork cost a small fortune?" Investigator McGuire interjected.

"Not if *I* do it, it won't."

"You can do that kind of work, Miss Sinclair?" Lincoln Porter asked, surprise evident in his voice.

"With the help of an overhead projector—yes I can."

"And where would you come up with the money this town would need to protect itself when we get slapped with a lawsuit over copyright infringement?" Dixie Dunn challenged with glee.

All eyes left the surrounding walls to focus on Tori.

"Miss Sinclair?" Winston prompted.

"My plan for bringing these scenes to life would not infringe on any copyrights whatsoever." Tori met Dixie Dunn's smug smile with one of her own before bringing the rest of her ideas to the crowd. "So other than some paint and some inexpensive carpet, there would be no expense."

"We already have the books to fill the room," Debbie Calhoun stated happily.

"We most certainly do. Our library has a wonderful collection of children's books. This room would just enhance what we already have."

"Do you have any other plans?" a man in the back asked.

Tori nodded. "I want to put together a trunk of dress-up clothes, outfits worn by the characters in many of the kids' favorite books. You know, Red Riding Hood, Peter Pan, Cinderella, that kind of thing. In fact, we already have our very first costume thanks to Rose Winters." She reached for the bag she'd placed in the room earlier in the day, unfolded the dress and bonnet for all to see. "I want the kids to be able to come in here—where they won't be a disturbance to our other patrons—and act out their favorite scenes and, perhaps, create new ones."

"Won't those kind of costumes cost money?" Lincoln Porter asked as he took the costume from Tori's hand and examined it closely.

She flashed a look at Rose and Debbie, saw the nod of encouragement from Margaret Louise. "No. It won't. There is a group of women here in Sweet Briar who would love to sew the costumes for the library's dress-up trunk. And their attention to detail will far exceed any store-bought costume we might find."

"I could build a small stage right here," a man said as he pointed to the very corner Tori had been envisioning for such an addition. "Free of charge."

The board members converged in a small circle as the rest of the crowd talked amongst themselves about various mural and costume possibilities. Milo had been right. Letting people's imaginations run free was far more powerful than any typewritten presentation could have ever been.

"Miss Sinclair?" Winston Hohlbrook and the other board members broke from their impromptu conference. "We have one question for you."

"Anything." She nibbled her lower lip inward as she stole a glance in Milo's direction, his attention focused on the board president.

"How soon do you think you could have Sweet Briar Public Library's very first children's room up and running?"

"You mean—" She stopped as her mouth stretched into a smile too wide to stifle.

"You've got your room!" Winston bellowed proudly as he smacked his fellow members on the back. "Think we can see the finished product by next month?"

Inhaling deeply she skimmed the crowd, her gaze falling on Rose. "Think we can stock the trunk in four weeks?"

Rose looked at Tori over the rim of her glasses. "We can stock it in one."

She glanced back at Milo. "Can I borrow your students' artistic abilities on Friday?"

"You most certainly can." He winked back.

She found Nina on the other side of the room. "Think you can tape this weekend?"

"I know I can," her assistant said.

The man who'd volunteered to build the stage stepped forward. "I can build a suitable platform in just a couple of hours. And yeah, I'm free this weekend."

Looking back at Winston Hohlbrook and the other two board members, Tori hugged the picture book to her chest and squared her shoulders. "It looks to me like we can host the grand opening of our new children's room a week from Saturday."

A smattering of applause broke out across the room as Tori made her way over to the board members.

"Very nice work, Miss Sinclair."

"Thank you, Mr. Polk."

"Victoria, this is exactly the kind of thing I saw in you during that very first interview." Winston Hohlbrook extended his hand and shook hers firmly. "We're so glad to have you on board."

"A sentiment that will change when she's unable to attend the grand opening," Dixie said from her spot along the east wall.

Winston's brows furrowed as he looked at Tori. "You won't be able to attend?"

"Of course I will." Tori shot Dixie a look of disbelief, unsure of where, exactly, the ex-librarian was going with her comments. "I wouldn't miss it for anything."

"Being behind bars on murder charges might make your absence unavoidable." Dixie waggled a finger at each board member, her tone morphing from mean to bitter in mere seconds. "But you wanted new and fresh, didn't you?"

"Dixie!" Leona chided as she released her hold on the investigator's arm and tugged the elderly woman backward. "That's enough." Turning to the man beside her, she gestured a hand in Tori's direction. "Daniel *say* something. Please."

The uniformed officer simply crossed his arms and shrugged. "I think Ms. Dunn did just fine on her own."

Chapter 15

She sat on the floor and flipped through each and every drawing Milo's students had done that morning. Jennifer's castle was quite good—the turrets well drawn and the stained glass windows boasting an assortment of cheerful colors. Erin's rendition of the dwarfs' beds was precious, all seven boasting the peculiar name of its inhabitant. Quinton's forest was amazing, his detailed trees as good as any adult could draw. His picture alone opened up a wide range of placement possibilities alongside any number of famous tales.

And then there was Lulu's log cabin, a picture she'd slaved over from the moment Tori had explained what she needed and why. Logs were drawn and erased and drawn again, over and over, until they were perfected. The perfect color for Laura's first home was agonized over in a careful head-to-head comparison of the many shades of brown in the crayon bin. But she'd finally gotten it the way she wanted, her picture proudly presented to Tori just moments before her class was scheduled to leave.

The pictures were everything she'd imagined and more, the students' enthusiasm for the project something she wouldn't forget anytime soon. Yet there she was, sitting on the floor, unable to make any headway on the wall—

"Something told me I'd find you here." Milo tapped his knuckles against the open door. "How's it going?"

"It's not." She leaned against the wall and lifted the stack of pictures into the air. "I've got all these amazing drawings and no way to get them onto the wall."

"I thought you were going to use an overhead." He stepped into the room, studied the freshly painted basecoat on each wall.

"I was."

"Was?"

Nodding, she set the pictures on the ground by her knees and released the sigh that had been building inside her since she walked in the building ready to paint. "I brought the projector in here myself after lunch. I even stopped by the hardware store and bought a new extension cord. But now"—she gestured around the room—"it's gone."

"Why does this conversation seem familiar?" Milo asked, his lips tugging upward.

"Because we've had it before. About Popsicle sticks and pitch binders."

"And lightbulbs. You can't forget the lightbulbs."

"As if." She leaned her head against the wall and looked up at the ceiling, objectively considered the puffy white clouds she'd painstakingly painted the night before. "I swear I think someone is out to get me."

"It sure seems that way." Milo crossed the rest of the room and slid his back down the wall, claiming a resting place mere inches from her own. "I was really impressed with how you handled the board the other night. You made this place come alive."

"Thanks." She pulled her knees upward and rested her head atop them.

"And you didn't let Dixie get to you even though she gave it her best shot."

"Thanks."

Milo scooted away from the wall, turning his body so they were facing one another. "And for the record, what she did at the end . . . what the investigator said . . . it was complete rubbish."

"Rubbish?" Lifting her head, she met Milo's gaze. "I haven't heard that word since I was a little kid—watching *Sesame Street*."

He shrugged. "Stick around here for a while and you'll hear all sorts of expressions that'll make you shake your head."

"Oh, I already have. And they think *I* talk funny."

"Well you do." He ducked as she reached out and smacked his arm. "But it's endearing."

Endearing?

A flash of red lit his cheeks and she looked away, certain her own were no different. Milo Wentworth was a nice guy. A handsome guy. A great listener. A fun person to hang out—

"Did you ever ask Nina whether she saw Tiffany Ann that last day?" Milo cleared his throat as he grabbed hold of the stack of pictures and began looking through them as he waited for her response.

"I did. And she *did* come in here." She lowered her knees a few inches and straightened her back. "She spent some time in the local section and apparently wasn't a whole lot different here than as Emma at the bakery described her. Then after a while she got up, asked if she could go out the back door . . . said she wasn't feeling well. And we know what happened then."

He nodded as he pulled his favorites from the pile, his selections a perfect match to her own. "I see."

"I asked Nina if she thought drugs were possible and she—"

"Drugs? Tiffany Ann? No way."

"Why is everyone so sure that wasn't the case?" she asked, the exasperation in her voice evident to her own ears.

"Because she was a good girl. A little misguided? Perhaps. Desperate for attention? Most definitely. But good at heart nonetheless. And besides, the traces were found in her coffee cup." Milo stopped sifting through pictures and simply looked at her, his intense gaze far more comforting than unsettling.

"I know that. But couldn't she have put it in there herself? You just said she craved attention. Maybe she simply misjudged the amount."

"I don't think anyone craves attention enough to mess with potassium cyanide."

"Cyanide?" she asked, the pitch of her voice bordering on shrill. "Who said anything about cyanide?"

"Apparently the medical examiner. At least that's what I'm hearing."

She swallowed hard. "Okay, but couldn't she have still tried?" She shook her head. "Scratch that. I know it sounds ridiculous. It's just—I don't know."

He reached out, touched her arm, his warmth lingering along with his hand. "Hey. It's okay. You're tired of all eyes looking at you. I get that."

She blinked back the tears that threatened to slip down her face if she uttered a word of response.

"But you have to know that all eyes *aren't* looking at you. They really aren't." He released her arm, tilting her face upward until their eyes met. "I'm not. Nina's not. Debbie Calhoun's not. Rose Winters isn't. And neither is Margaret Louise Davis."

"I know but—"

"Leona Elkin isn't and the board members aren't."

She knew her laugh sounded hollow, bitter even. But it was all she could do to keep from screaming. *Leona?* Leona was probably readying the jail for her stay at that very moment.

She said as much to Milo.

"I think you're wrong. You see, you were reeling from the investigator's words Wednesday night . . . as anyone in your position would have. But *I* saw the way Leona looked at him. She was not impressed. Not in the slightest."

A brief ray of hope zipped through her body before she squashed it like a bug.

"That meeting was forty-eight hours ago, Milo. She couldn't have been too outraged."

His hand dropped from her face, scooped her hand from her lap, and held it tightly. "People do things at their own pace, Tori."

She shrugged, her senses all too aware of his hand on hers. "I suppose. Though I sure wish Investigator McGuire would pick up the pace in his investigation a little bit more. I'm not sure how much longer I can handle the constant scrutiny and never-ending looks."

"He just needs to find the right person."

"You mean, *I* need to find the right person." She traced the fingers of her free hand across the top of his, pulling them back as she realized what she was doing. "I can't help but feel as if Tiffany's mood the day of her murder is the key to all of this. I mean, wouldn't *you* be jumpy and edgy if you were afraid for your life?"

He stared at her. "You think she knew someone was after her?"

"Well why not? I mean, if you listen to everyone talk, she was this sweet-as-pie, picture-perfect local girl whom everyone loved, even if they didn't always believe what she had to say. I can't imagine someone would kill her for no reason. And if she was suddenly acting all weird and out of character doesn't that make you wonder—even a little bit?"

"Yeah, I guess it does. But it's like you said—everyone loved her."

"Maybe the love wasn't as strong for some as it was for others." She thought back on her conversation with Emma Adams, the way the girl had obviously been jealous of Tiffany Ann's good looks. She recalled the obsessive nature Cooper had displayed when he talked about his ex-girlfriend. . . .

"It will work out somehow." Milo turned her hand over in his and peered down at it, a shy smile teasing his lips.

"Oh, Milo, I hope you're right."

"What's going on in here? I thought the room would be ready to go by now." Margaret Louise breezed into the room, her lips twitching at the sight of Tori and Milo sitting on the ground together. "Didn't your parents ever lecture you guys on holding off the hanky-panky until *after* you got your work done?"

"*Hanky-panky*—Margaret Louise, there's nothing going on." Tori pushed Milo's hand from hers and stood. "I was trying to work on the room and—"

"Miss Sinclair, Miss Sinclair, have you done my picture yet?" Lulu ran around the corner and stopped, her face falling at the sight of the near empty room.

"Not yet, Lulu." Tori scrunched her brows together. "Remember our mystery?"

The little girl nodded. "About the missing sticks and stuff?"

"Exactly." She reached out and smoothed the child's hair from her face. "Now there's another one."

"Really?" Lulu's eyes grew wide as saucers as she bent her head close to Tori for more details.

"The overhead projector I need to put your pictures on the wall has disappeared. Poof! Just like the sticks. Only this time I'm not sure your dad can help me out."

"What's a pro—a pro—"

"A projector," Margaret Louise and Milo supplied in unison.

"Yeah, *that*." Lulu lifted her face expectantly as she waited for Tori to explain.

"It's a box about this big." Tori motioned with her hands to show the approximate size of the object in question. "And it has a little arm that comes out of the back and shines a light onto a picture and then magnifies it onto the wall." She grabbed a piece of blank paper from the stack of pictures beside Milo and drew a sketch of a projector. "It looks like this."

"Oh." Lulu looked around the room, her gaze lifting upward until it focused on the ceiling. "Whoa, Mee-Maw, look—clouds! Big puffy clouds!"

"You like those?" Tori asked, anxious to get some initial feedback on the progress she'd made.

"I love 'em! Wait 'til Jennifer sees those. She loves clouds, too!" Lulu began skipping around the room, her initial excitement resurrected. "And when we find your pro—your pro thing—you can make the walls all pretty, too."

Tori's shoulders slumped as she turned and looked at Margaret Louise. "You wouldn't by chance know anyone who could spare a projector for a few days, do you?"

"I most certainly do. Colby Calhoun has a projector. It's one of those portable ones. He uses it when he gives talks. I've seen it myself a half dozen times or more."

Her hope lifted. "Do you think he'd let me use it?"

"Of course he will. Colby and Debbie are cut from the same cloth. Knowing him, he'll deliver it himself before we're even off the phone."

"Oh Margaret Louise, that would be perfect."

"You want it now?" Lulu's grandmother pulled a cell phone from her overly stuffed purse and flipped it open.

Tori glanced at her clock. "How about tomorrow by noon? I'll be in Ridge Cove first thing in the morning hitting up flea markets."

"Whatever for?" Margaret Louise asked.

"A trunk for the storybook costumes. Nina thinks I should be able to find one for no more than twenty-five dollars."

"You'll find aplenty for that kind of money." The woman took hold of her granddaughter's hand and headed toward the door. "And it's a good thing you're getting it now because Rose has handed out costume assignments and accompanying threats if they're not done by Friday."

"Threats?" she asked, amusement mingling with her words.

"Mine is no new recipes from anyone in the circle for a year if I don't get my Little Red Riding Hood outfit done in time."

A low whistle escaped Milo's lips. "No new recipes? Man, that woman is tough."

"Tough will be the conniption fit she'll throw if we don't produce." Margaret Louise and Lulu waved as they stepped into the hallway. "I'll call Colby first thing in the mornin' after I drop Lulu and her brothers and sisters off at Dixie's house. Dixie is havin' a birthday party for her granddaughter and every one of Jake's kids are invited, bless her heart."

"Thanks, Margaret Louise." Tori walked over to the door and poked her head into the hallway. "Have fun, Lulu."

"I will."

Margaret Louise looked back over her shoulder and winked. "I'd tell you the same thing but I think you're a little too old to need permission."

"Permission for wh—" The woman's words turned in her thoughts, the reality of their meaning bringing a flush to her cheeks and a tickle to her throat. "Margaret Louise! There's nothing going on."

"Well maybe there *should* be."

Chapter 16

She hadn't realized just how much she'd been craving a little distance from all things Sweet Briar until she turned her car north on Route 190, the white picket fences and moss-draped trees that surrounded the town square disappearing in her rearview mirror. But as she maneuvered the narrow two-lane route that led in and out of her new hometown, the need she'd been unaware of was suddenly undeniable.

The possibility to love Sweet Briar was there, its small-town charm and picturesque setting hard to ignore. But being singled out as a murder suspect because you hadn't grown up with everyone else was more than a little disheartening. Especially when she'd just come from a town where no one knew anyone yet trust was easier to earn.

Flipping on the radio, Tori scanned her way from station to station, her choices limited to country, bluegrass, and their various offshoots. It was the kind of music she could learn to like, each song telling a story of some sort.

But not today. Today she needed to be true to herself, to stop trying to fit herself into a box made by other people's expectations. And, even more importantly, she needed a break from the worry of whether people believed in her or not.

Pulling her eyes from the road for just a moment, she grabbed her travel CD case and unzipped it, her hands instinctively finding the page that held her favorite pick-me-up music of all time and extracting the disc from the fabric sleeve. With a flick of her wrist and the push of a button, the dance track she'd compiled back in college wafted its way through each of the car's four speakers, and she began singing along at the top of her lungs.

She bypassed the air conditioner in favor of open windows, savoring the feel of the wind against her arms and face as she bopped along to the music. Suddenly the stress of lost objects and the humiliation of being a suspect in Tiffany Ann's murder seemed a million miles away, the deserted road and rapid speed putting much-needed distance between herself and events she couldn't control. It also gave her time to think, to remember Jeff's betrayal and to realize the pain wasn't nearly as raw as it once was. Somehow, someway, her aching heart had started to heal, a fact that surprised as much as it pleased.

Were the events of the past week that all-encompassing? Had she simply traded one hurt for another? Or was it something more?

Like Milo?

Gripping the steering wheel more firmly, Tori forced herself to focus on the lyrics of the song she had cranked up as high as it could go, to hit every note the artist hit at just the right time. The last thing she needed on top of everything else was to fall for a man. A man who'd already married his soul mate only to lose her much too soon.

What difference did it make that he was good-looking

and sweet, honest and caring, and supportive as all get-out? Jeff had seemed to be all those things at one time, too. And look how *that* turned out.

The ring of her cell phone cut through her woolgathering, snapping her mind back to the present. "Who the—" She lifted her phone from the center console and stared at the unfamiliar number on the caller ID screen, her curiosity winning out over the desire to keep singing. "Hello?"

"Victoria?" She strained to pick out the voice, to put a face to its sound, but other than her late great-grandmother no one called her by her given name. Except, of course, the people of Sweet Briar.

Ooooh. Maybe, if she were really lucky, Dixie Dunn was calling to complain about a page in one of the library books that looked as if it had actually been *turned*.

"Victoria, it's Debbie. Debbie Calhoun."

With any luck the wind in the car softened the sigh of relief she exhaled into the woman's ear. "Debbie, hi. Is everything okay?"

"Everything's fine. I hope you don't mind, but I asked Nina for your number when I called the library this morning."

"You asked what? Wait—wait one minute," she said as she muted one of her favorite songs, "Holding Out for a Hero." "I'm sorry, I tend to play my music a little loud in the car."

Debbie's staccato laugh filled her ear for a moment before she began singing a few bars of the song Tori had just stopped. "I understand. I do the exact same thing when the kids aren't with me. It's the only time I get to listen to my stuff."

Tori glanced out the window at the small green sign on the side of the road—Ridge Cove, fifteen miles. "So, I'm sorry, what were you saying before I turned it down?"

"Just that I got your number from Nina and am hoping you don't mind."

She pulled her eyes back to the road, instinctively shook her head. "Of course not. What can I do for you?"

"Not a thing. I just wanted you to know that Colby will be dropping off his projector with Nina in about thirty minutes."

"Oh, Debbie, you guys are lifesavers—thank you so much." She switched her cell phone to her left hand and guided the car with her right. "I take it Margaret Louise called?"

"First thing this morning." A shriek in the background made Tori pull the phone from her ear momentarily. "I'm sorry, Victoria. Jackson is having a minor meltdown. It happens sometimes. Anyway, what's with all your stuff disappearing?"

"Margaret Louise told you about that?"

"Uh-huh."

"I don't know. Just a few extra little treats to try and drive me over the edge." As soon as she spoke the words, she wished she could take them back. Instead, she engaged in a hefty dose of backpedaling. "Not that I'm close to the edge or that I'd do anything crazy. I'm really a very mild-mannered person. Really."

Could she sound any more lame? She groaned inwardly.

"Victoria, please don't worry about everything you say. I've been driven over the edge so many times I think I've worn a path. But that doesn't mean I'm going to kill someone. I *know* that."

Tori sighed. "Thank you, Debbie."

"Look, you've been through a lot. And I'm not just talking about the gossip surrounding Tiffany Ann's death. I mean, I couldn't believe how nasty Dixie was at the library meeting Wednesday night. I was almost ashamed to call her my friend." Debbie's voice grew muted as she addressed someone in the background before continuing. "She was way out of line."

Tori didn't need any help remembering. In fact, she'd have to be an idiot not to realize she was on Dixie Dunn's despised enemy list. The woman had flashed more than her share of dirty looks in Tori's direction. She'd created a scene over a faded coffee stain in a library book. And she'd done her best to make Tori look like a fool in front of the library board.

"She's just hurt, I guess," Tori offered, the pick-me-up of her music beginning to descend—rapidly. "And it's not like anything she's done has swayed the community as a who—"

She stopped midsentence, her free hand leaving the steering wheel to cover her open mouth.

Oh my God. Did Dixie set me up?

It fit. All along she'd assumed Leona was the one feeding conversations to Investigator McGuire. But Dixie had been at the sewing circle meetings, too.

"At least the second and third one," she mumbled as her hand returned to the wheel.

"What was that, Victoria?"

"What? Oh. Never mind." Her thoughts rewound through the board meeting, stopping to replay each of the moments Dixie had tried her best to ruin. "Debbie?" She swallowed over the lump that sprang to her throat, willed her nerves to calm long enough to speak coherently.

"Yes?"

"Do you think Dixie hates me enough to set me up?"

"Set you up for what?"

"Murder."

Debbie's gasp in her ear was all the answer she needed and she rushed to smooth any rumpled feathers. "I'm sorry. I shouldn't have asked that. I guess I'm just grasping at straws."

"No, I understand. I'd probably be doing the same thing. But, Victoria, just because Dixie is hurt over losing her job to you doesn't mean she'd kill an innocent young woman."

"I didn't mean to say she murdered Tiffany Ann." She tightened her grip on the phone.

"But in order to set you up she would have to have done it herself, wouldn't she?"

Feeling suddenly foolish she pulled over onto a short stretch of shoulder five miles outside Ridge Cove. "You're right. I'm so sorry."

"It's okay." Silence filled Tori's ear as she waited to see whether Debbie was truly okay with her misguided thoughts. But the longer the awkwardness continued, the more sure she was she'd alienated yet another member of the Sweet Briar community.

"I'm sorry," she repeated.

"Really it's okay. Anyway, Margaret Louise said you're off to Ridge Cove to hit some flea markets?"

It was painfully obvious it wasn't okay, but at least the woman was trying to make polite conversation. What she did once they hung up, though, was anyone's guess.

"Nina mentioned two different places I should check out for the costume trunk. I'm hoping I find a really nice one for a steal."

"Ridge Cove may be backwoods . . . and by back-woods, I mean *backwoods* . . . but they've got the best flea markets around." Debbie's voice faded momentarily only to strengthen once again. "Colby says it's the only thing that makes him even consider making that drive."

"So if the place is that bad, how could Tiffany Ann have seen it as a potential launchpad for her career?"

"I'm not sure. She said it was a start. Her enthusiasm the morning she was heading to Ridge Cove was contagious. She reminded me of myself when I got the idea to open my own bakery."

Tori checked the side and rearview mirrors and pulled back onto Route 190. "She wanted to be a fashion designer, right?"

"No. An interior designer. She loved helping people put things together—whether it was as simple as a bouquet of wildflowers or the remodeling of an entire room. And it didn't just start when she was a teenager. Oh no. Long before that child started designing floats for the annual Sweet Briar Sweetheart parade she was dabbling with presentation and style. In fact, from the time she was five years old, that child had a flair for color. Her bike was always the blue-ribbon winner in the Fourth of July fair each year. Forget about red, white, and blue streamers hanging from handlebars. This child had flags and sparklers and pictures hanging from every piece of metal she could find."

"Wow." It was all she could think to say at the moment. No wonder everyone loved Tiffany Ann. How could they not? She'd never even met the girl yet couldn't help but feel as if she'd missed out on someone special.

"Yeah. It still gets me teary-eyed. The whole thing was just so senseless, you know? I can't help but wonder if the poison hit real fast or if she felt funny first. And if she did, would she have asked for help? She was so determined to handle her own affairs . . . to try and become the kind of grown-up woman she hoped Milo would finally notice . . . to prove she'd outgrown her attention-seeking ways. It's just so sad. All of it." A raspy quality found its way into Debbie's words, her genuine sadness impossible to overlook. "Anyway, I better head off. I've got a headache brewing."

"Okay. Please extend my thanks to your husband for the projector. I'll get it back to him in the next few days." Tori slowed as she reached a four-way stop, her eyes sliding from left to right as she crossed. "And Debbie, thanks for listening. Even when what I'm saying makes no sense."

"My pleasure. Have a safe trip home." Debbie pulled

the phone from her mouth and spoke to someone in the background, a tiny voice rising up in protest. "Oh. And make sure you check out Stu's. His flea market is just off Route 190 on Clover Street. He seems to actually have some good stuff."

"Stu's on Clover Street—got it," Tori repeated aloud, commending the name and street to memory. "I'll see you soon."

"Oh and Victoria?"

"Yeah?"

"Don't worry about the Dixie thing. She'll come around."

Tori snapped the phone shut in her hand, her spirits buoyed somewhat by Debbie's final comment. Maybe she wouldn't pass on Tori's crazy accusation about a longtime member of the sewing circle, after all.

She could certainly hope, anyway. Because if Debbie *did* share that portion of their conversation, it was pretty much a safe bet Rose and Margaret Louise would disappear from her group of supporters.

Her meager four-person group of supporters.

But was it truly out of line to add Dixie Dunn to her potential suspect list? Sure, the woman was in her seventies, but that didn't preclude her from tossing something into a person's coffee and giving it a quick stir.

The key though would be whether she'd even been in Debbie's Bakery on the day Tiffany Ann Gilbert was murdered. A question Emma Adams could surely answer.

Tori crested the top of a windy hill and proceeded down Route 190, the pavement becoming more and more rough with each passing mile. Debbie wasn't kidding. Ridge Cove was barely a blip on the road, the occasional house she passed nothing short of dilapidated.

Who lived in a place like this? And what on earth did Tiffany Ann hope to accomplish—career-wise—in a spot so far off the beaten path? Would she have told Cooper or one of her girlfriends? Would she have mentioned it in passing to Milo?

Or did she want it to be a surprise? One she sought to shore up before telling a soul?

Stu's Flea Market appeared on Tori's right as she rounded a curve canopied by massive moss trees. The building itself wasn't in awful shape but it wasn't in a league with the series of newly constructed hutlike structures that stood not more than three hundred yards away. Each of the five smaller structures boasted the kind of storefront exterior not easily found in an age where the sterilized look and feel of big chain businesses was the norm.

Curious, Tori stepped from her car, bypassing the flea market in favor of a closer look at the old-fashioned shops.

"Interested in rentin' one?"

Tori whirled around, her heart beating double time.

"Whoa. Didn't mean to up and scare you, ma'am." A man, standing about six feet tall, pulled a green John Deere hat from his head, revealing a receding line of salt-and-pepper hair. "I noticed you headin' this way and figured I'd offer a little help."

Holding her hand to her chest she inhaled and exhaled before finally answering. "I just wanted to take a closer look, maybe peek inside one of the windows." She looked back over her shoulder at the charming outer buildings. "They're really quite darling."

The man replaced his hat and nodded, his flannel-clad arms crossing casually across his chest. "Thank you."

"What are they for?" Tori asked as she resumed her path, the fifty-something man at her side.

"Whatever people want to use them for. A seasonal fruit shop, a place to sell jams and jellies, a small appliance repair shop." He walked alongside Tori as she peeked in each building, her hand covering her eyes in an attempt to block the morning sun. "I actually have a renter for this buildin'. I tell you, Travis can fix just about everythin' under the sun . . . no matter how bad broken it is. He's sick and tired of his wife naggin' him about parts being all over the house and yellin' at him for grease stains on all the furniture. So he's rentin' this place to get away from her." He waited as she peered inside, rubbed his chin between his thumb and index finger. "That is, unless he's really run off the way his wife is squawkin'. Seems he disappeared about a week or two ago. Frankly"—he looked both ways, a gesture that was futile considering they were the only two people for miles—"I think he just needed to give his head a break from all that naggin' and who can blame the fellow?"

She ducked her head to the left, the large wooden counter and bay of shelves reminiscent of a mom-and-pop style market she used to visit with her parents. "Aren't people worried about getting business out this far?"

He shrugged. "I do pretty well on Saturdays."

"But people are coming here specifically for your flea market." She wandered to the next building, a more cottagelike version of the two on either side.

"And they'll come specifically for whatever is offered in these here buildings, too." He pulled his hat off with one hand and scratched the top of his head, his face contorted in a momentary grimace. "I've got a young woman who's planning on taking this one and turning it into one of those fancy home places. You know, the kind that people can visit to get ideas for fixin' their homes up all pretty like. I told Travis the last time I saw him that I had a woman comin' in to rent a place that very day—one who could help him smooth his wife's feathers. Though, come to think of it, if his wife had seen Miss Gilbert she'd be squawkin' about a helluva lot more 'n a dirty house."

She froze.

"Did you say, Miss *Gilbert*?"

"I sure did." He popped his hat back on his head and

rubbed his hands down the sides of his worn jeans. "Do you know her?"

"I—uh—no, not really." She knew she should probably tell him Tiffany Ann was dead, but she didn't. Why, she wasn't quite sure.

"She sure is a pretty one. Sweet, too. When I asked if she thought she'd get customers out here, she said she was confident she would. Even said something 'bout setting up one of those computer things so she could reach even more customers." He pulled a key from his back pocket and gestured toward the door. "I can't let you have this one because it's Miss Gilbert's, but you can take a look-see if you'd like."

"Uh—yeah, okay, sure." She followed the man into the building, her eyes drawn to the sun-filled front room and wide-open space. It wasn't hard to see what had drawn Tiffany Ann to this building, why she'd felt it a perfect place to begin her career. But could a business—even one that was website accessible—survive in the middle of nowhere? "Did Miss Gilbert actually sign papers on this place?"

"Not quite. She took a walk down by the creek out back so she could think. 'Bout the time I went to check on her she was peelin' out of my parking lot like a world-class race car driver. Guess somethin' came up. But she'll be back. Miss Gilbert was so excited that day, so full of plans. She reminded me of my own daughter, though Maria felt New York City was the only option if she wanted to be someone. But I think that's baloney."

"How come Ridge Cove isn't more developed to begin with . . . even to the degree of what Tom's Creek or Sweet Briar has achieved?"

"Businesses don't want to come where there isn't any po-lice."

"You don't have a police department?" she asked, her thoughts flitting between the man's words and her sadness for Tiffany Ann.

"We fall under county jurisdiction out here, which is 'bout the same as having no po-lice. But I'm gonna change that, one step at a time."

"How?"

"By buying me some po-lice."

"Buying police? I don't understand—do you mean hiring a security guard or two?" She pulled her thoughts from Tiffany Ann and focused them on the man standing on the other side of the dead girl's dream.

"No, ma'am. I mean buying po-lice. Gun-carryin', car-drivin' po-lice."

"Can you do that?"

"Of course I can. I already have. And it's why Travis and Miss Gilbert are taking these buildings seriously. Heck, Travis asked me that last day I saw him if he could see the paperwork." He peered out the large front window and pointed at two new additions to the parking lot. "We best be heading back, I got some customers to take care of."

She followed him into the bright morning sun. "Can I ask one last question?"

"Rent for the first year is just two hundred dollars a month. After that it will double." He strode toward the larger building, Tori half jogging to keep pace. "You thinkin' about rentin' one? Because we'd sure love to have you."

"Two hundred dollars? How can you survive on that?"

"It's about faith, ma'am. I believe Ridge Cove is going to take off now. And I need to be willin' to pony up a little money to back up that faith."

She considered his words. "Actually I wanted to ask about the police. I mean, who are you buying police from?"

"A little town about twenty-five miles from here. I imagine you drove through it on the way here."

Mentally she reviewed her drive, tried to recall the

towns she'd driven through between Sweet Briar and Ridge Cove but could recall none.

"What town is that?" she asked, her attention thwarted momentarily by a large trunk displayed just outside the flea market's main entrance.

"Sweet Briar."

Chapter 17

She slipped Lulu's log cabin onto the screen and shone it onto the far wall, the picture magnified to proportions that coincided with Quinton's forest. Once she was satisfied with its placement, Tori stepped out from behind Colby Calhoun's portable projector and began tracing the building onto the base-coated drywall.

Little by little the drawings Milo's students had created were being brought to life on the walls of the new children's room, pictures that would invite curiosity and ignite a passion toward books. It was the kind of library she'd dreamed of as a child, the kind of library she wanted to offer as an adult.

And thanks to Winston Hohlbrook and the rest of the board, it was finally happening. In just one week, her dream would officially move from the recesses of her brain into the epitome of reality.

A reality that would blow the residents of Sweet Briar away—with Dixie Dunn the most flabbergasted of all.

Tori'd never seen herself as the type who gained enjoyment from another person's downfall, but things were different now. Dixie Dunn and the rest of Sweet Briar were in dire need of a healthy wake-up call about what did and didn't define a person. And last she checked, birthplace wasn't anywhere in that definition.

"Would you look at who I found outside?"

Tori pulled her pencil from the wall and turned around. Milo and Lulu stood just inside the doorway, a silent and pale-faced Margaret Louise less than five feet behind.

Lulu squealed as she ran over to Tori. "You're making my log cabin, you're making my log cabin!"

Squatting down to the child's eye level, Tori nodded. "You bet I am. And with any luck I'll get it painted before I go home for the night."

"Wow, Tori . . . the trees look spectacular!" Milo approached the wall, his eyes skimming the wide trunks and gnarled limbs she'd transferred from Quinton's paper to the wall. "The colors you picked are amazing."

Her cheeks grew warm as she stood once again, Milo's sincere praise tugging at a place in her heart she'd put in mothballs months earlier. "Thanks."

Lulu's teacher took a step closer, his focus no longer on Quinton's trees or any other part of the children's room for that matter. "Did you find a trunk?"

"A trunk?"

"Yeah. For the costumes."

"I—uh—"

"Miss Sinclair?" Lulu tugged on her paint smock.

She looked down, her head grateful for the distraction her heart obviously needed. What was wrong with her? Had she not learned a valuable lesson about relationships?

"Miss Sinclair?" Lulu repeated.

"Yes, sweetie, what can I do for you?"

"I solved the mystery, Miss Sinclair." The child hopped from foot to foot, her attention obviously at war between what she wanted to say and the allure of the room taking shape around her.

"Lulu, why don't you give Victoria a chance to get her work done. Maybe she can stop by on the way home . . . and you can tell her *then*." Margaret Louise's usual peppy demeanor was gone, in its place a curious mixture of reluctance and disappointment.

She looked from Lulu to Margaret Louise and back again. "No, it's okay. I could use the break." She reached down and lifted Lulu onto the table she'd dragged into the room for the sole purpose of housing her various paints and brushes. "Did Mr. Wentworth give you one of Cam Jansen's books?"

"Who's that?" Lulu asked, her face scrunching in confusion.

"She's a little girl in a series of mystery books. She solves crimes by utilizing her photographic memory."

"What's pho—pho-pho memory?"

Tori laughed, the happy sound mingling with Milo's. "Photographic memory. It means she can see something . . . like a scene or a person or a thing, and then recall it by memory at a later time."

"Oh." Lulu peeked around Tori's shoulder, a smile stretching across her face at the sight of her log cabin on the wall. "Will you paint mine, too? Like you did for Quinton's trees?"

"Of course." Tori plucked a can of weathered brown from the other side of the table and held it up for Lulu to see. "I even have the perfect color all picked out."

Lulu's smile grew even larger. "You don't need that thing anymore."

She let her gaze follow Lulu's to the projector in the middle of the room. "What thing? The projector?"

"Uh-huh."

Tori looked a question at Milo, who simply shrugged in response.

"I do need Mr. Calhoun's projector. It's how I'm going to finish your cabin—"

"*Laura's* cabin," Lulu corrected.

"You're right. *Laura's* cabin." Tori touched her index finger to the tip of Lulu's nose and gave it a gentle push. "I can't finish Laura's cabin or Cinderella's castle or the dwarves' beds or any of the other wonderful pictures your classmates made for me if I don't have that projector."

"You can use your own." Lulu swung her feet back and forth from the knee, the flow of air they created a welcome relief in a room that had grown all too warm thanks to the projector.

She extended her confusion toward Margaret Louise only to have eye contact diverted.

O-kay.

"I don't have my own, remember?"

"I know where it is." Lulu turned her body a hairbreadth so she could run her fingers across the tops of the various paint cans. "*Ooooh.* I love purple."

"I do, too." Tori took hold of the child's hands and held them gently until they regained eye contact. "You know where my projector is?"

"Uh-huh. Your Popsicle sticks, too." Lulu's eyes widened. "And it sure is a great big box. I bet you have five million Popsicle sticks in there. Maybe even *six*!"

"Where did you see—"

"I saw lots and lots of lightbulbs, too. And a book—with big squares and numbers in it . . . like a calendar." Lulu hopped off the table and skipped over to her grandmother, the pure joy on her face at complete odds with her kin's.

She glanced at Milo once again, his latest shrug accompanied by a look of confusion he, too, cast in Margaret Louise's direction.

"What's she talking about, Margaret Louise?" Milo asked, his audible question a near perfect match to the mental one making a constant loop in Tori's head.

"Now she could be mistaken. She has a vivid imagination whether she's holding a book or no—"

"Mee-Maw, I told you I'm not lying."

"Hush, Lulu. I'm not accusing you of lying. I'm just thinking maybe you saw what you wanted to see. You'd had a lot of excitement at the party, remember?"

What were they talking about?

"But Miss Dixie had all those things in a big shed in the middle of the woods, Mee-Maw. I saw it with my own two eyes."

Tori's gasp echoed Milo's.

"*Dixie?* Did you say Dixie?" she asked, her voice bordering on shrill.

"Yes, Miss Sinclair. She's been taking good care of your things."

"I'll bet she has," she bit out through clenched teeth. "That woman's sole goal in life since the moment I set foot in this town has been to make me feel unwelcome and—and completely *incompetent*."

She felt Milo's hand on her arm, a steadying gesture that was probably meant to calm her down, but she didn't care. Nothing could stop the flow of words as they escaped her lips. Not Margaret Louise. Not Lulu. Not Milo. And not even Nina, who had the misfortune of making her entrance at that very moment.

"She did everything in her power to sabotage my work here—she stole the appointment book that made me look ridiculous in front of Milo, she screamed at me over a coffee stain in a book she probably put there herself, she tried to make me look like an idiot in front of the entire library board, and she made me question my sanity every time I replaced another missing bulb on my front porch."

Margaret Louise finally looked up, her eyes hazy and tear-filled. "What are you going to—"

"And you know what hit me like a ton of bricks during my drive to Ridge Cove this morning? Do you know what thought I shoved down simply because I was ashamed for thinking it about a woman of Dixie's age and status in this town? Do you?"

Milo's hand tightened on her arm as he moved in behind her, his lips nearly touching her ear. "I know what you're going to say and it's worth investigating but—"

She spun around, her rant continuing at full voice. "Worth investigating? You think it's worth investigating? Does that mean I have Sweet Briar's permission?"

He grabbed hold of her shoulders and brought his face to hers. "Do not say it in front of Lulu. Please."

And just like that the air gushed from her balloon. Inhaling deeply, Tori closed her eyes, fought with herself to regain some semblance of composure before she faced Margaret Louise's grandchild, a child she adored as if she were her own.

Slowly she turned, her eyes frantically blinking away the enraged tears that burned their way from the inside, out. "Lulu, I'm sorry. I shouldn't have spoken like that in front of you."

Lulu shrugged. "Miss Dixie took real good care of your stuff, Miss Sinclair. I promise she did. Not a single thing looks broke. Not even a lightbulb."

Chapter 18

She turned the pen over and over on her desk, the fingers of her right hand sliding from top to bottom. So much had happened that day it was hard to know what to focus on, which tidbit of information could be the key to removing her name from Investigator McGuire's list of suspects once and for all.

"Do you think I made the right decision letting Margaret Louise confront Dixie?" Tori stopped the pen midturn and looked from Milo to Nina and back again. "You know she's going to end up letting her off easy. They've been friends for more years than I've been alive."

"I think it was a good call, Tori, I really do." Milo stretched his legs in front of the same chair she'd sat in to read with Lulu. "Dixie Dunn is threatened by you—to a much higher degree than any of us imagined. She's not going to let her guard down if you're in the room as part of the confrontation team."

She stole a glance at her assistant, saw her head nod in agreement.

"But what happens if she *did* try to frame me? Do you think Margaret Louise will be open-minded enough to listen for any clues that might point in that direction?"

"I think she will be. But if she can't, then Rose Winters will." Milo rested his elbow on the armrest of the chair and balanced his chin atop his knuckles. "Rose Winters doesn't let much go. She's a stickler for rules. Like Georgina."

"Yeah, but she's been friends with Dixie for even longer than Margaret Louise has been." She knew she sounded paranoid, but really, how could they blame her?

"There's plenty of good people in this town. No one is going to turn the other cheek on someone who's tried to frame an innocent person." Nina's voice, shy but firm, struck a chord.

Then again, everyone thought Dixie Dunn was a relatively decent person, and look at the problems she'd caused already—regardless of whether she had a hand in Tiffany Ann's murder or not.

Tori voiced those feelings aloud. "I can't believe she did all those things. Stealing lightbulbs night after night? Sneaking in my house and removing a box of craft supplies I needed for a visit with your students," she added, pointing in Milo's direction.

"I know."

"And, Milo, can you imagine someone being so angry at a person they'd lift an appointment book just to make them look bad even knowing innocent children would lose out as well?"

Nina leaned against the wall, bending her left leg at the knee. "Nobody was the wiser though. You pulled off that first visit in a way not many people could have done *with* notice."

"And the projector? That was nothing short of wanting to make me go down in flames in front of the library board when the room wasn't completed by the date I promised." She slid her thumb and index finger down the pen again, the repetitive turning motion a mind-numbing release.

"You got Colby Calhoun's though, and I can't believe the progress you made on that far wall in just one afternoon. You'll have no trouble being ready by next week if you keep that same pace." Milo raised his arm, swept his hand through his hair, the unruly result stopping her pen-holding hand once again.

Stop it, Tori.

She made herself look at Nina, the wall clock, Lulu's chair, anything and everything besides Milo Wentworth. She needed to stay focused, to examine the revelations of the past few hours.

"And you—you didn't see how she nearly bit my head off over that book with the coffee stain in it." Pushing her chair back several inches, Tori stood and paced around the room. "I swear, if I find out she put that there herself, I will impose a fine on her so fast her head will spin."

"Ms. Dunn didn't make that stain, Miss Sinclair. Tiffany Ann did." Nina's foot dropped back down to the ground. "She just knew it and came back looking for it."

Tori spun around, her eyes narrowing on her assistant. "What did you say?"

"I said—I, uh, *Tiffany Ann* made the stain in that book. Ms. Dunn knew it because she'd been here that morning, too."

Tori saw Milo straighten up out of her peripheral vision, his curiosity piqued by the assistant's words as well.

"What morning, Nina?" She closed the gap between her and Nina in five quick strides. "*The* morning? The morning Tiffany Ann was murdered?"

"Yes, Miss Sinclair. The only day Tiffany Ann was in here." Nina shifted uncomfortably. "I told you she was in here when you asked me just the other day."

"I know you did. I just didn't realize the stain was hers." Not that it mattered. Who cared whether it was from

Tiffany Ann Gilbert or some resident of the local senior center? A stain was a stain.

But still.

"What do you mean the *only* day Tiffany Ann was in here? Surely she came into the library from time to time, right?" She glanced from Nina to Milo and back again, their heads shaking in unison. "What? She had something against the library?"

"She wasn't a reader," Milo offered. "I had a lengthy discussion with her parents one day about how pleased they were to see Tiffany Ann's nieces and nephews devouring books after being in my class. They said Tiffany Ann had never been like that. That's why they asked me to tutor her. But she just didn't love books. Not before I came along and not after."

"I've been here four years and I've never seen her in this branch . . . ever," Nina added quietly.

"So what made that day different? Why was she knocking into people in line at Debbie's Bakery just to come to a place she didn't like?" Returning to her desk chair, Tori rested her elbows on her desk and cradled her head in her hands. "I just don't get this. I don't get any of this."

She heard Milo's feet as he crossed the room to her desk, felt his strong hands as they began to knead her shoulders. Slowly, hesitantly, his long capable fingers rubbed at the tension that had knotted itself into her body.

"You'll figure it out . . . *we'll* figure it out." He continued working her shoulders with his hands, his touch warming her body from top to bottom.

As much as she tried to discount his words and offer of support, there was something about Milo Wentworth that made her believe it was possible. That a man could truly want to follow his words through with actions.

"Miss Sinclair, if it's okay, I'd like to head home to

Duwayne. He's probably as hungry as a racehorse 'round 'bout now."

Tori lifted her head as Milo's hands stopped moving and he stepped to the side. "Of course, Nina. I'm sorry you got wrapped up in this afternoon's drama." She pushed her chair back once again, this time crossing the room for the sole purpose of hugging her assistant. "I don't know how and I don't know when . . . but I promise you we will be able to focus purely on library things sometime soon."

"I know we will." Nina stepped back from Tori's embrace and grabbed her lunch sack from the narrow table beside the office door. "I can see now why the board picked you. I wasn't ready no matter how badly Duwayne thought I was. But one day, dab by dab, I will be."

"I don't doubt that for one second." As Nina walked out the door and into the hallway Tori turned and faced Milo. "A *dab*?"

"A little bit. A small quantity." He returned her stare with a smile, one that started in his eyes and spread to his mouth. "I know. I know. But when you learn it, you'll be good to go."

"Any chance I could talk Debbie's husband into abandoning his latest writing project in favor of a dictionary of southern expressions? I'd buy a copy—maybe even several. One for my house, one for my office, one for the branch."

"You wouldn't need one in the branch." Milo peeked out the window into the night, the blanket of darkness broken by a smattering of streetlamps and a few stars. "Everyone in Sweet Briar knows the talk."

She set her hands on her hips. "What about the poor soul who moves here and needs a little assistance learning— wait, scratch that. No one in their right mind would move into this town. They'd have their possessions disappear into thin air and they'd be accused of every crime known to mankind that happens in this tow—*what*? Where are we going?"

His hand sent a charge through her body the second he took hold of her arm and started guiding her toward the hallway. "For a walk."

"A walk?" she protested feebly.

"Nights don't get much more beautiful than this, and I don't want to waste another second of it sitting inside your office listening to you rant about the many pitfalls of life in Sweet Briar."

"Rant? Me?" She felt her heart sink as his words took root in her thoughts, highlighting the many examples of his accusation. "I'm sorry. Why don't you head home? Get as far away from me and my pity-party as you possibly can?"

"Oh I'm not in any hurry to get away from *you*." He cleared his throat, his hand shaking ever so slightly as he pulled the door shut behind them and led her into the library's parking lot. "I just think we both could use a little fresh air."

She couldn't argue. In fact, the cool night air felt good against her flushed cheeks. It slowed her down, made her breathe a little more deeply.

And it gave her some quiet time alone with Milo. Time that didn't include other people's children or a project in the library.

Unfortunately, now that they had the time, she had no idea what to say. She hadn't done much of anything since moving to Sweet Briar. And she'd already ranted about her role as a suspect long enough.

"Did you enjoy the fair last week?" he asked as they strolled around the library and headed down the sidewalk that lined the town's square.

She looked up at the stars, found the Little Dipper, and made a wish. "I did. Much more than I thought I would."

He nodded as they walked, the gesture an obvious ploy to make her elaborate.

"I think it's kind of neat to be in a place where everyone knows each other. They know each other's children and grandchildren. I've never really lived in a place like this before." She stole a glance in his direction as they passed the playground and the center gazebo, hoped her answer smoothed some of the sting from her earlier words. Sweet Briar was Milo's home and it wasn't polite to trash it simply because it wasn't necessarily the right place for her.

She said as much to him.

"Why don't you hold off just a little while longer before deciding whether Sweet Briar is right for you." He placed his hand on the small of her back and led her to a large rock at the far edge of the square. Removing his hand from her back he lowered it to the rock and patted the flat surface. "You like your sewing circle, right?"

She nodded. "I did. I mean, I do. But"—she exhaled a pent-up burst of air that begged to be released—"sewing just does that. It calms you. It forges an instant bond with others who sew, too. I could find a circle anywhere."

"You could," he agreed. "But you already *have* one here."

"True."

"Tell me about it," he prompted.

"About what?" she asked.

"Sewing. Why you like it so much."

"I don't know." She shrugged. "I guess it's about bypassing the easy store purchase and doing it yourself. With your own vision, your own tastes, your own hands. It's special in a way I'm not sure I can fully explain. And to be around other people who feel the same just makes it even more special."

He tilted his head ever so slightly as he studied her, tiny crinkles forming beside his eyes as he smiled and patted the rock once again. "Oh, Tori, once this whole mess is settled, I suspect Sweet Briar is going to embrace you."

Claiming the spot he indicated, Tori set her back against the rock and lifted herself to a sit with her forearms. "You and Nina sound so sure of that."

"Because we are."

She turned her head away from him, focused on the tiny white lights that trimmed the gazebo. "But you can't be. Neither of you even really know me. So how can you be sure you're right and Investigator McGuire and the rest of Sweet Briar are wrong?"

He guided her focus back with a gentle touch to her chin. "First of all, I'm good at reading people. Always have been. I suspect Nina is as well. It's the positive side of being"—he raised the index and middle fingers of both hands into the air—"*shy*. We can observe while everyone else is talking."

Dropping her gaze to her hands she waited for him to continue, her psyche suddenly desperate for the reassurance he offered.

"Second of all, you don't know what all of Sweet Briar thinks."

Her head popped up. "But Leona and Georgina and the investigator and the parents of your students—"

He held an index finger to her lips. "A few parents is not all. There were more kids *in* school that day than *out* and those families were every bit aware of what was going on as the others were. They just believe in waiting for the facts. Like Nina does. And Margaret Louise. And Debbie. And Colby Calhoun. And—"

"I've never even met Colby," she offered in protest.

"He sent his projector, didn't he?" Milo slid his finger back to her chin, forced her gaze to meet his. "And no, he wouldn't have sent it over just because Debbie told him to. Colby is an independent thinker."

She weighed his words, allowed her heart to try them on for size. Milo was right. She had people who believed in her and she knew that. So why was it easier to focus on the handful of people who felt differently?

"It's easier to believe the bad stuff sometimes, isn't it?"

She stared at him, her mouth agape. "How-how did you know I was thinking that exact thing?"

He shrugged, a mischievous gleam in his eye. "I'm really a psychic posing as a third grade teacher."

It felt good to laugh, to surrender her body to a little fun after the mammoth-sized mountains and unending obstacles she'd been maneuvering for days. "Thank you, Milo," she said, her voice not much more than a whisper.

"For what?"

"I don't know . . . for everything, I guess." She pulled her knees to her chest and hugged her legs tightly as she took in the stars overhead. "For being open to the fact that I might actually be an okay person, for letting me read with Lulu, for making Heritage Day even more fun, for giving me pep talks when I need them most."

"Wow. You make me sound like a pretty nice guy." He rocked his body to the side, his head gently grazing hers before straightening up once again. "But you make it easy. You're truly a gift to my students . . . and to me."

"Even if I'm the reason you no longer get apples?" She kept her face directed toward the stars despite the distinct feeling that he was studying her closely.

"*Especially* because I no longer get apples." He pushed out his fairly muscular stomach and patted it soundly. "I'm much more of a butter kind of guy. It's easier to spread on bread."

A whistled melody cut short their laughter and made them both turn. A single solitary figure strolled down the sidewalk in their direction, the familiar swagger a dead giveaway as to the man's identity.

Investigator McGuire.

She felt Milo's hand cover hers as her body tensed in reaction.

"It's okay," he mumbled under his breath as he hopped down from the rock and extended his hand to the police officer. "Investigator McGuire, what brings you around this time of night?"

The officer's steel gray eyes left Milo's and focused squarely on Tori. "Just keeping my eyes and ears open for any potential issues."

"Issues?" she challenged.

"The kind of things that threaten Sweet Briar's way of life." The officer rested his hand on the top of his gun belt, his fingers wrapped casually around the black baton.

"Don't you mean the kind of *people* who threaten Sweet Briar?" she asked through clenched teeth.

"I mean both. I have my eyes open at all times."

She knew she shouldn't laugh but she couldn't help herself. Investigator Daniel McGuire was a perfect carica-ture of the narrow-minded cop found in all too many bad movies. Unfortunately, in this case, the movie was her life.

"Well, we were just getting ready to continue our walk so we'll leave you to your work, Investigator." Milo reached a hand in Tori's direction, pulling her off the rock the moment she took hold. "Good night."

They walked a few hundred yards before either glanced over their shoulder or uttered a word.

"I'm sorry about that; if I knew we'd run into him I never would have suggested a walk." Milo dug his hands into his pockets as they crossed the center of the square and turned toward the library.

"No. It was fine. *Great*, actually." She inhaled deeply, willed herself to focus on how much she'd enjoyed their time together rather than the minor irritation that was In-vestigator McGuire. "One day very soon I'll figure out what happened to Tiffany Ann and he won't be able to harass me any longer."

"Any progress yet?" Milo's words trailed off into the air as a police car drove slowly down the road just inches from where they stood.

"Will it ever stop?" she said, the sudden influx of tears evident in her voice.

His hand, warm and strong, took hold of hers as they watched the car pass. "Oh, wait . . . never mind . . . that's one of our cars. McGuire's been driving his Tom's Creek car."

She forced her body to relax as they continued walking, his hand still entwined with hers. "How many cars does Sweet Briar have?"

"Two or three. Though we only have one officer—Chief Dallas. We had a part-time patrolman at one time but we just didn't need him. It's about as quiet as it comes here in Sweet Briar. At least it *was*."

"So who's driving the cars?" she asked.

"Probably Thomas. He seems to be doing that more lately, particularly at night." Milo shrugged. "Perk of being married to the mayor, I guess."

"Driving a police car is a perk?"

"Every little boy's dream." He flashed a smile at her as they walked, two dimples appearing in his cheeks.

"Even you?"

"Nah. I thought the garbage trucks were cooler."

As they approached the library from the west he stopped and gestured toward a quiet residential street on their left. When she nodded, he turned in that direction, a move she couldn't help but see as an intentional effort to elongate their time together.

"With Tiffany Ann's death and everything I can't help but think this town could probably use a few more officers, don't you?" She reveled in the feel of his skin against hers, willed his steady confidence and positive attitude to seep through her skin.

"Nah. Stuff doesn't happen here. Not usually anyway. And if Dallas needs help, then Tom's Creek sends an officer."

She pondered his words, a question forming on their heels. "Is that what we do for Ridge Cove, seeing as how they don't have a police force at all?"

"They're covered by county, which isn't a good thing for anyone, even a place as dinky as Ridge Cove. The response time is pathetic." Milo pointed at a pale yellow house on the left side of the road, a For Sale sign gracing its front lawn. "I love that place. I even checked it out with a realtor last week, and it's even more charming inside."

"Are you going to buy it?" She looked from Milo to the house and back again, his enthusiasm for the structure bringing a smile to her lips.

"I wish. But it'd be silly for a single guy like me. Besides, there's nothing wrong with my place." He pointed at a large tree in the front yard. "But can't you just see kids hanging from that tree?"

"And breaking their necks?" Her laughter was met by a squeeze of her hand and a flush on her face. "But if there's nothing wrong with your place why would you want to move?"

"To have a fresh start, I guess. A place where the only memories are ones to be made . . . now and in the future."

They continued on in silence, the sound of their feet on the sidewalk the only noise to be heard as they retreated to their own private thoughts and dreams.

Finally she spoke, her words tumbling from her mouth at the very same moment the question formed in her thoughts. "So Ridge Cove would be better off receiving police coverage from Sweet Briar than from the county?"

"Of course they would. It would take far less time and

from what I've heard they'd be in a lot better hands." He looked down at her as they walked, his brows slightly furrowed. "Why do you ask?"

"I don't know. I guess the guy made a smart decision." Wordlessly they turned around at the end of the street and headed back toward their original destination, the sound of an occasional cricket peppering the air around them.

"What guy?"

"The guy who runs one of the flea markets in Ridge Cove." She thought back to the sign over the store and the way customers had greeted him the moment they arrived. "I guess he's Stu . . . of Stu's Flea Market. I met him this morning when I went trunk searching."

"Okay, so what decision did he make?" Milo pulled her hand closer as he guided her around a raised tree root that had buckled the sidewalk and created a potential tripping hazard.

"To buy police coverage from Sweet Briar." She glanced at the home Milo wanted as they passed by it once again, the wide front porch and large front windows beckoning to all who passed.

She felt his hand release hers as he stopped in the middle of the sidewalk, his eyes narrowed on hers in confusion. "Buy police coverage from Sweet Briar? Tori, you must have misunderstood. Ridge Cove can't buy those kinds of services and Sweet Briar most certainly can't sell them."

"But Stu said—"

Milo shrugged and shook his head, his hand finding hers in the dark once again. "I don't care what this guy said. It simply can't be done."

Chapter 19

She was grateful for the distraction painting afforded. It gave her a way to escape the troubling thoughts that plagued her subconscious and left her tossing and turning throughout the night.

Finally, just before dawn, she'd given up trying to sleep and made her way over to the library where she could make optimal use of her time. Still, she found herself wading through the past few weeks in Sweet Briar—the people she'd met, the gossip she'd heard, the experiences she'd had, and the conflicting things she'd learned.

While some had attributed Tiffany's bizarre behavior during the final days of her life to drugs, others had dismissed the notion as absurd. While some were eager to see Tori for who she was, others seemed every bit as unwilling to consider her as something other than a murder suspect. While she'd thought she was building a solid friendship with Leona Elkin, Leona was simply humoring her, biding her time for something bigger. And in uniform.

Shaking her head, Tori forced herself to focus on Jennifer's stained glass castle windows as she applied a splash of red and a splash of yellow paint. The room was coming out better than she'd dreamed. Quinton's trees, which she'd used in several places throughout the room, enhanced the artwork of the other students. The varied colors and scenes drew the eye around the room, hinting at the many possibilities that could come from reading.

Yet she wasn't happy. Not the way she should be after realizing a dream she'd had since childhood. But how could she be with everything that was going on around her on a daily basis—not the least of which was Milo's contradictory statements regarding Stu's claims?

"Oh, Victoria, this is—this is wonderful." Rose Winters stepped into the room, Margaret Louise at her heels. "I had no idea you could—" Her voice trailed off as she set her glasses firmly onto the bridge of her nose and walked from mural to mural. "I had no idea you could make a room so . . . so wonderful. The children are going to love this, absolutely *love* this."

Tori inhaled sharply, letting the subsequent outtake of air clear her mind of the incessant thoughts that had nagged and pulled at her for hours. "You really like it?"

Rose wandered around the room as she attributed the correct book to each and every picture Tori had painted onto the wall. "How could I not? How could *anyone* not?"

Tori stole a glance at Margaret Louise, a name burning on the edge of her tongue that could contradict Rose's rhetorical question. The woman clasped her hands together, her head moving slowly from side to side.

"We tried your house first, but when you didn't answer we figured you'd be here. Working. Can you take a break?" Margaret Louise asked as she ventured into the room and stopped between Tori and the window she was painting. "For just a little while? Rose and I would like to talk to you."

"Sure, I guess." She dipped the brush in a cup of mineral spirits and wiped it with a paint-spattered cloth. "I take it you talked to Dixie?"

"We did." Margaret Louise looked around the room, her shoulders slumping. "No chairs?"

"Not yet. But by Saturday we'll have a colorful assortment of beanbag chairs to choose from." She knew her answer was bordering on ornery but she didn't care. Dixie Dunn had gotten too much blind support when it was anything but justified.

"There's a step stool right there, Margaret Louise, sit on that." Rose made one last turn around the room before finding a stable enough table to lean against. "I heard what Lulu found in the shed and I want you to know how sorry I am. You deserved better than we gave you when you first came."

Tori swallowed over the sudden lump in her throat that made it impossible to speak.

"I started to see Dixie's part at that second circle meeting. And it was impossible to miss at the board meeting. If it matters any, I was disgusted." Rose lowered her glasses a half inch and peered at Tori over the top rim. "And I let Dixie know that when we confronted her in her home yesterday."

It was a start. Tori leaned against an unpainted section of wall and waited for more details, her mouth untrusting of what her heart might blurt out.

"She denied it all—taking the sticks, stealing your lightbulbs, hiding the library's desk planner, all of it." Margaret Louise eyed the stool for a moment before looking over her shoulder at her lower half and shaking her head, opting instead to stand against a wall as Tori did. "She even went so far as to say you planned it to make her look bad."

Tori's gasp was cut short by Rose's hand. "We didn't let her get away with it, Victoria, you must know that."

"Good."

"Though, in the end, we realized she was telling the truth." Rose studied her from across the room, her eyes magnified to twice their size by the bifocals she wore.

Telling the truth?

They couldn't be serious.

"You're kidding, right?" she finally uttered. "She had my things in her shed. You heard what Lulu said."

"We heard what Lulu *said*," Margaret Louise stated.

"What she *said*? Oh . . . no." She flashed a look of understanding at the child's grandmother. "She seemed so sure she'd seen everything. Was she crushed to have you realize she was wrong?"

"She wasn't wrong," Rose said flatly. "Everything she saw was exactly where she saw it."

"Then I don't understan—wait. Tell me this isn't going to be swept under the carpet because Dixie's lived here her whole life." She looked from Rose to Margaret Louise and back again. "This town can't be that narrow-minded, can it?"

"We have eyes, Victoria. And we don't shut them from things simply because we don't want to see."

"But isn't that what you're doing, Rose? By taking her word for something that's as plain as the nose on my face?" She could hear the anger in her voice, knew it was getting out of control, yet it was hard to stop.

"Sometimes there's more to the story." Margaret Louise shifted her weight from one leg to the other. "An unexpected detail or twist that changes everythin'."

"You mean like just how far she was going to take this before waving the white flag?"

Rose ignored her flippant comment. "It took a while but I think Dixie will admit she's been overly hard on you. But she was hurt and angry at the way she was removed from her job."

"She'll *admit* that? Wow. I should feel so relieved."

"Victoria, just hear us out." Margaret Louise peeked

her head into the hallway and then pulled it back in. "Is Nina here?"

"No, why?"

"Because this concerns her . . . or rather . . . her husband, Duwayne."

"No, this doesn't. I'm so tired of everyone handing Dixie Dunn a pass for her bad behavior. She was nothing short of nasty during the meeting the other night and—"

"And Leona called her on it," Margaret Louise interjected.

"True. But even at the circle meetings she's been more than a little unfriendly."

"And I've spoken with her about that as well," Rose said.

"And the things she stole? The way she has done her best to sabotage me since day one? Did you talk about those things?"

"We started to."

"What stopped you, Margaret Louise?" Tori willed herself to take several long, deep breaths, to find a way to settle her heart and her stomach.

"The shed isn't hers."

She stared at Margaret Louise and then Rose. "The shed isn't *hers*?"

"It's Nina's," Rose said softly.

"Nina's? It can't—wait. Did you say, *Nina's*?"

"Her property backs up to Dixie's with a stretch of woods in between. Lulu assumed the shed belonged to Dixie but it really belongs to Nina and—"

"Nina? Nina has been trying to sabotage me? But wh—" And at that moment, she knew. Nina had wanted her job. Nina had been forced to remain the assistant librarian so she, Tori, could take the lead. "Oh no . . . how could I have missed that?"

"You didn't." Rose linked her arms across her sweater-clad chest. "It wasn't Nina."

Were they *trying* to confuse her?

Exasperated she pushed her hand through her hair, exhaling loudly. "But you just said the shed was Nina's."

"Nina and *Duwayne's*," Margaret Louise corrected.

"Nina and—wait. You think *her husband* stole everything?"

"We did. And now we know."

She pinned Rose with a steady gaze. "You know?"

"We confronted that young man and he fell apart. Admitted the whole thing." Rose nodded at Margaret Louise to pick up the story.

"He didn't mean any harm, not in a malicious way. He just wanted Nina to shine." The heavyset woman tossed her hands in the air. "He said he knew it was wrong, felt it more strongly each time Nina came home bragging about you . . . but he couldn't stop. It just spiraled out of control."

I'll say it did.

"You need to do what you need to do, but he's sorry. And he's afraid Nina will leave him if she finds out."

Her heart twisted for just a moment before another possibility—too glaring to ignore—reared its head and brought the anger back again. "What if the mistakes he's made extend to . . . this-this cloud of suspicion I've been living under for the past few weeks?"

"They don't."

"How do you know, Rose?" she spat.

"Because I had Duwayne Morgan in my classroom all those years ago and he doesn't have it in him to hurt a flea."

"He hurt *me*."

"Psychologically, yes. Physically, no."

She'd been so sure—so hopeful the missing objects would lead to her being absolved from Tiffany Ann's murder. But if it wasn't Duwayne—

"You've seen the outrage Dixie has shown me . . . what if that anger extends beyond mean-spirited barbs and threatening glares? What if all this scrutiny I've been under is *her* doing?"

Rose struggled to a stand from her spot against the table and slowly closed the distance between them, her hand grazing Margaret Louise's arm as she passed. "Dixie Dunn did not murder Tiffany Ann Gilbert."

"Did she say that?"

"No, Victoria, she didn't." Rose stopped a few feet from where Tori stood and stamped her sensibly clad foot. "Because we didn't ask."

"You—you didn't *ask*?"

"No. We didn't," said Margaret Louise. "We talked about it, even considered it, but . . . in the end . . . we decided it wasn't fair."

"Wasn't fair? Wasn't fair? That woman has been anything but fair to me from the moment we met." She could feel the stinging sensation building behind her eyes, could taste the bile that threatened to rise further up her throat.

"We see that now. We've admonished her for it. But murder? No, Victoria. Dixie is no more capable of murder than you or Duwayne Morgan are. For you to think otherwise—based on a few jealous little acts—is not much different than what that McGuire fellow is doing to you simply because you're new to Sweet Briar." Rose shot her hand out and gently squeezed Tori's wrist. "I believe in her innocence in Tiffany Ann's murder as strongly as I do in yours."

Suddenly deflated, Tori closed her eyes and leaned against the wall once again, Rose's arm still holding her wrist. "I thought maybe this was it. The answer that would make everything right again."

"Well this isn't it. Of that I'm sure." Rose stepped closer, her hand gently touching the side of Tori's face.

"But Victoria, there *is* an answer. There has to be. Because you did not kill that girl. And neither did Dixie. Or Duwayne."

The sincerity in Rose's eyes, the mirror emotion in Margaret Louise's face buoyed Tori's spirits somewhat, lifted the cloud of hurt that had descended on her heart as she realized Dixie wasn't guilty either. No, she wasn't any further in the whodunit process, but she could cross one suspect off her own imaginary list. And another who'd never even entered her mind. Even if the lines were drawn with a measure of reluctance and a hefty dose of lingering anger.

"So what do I do? This keeping-my-eyes-and-ears-open stuff has done little in the way of getting me out from under Investigator McGuire's thumb."

"We keep looking. And we keep listening. And we keep searching. Tiffany Ann's killer is out there, *somewhere*." Margaret Louise backed her way to the door, her gaze trained on Rose's. "But you can't let it consume you, Victoria. You need to relax, take some comfort in what you're creating right here in this room."

"If only it were that simple," Tori mumbled as Rose pushed a strand of hair behind her ear before heading in the direction in which Margaret Louise had just disappeared.

"Let us help you." Rose reached out for one of two parcels Margaret Louise held in her hands as she reappeared in the room.

"What are you two up to?" Tori asked, curiosity infusing a little much-needed energy into a voice that had grown bland and defeated.

"Take a look for yourself." Rose handed her package to Tori then crossed her bony arms across her frail body. "I hope you like it."

Slowly, Tori unwrapped the package, a dark green piece of fabric appearing in her hands. "What's this?"

"Robin Hood."

She felt her mouth gape open as she unfolded the perfectly costumed rendition of a boyhood classic. "Oh, Rose, it's perfect. The boys are going to love this."

The elderly woman beamed. "I'm glad."

"I've got something for you, too," Margaret Louise boasted as she held out the package she carried. "I *know* you'll like it."

Seconds and layers of paper later, a red dress with a matching cape and hood emerged in Tori's hands, the tears from earlier finally making their escape. "Oh, Margaret Louise, I've never seen a finer Red Riding Hood costume."

"See, Rose, what'd I tell you? It *was* worth it."

"Worth it? What was worth it?" Tori pulled her attention from the costumes in her hand and bounced it between her two friends. "What did I miss?"

Rose's head dropped downward as it shook from side to side. "A woman who doesn't listen any better than you do."

"I listen," Tori protested. "Unless—*wait*. Margaret Louise, did you confuse a statement for a question, too?"

"I suppose." Margaret Louise pried her lips open to reveal a noticeable chip in her front tooth.

Tori looked back down at the dress in her hands and back up at Margaret Louise. "You forgot the scissors, didn't you?"

"Forgot would be to imply *thought*, Victoria." Rose lifted her head and shook a finger at Margaret Louise. "I tried to warn you."

"Eh, that's okay. It was all for a good cause. Right, Victoria?" Margaret Louise let her head fall backward just a little as a laugh began somewhere deep inside her soul and burst out into the children's room.

Tori looked around the room, her eyes skimming across the murals she'd painted and the costumes she'd collected thus far thanks to the two women in the room with her at that very moment. Friends she'd never have met if she hadn't moved to Sweet Briar.

"Yeah," she finally answered, her accompanying smile warming her body from within. "It's worth it."

"That's my girl," Rose whispered as she took hold of Margaret Louise and nearly dragged the heavyset woman toward the door. "We've taken enough of your time already, but we'll see you tomorrow night, right?"

Tori looked down at the costumes in her hand. "Not this week."

"Victoria . . ."

"I know it wasn't a question, Rose. But I have something important I have to do after work tomorrow. Something I can't put off."

"Does this something have to do with a certain someone?" Margaret Louise teased until Rose jabbed her with a well-placed elbow to the side. "Ow. Watch those bony elbows, old woman."

Tori couldn't help but laugh as she waved off two of the truest friends she'd ever known. Women who were determined to stand by her through thick and thin, supporting her every step of the way. "No, it's not about Milo or any other man for that matter. It's about finding answers. For *myself.*"

Chapter 20

In the light of day, Stu's Flea Market in Ridge Cove had seemed inviting in a rustic sort of way. In the gathering dusk, however, the one-story weathered building conveyed utter isolation and suffocating loneliness—feelings that made Tori's stomach more than a little bit squeamish.

She should be home, gathering up whatever recipe she might have made and heading off to Leona Elkin's home for the weekly meeting of the Sweet Briar Ladies Society Sewing Circle. But instead, she was sitting alone, in a deserted parking lot, staring at a row of old-fashioned one-room stores and contemplating what may very well have been one of Tiffany Ann Gilbert's last moments of pure happiness.

The girl had been reaching for a dream, taking her first real independent steps toward making it a reality. Yet five days later she was dead. A victim of foul play.

It was a thought she simply couldn't dwell on at the moment. Not when she was trying so desperately to make sense of the troubling thoughts that kept teasing her sub-conscious, nagging at her for missing something big.

What that something was, though, she had no clue.

Stepping from her car, Tori squared her shoulders and inhaled deeply. It had been a gamble making the drive to Ridge Cove on a Monday evening, but waiting until Satur-day wasn't an option. Something had changed Tiffany Ann's demeanor while she was there. How else could one explain a happy and upbeat woman taking off in a rush without so much as a word to the owner of the property? Had she re-ceived a call on her cell that sent her running? Had she been scared off by something? Was she angry? Was she sad? Was she hurt?

They were all questions Tori had pondered on the drive from Sweet Briar. The kind of questions she knew she might never be able to answer yet couldn't ignore until she did a little digging.

She tugged her backpack purse onto her shoulder and set out for the main building, a single solitary lamp in a western window giving her hope that Stu was nearby. Al-though their initial encounter had been fairly brief, she'd seen enough to know he was a decent man or, at the very least, someone who wouldn't do her any harm.

As she approached his front porch the door opened and a shadowed figure emerged from a dimly lit foyer. "Who's there? What do you want?"

"Mr. Stu? I met you over the weekend and you showed me your new buildings."

The man didn't move. "It's a little late to be shoppin' for an office buildin', don't you think?"

"You're probably right. And I'm sorry. I just wanted to talk to you a little bit more about the day Tiffany Ann Gilbert came to see you."

He stepped out onto the porch, the early moonlight picking out the silver strands in his otherwise dark head of hair. "Oh, sure, I remember you . . . though I'm not sure you ever gave me your name."

Tori extended her hand and smiled. "I'm Tori Sinclair. I imagine you're Stu?"

"Yep. Stu Walker." He lifted his hand to his chin and rubbed it along stubbled skin. "Miss Gilbert isn't going to rent with me, is she?"

Dumbfounded, she shook her head. "Um, well, I can't answer that. I di—don't know her." She cringed inwardly at the lie, mentally chided herself for being so evasive. But she couldn't find the words to wipe away Tiffany's dream.

"I feel like I lost two clients on that same day." Stu slid his fingers farther up his jawline. "One I have money from, the other I thought was a done deal."

"Two? Oh—wait. There was the other guy, too, right? The repairman." She pulled her purse from her shoulder and set it on the porch floor. "Now what happened with him again?"

Stu shrugged. "That's just it. No one seems to know. To hear his wife rantin' 'n ravin' he's probably run off with some little hussy. And after seein' his wife, I can't say as I'd blame him."

"His name was Travis, right?" she asked, her voice quiet against the constant chatter of crickets.

"Travis it is." He crossed his arms and leaned against the back wall of the porch, a swarm of moths and late fall bugs taking advantage of the still-open door and lighted foyer. "He was a stickler that one. He read every single paper five times each before he'd sign anythin'. Wanted to see the papers I signed guaranteein' my tenants a nightly po-lice presence."

"About that paperwork . . . I was wondering how that really works, how Sweet Briar can promise—"

"Now you sound just like Travis. He had questions,

too. And since I was busy givin' Miss Gilbert a tour and explainin' it all to her, my contact took a few moments to answer his questions once and for all."

She considered the man's words as she looked out into the night, five outlines drawing her gaze and her thoughts back to Tiffany Ann. "Would it be possible if . . . well . . . for me to take a look at those papers?"

A smile crept across his face. "You're thinking about rentin' aren't you? Why else would you come out here after supper? Flea market's not even open."

She shrugged quickly, guilt over the mounting lies nagging at her soul. But what else could she do?

"I'll be right back." The man disappeared inside the open door only to return less than a minute later. "Here you go, Miss—now what was that name again?"

"Sinclair," she offered as she studied the document he'd placed in her hand. Sure enough, it was an official Sweet Briar contract offering police coverage to the people of Ridge Cove. The paperwork itself was fairly easy to read, the language more palpable than any legal text she'd ever seen.

"Who signed off on—" She flipped to the last page, her gaze seeking the signature at the bottom. "Oh, Georgina Hayes, the mayor."

Stu puffed out his chest in pride as he retrieved his contract from Tori's outstretched hand. "That's right. It doesn't get much more official than that now does it?"

"I guess not." She pushed her hands into the front pockets of her jeans and rocked briefly onto her toes, her heart saying it was time to go despite her head's gnawing argument to stay.

What was she hoping to find? A golden pathway leading to Tiffany's killer?

Exhaling and blowing a stray piece of hair from her forehead, she looked out at the buildings once again. "Can I ask one last question?"

"Shoot."

"If Tiffany Ann—I mean Miss Gilbert—was so excited about the building you showed her, why do you think she took off like she did? Did she have an explanation?"

"Nah. When we were done she mentioned wantin' a little time. I suspect she was wantin' to play a little hardball . . . make me think she had other prospects. So I played along. Even pointed out back to the creek bed that runs parallel through my property. When she headed that way, I went back inside. Next thing I knew she was heavy footin' it out of my parking lot. Last I seen of her."

And the last you will.

"Thank you for your time, Stu." She lifted her purse back onto her shoulder and turned toward the parking lot, her gait slow and preoccupied as she descended the porch steps.

"If Miss Gilbert doesn't get in touch with me by Friday, you can have the one in the middle if you want."

On impulse she turned back toward the man as she lowered her purse into her hands. "If I give you my card, would you call me if something comes up—on any of the buildings?"

"I'd be happy to. Seems to me you know a good thing when you see it." He extracted the card from her hand and looked down at it, his hand tipping back and forth in the poor reading light. "Victoria Sinclair—Sweet Briar Librarian." The man glanced up, her card still held outward in the few stray rays of light from the open doorway. "What kind of business would you be openin' up?"

"Uhhh, well, I was thinking about maybe opening a—a *bookstore*." It was a bold-faced lie but it was all she could come up with on short notice. And, considering her background, it wasn't too far outside the realm of possibility.

Assuming she was looking to open a business.

Which she wasn't.

After promising she'd be in touch and extracting the

same from him, Tori got back in her car and headed home, her favorite songs virtually unheard above the chatter in her brain as she sped along Route 190 on her way back to Sweet Briar.

But as she pulled into town she found herself bypassing her own quiet street in favor of the library, the one place she could always find answers. Though what answers she was hoping to find in the pages of a library book was anyone's guess. Sure, there were books that could offer a nifty escape or a ray of hope during a trying time. But a book capable of finding a specific person responsible for a specific crime? Not in her lifetime.

She let herself in the employee entrance with the key Winston Hohlbrook had provided on her first day as branch librarian. She'd been so proud that day, so excited to finally be running her own library—feelings that had faded into the background all too quickly as she realized she was an outsider in every sense of the word.

Yet there'd been hope along the way. Both before she'd discovered Tiffany Ann's body and after. Kind overtures from people who'd seemed happy to welcome her into the town. Leona had turned a lonely day around. Georgina had extended the invitation that put her in contact with her two truest Sweet Briar friends. . . .

Georgina.

What was it about those documents Stu had shown her that wouldn't let go of her thoughts? She'd seen the contract, read the basic agreement, noted the signature at the bottom . . . So what was her problem?

"Ridge Cove can't buy that kind of services and Sweet Briar most certainly can't sell them."

Milo's words flashed through her thoughts, the insistence with which he spoke them every bit as clear as it had been during their walk. Yet no matter what he'd said, she'd held the impossible contract in her own hand less than two hours earlier. . . .

Was Milo simply unaware of city policies or had Georgina done something illegal? She didn't know. Not for sure, anyway. Though, for some reason, she couldn't help but feel as if the latter was more likely than the former.

Grabbing the portable phone off her desk, Tori headed down the hallway and into the library, her hand instinctively finding the light switch despite the darkened room. As the fluorescent lights hummed to life she dialed Milo's number.

He picked up on the second ring.

"Hello?"

"Milo? It's Tori. Tori Sinclair." She wandered behind the information desk and settled herself onto one of the two stools. "I hope I'm not calling too late."

"No! Not at all." The obvious pleasure in his voice made her smile. He liked her, that was fairly obvious. And, judging by the butterflies that took flight the second he answered, it was impossible to ignore her similar feelings. "How was your sewing circle tonight?"

"I didn't go." She pulled the phone tighter to her ear and leaned her back against the counter. There was something about the presence of so many books that simply calmed her, made her feel as if everything would be okay.

"Why not?"

"I went back out to Ridge Cove instead."

"Alone? At this time of night?"

She nodded then put a word to the gesture he couldn't see. "I did. I wanted to talk to Stu again. You know . . . about buying police services from Sweet Briar."

"Tori, I already told you they couldn't do that. Why did you waste an unnecessary trip just to hear the same thing?" An awkward pause filled her ear momentarily before he asked another question, his voice much more hesitant. "Or were you *trying* to avoid your sewing circle?"

She couldn't help but smile. Milo Wentworth was an

observant man. Had she not felt such an overwhelming urge to talk to Stu, she probably would have avoided the weekly gathering if for no other reason than to keep from throttling Dixie Dunn.

"I truly wanted to talk to Stu. And he was right. He did sign a contract with the city for a nightly police presence and rapid response in the event of an emergency." She looked around the room, her mind making mental notes on little additions she wanted to make—a few more cushioned chairs, a few small end tables. "I saw it with my own eyes."

"You saw it? You mean you saw a contract for this supposed agreement?"

Again she nodded. And again she felt foolish. "Not a supposed agreement, Milo. A real one. Signed by Georgina Hayes herself."

"But she can't do that."

"Well, she did." Tori narrowed in on a far corner of the library, a section with countless shelves but no place to read. Perhaps a recliner would fit . . .

"But she can—"

Milo stopped midsentence only to speak again, his voice bordering on harsh. "What does Sweet Briar get in return for this little agreement? Did you happen to catch that on the contract?"

"Ten thousand dollars. Every three months."

"Ten thousand dollars?"

She pulled the phone from her ear and then replaced it, all thoughts of recliners and end tables gone. "You still think they can't do this?"

"I don't *think*, Tori. I *know*. Georgina Hayes can't do this."

Was Milo right? Had Georgina really done something illeg—

"And since I was busy givin' Miss Gilbert a tour and

explainin' it all to her, my contact took a few moments to answer his questions once and for all."

She heard herself gasp as the implications of what Stu Walker had said took root in her mind. He'd *told* Tiffany Ann about the agreement for police protection. Could she have realized it was wrong as well? Could that have been what made her take off without warning? And could that explain her strange moods prior to her death?

Her mouth grew dry as another question—one far more frightening—begged to be answered. . . .

Who could Tiffany Ann tell when the person responsible for breaking the law was the town's highest elected official? And with her supposed track record of tall tales, would anyone have believed her?

"Tori, are you okay?" Milo asked in her ear.

Could she tell the police? And if she did—would they believe her over the mayor, a woman who came from a long line of Sweet Briar residents and former mayors?

"Tori? You still there?"

Milo's voice redirected her internal questions. "If you knew Georgina had done something wrong . . . something illegal, who would *you* go to for help?"

The silence that greeted her question was comforting as she knew it meant he was giving his answer cautious thought—something that was desperately needed.

Finally he answered, his words carefully shared. "I would go to the next person in line . . . the one just below the mayor on the flowchart of authority figures. And I'd"—he stopped and cleared his throat—"hope against hope that person wasn't involved as well."

She couldn't even consider that possibility at the moment. It was outside her realm of comprehension. She needed to take it one step at a time.

"Who would that person be?"

"I don't know. I'd have to look at the town's setup,

probably something with the town's bylaws and ordinances."

"Something with the town's bylaws and ordinances," she repeated, her mind commanding his words to memory.

"I imagine you'd have something like that in the library. Something citizens could easily acc—"

"That's it!" she screamed. "That's it!"

"Wait. What? What's it?"

She jumped up and ran around the information desk, her body maneuvering around bookshelves like a skier on a memorized slalom run. A skier who slid her way to a stop in front of the local interest shelf and the lone book she sought.

Sweet Briar City Structure and Laws.

Pulling the book from the shelf she held it in her free hand, her eyes skimming back and forth across the cover. "The book."

"What book?" he asked in her ear.

"The book Dixie threw at me in my office because it had a coffee stain in it." She heard the words as they left her mouth, knew she'd finally put two and two together.

"O-kay. You lost me."

"The stain . . . in the book. Tiffany Ann made it."

"Come again?"

"Remember how she came here? On the day she died? And remember how Nina said Tiffany Ann had made the stain on the book that got Dixie so upset?"

"Okay, yeah . . ."

"Well, I'm staring at the book she was reading with the coffee that eventually poisoned her to death."

A long, low whistle filled her ear as she carried the book to the information desk and flipped it open, her left hand instantly seeking out the stained pages that had ignited Dixie's fury.

Sweet Briar Chain of Command:

Mayor
Police Chief
Council Member—section one
Council Member—section two

"Milo, this is it! Tiffany Ann did exactly what you said you'd do." She read the names on the list again and again, her thoughts trying to make sense of the printed words. "The chain of command is right here on the stained page."

"Who's next in line after Georgina?"

"The police chief," she answered.

"Okay. And he's been out of town for a few weeks on his annual fishing trip, which is why Investigator McGuire stepped in to cover the Tiffany Ann situation."

The Tiffany Ann situation.

"Well isn't that the same thing as what you're saying Georgina can't do with Ridge Cove?" She braced herself for his answer, afraid that maybe they were barking up the wrong tree.

"Not at all. McGuire is essentially on loan from Tom's Creek. A professional courtesy the two towns extend to one another when their respective chief is on vacation or too sick to work." He paused for a moment. "Okay, so after Chief Dallas, who's next?"

She read the next position aloud.

"Well that wouldn't work in this situation, as Lucas Blakely, the council member from section one, is Georgina's brother. Likewise for section two. Only in that case it's her cousin, Cooper Riley Senior."

"Georgina is Cooper Riley's *cousin*?" Suddenly the lack of attention given to any other potential suspects in Tiffany's death made all the sense in the world.

"In a roundabout sort of way. In fact, if I remember correctly, Georgina has kinfolk in authority positions in a few of the surrounding towns as well. I believe the mayor of Tom's Creek is somehow related to her ... a brother-in-law or an uncle, maybe." Milo took a sip of something. "You kind of get used to that around here."

"Isn't that considered nepotism?" she asked, her hand gripping the phone more tightly as Tiffany's reality flowed through her veins like ice water.

Milo laughed, a hollow sound that portrayed the noise for what it was—disgust. "In Chicago, yes. In New York, yes. In most cities and towns across the country, yes. But things are different here, Tori. They just *are*."

She tried his words on for size, allowed their meaning and various implications to roll around in her thoughts. "Then what do we do?" she finally asked.

"We sleep on it. Consider this from every angle we can possibly imagine."

"And then what?" she asked as she dropped her head into her hand and tried, futilely, to rub away the pain that pulsed behind her right eye.

"There's no school tomorrow, so I'm free. Any chance you can get Nina to cover you in the morning?"

"Uh—yeah, I guess. But why?"

"Let's meet at Debbie's Bakery at nine so we can try and figure out what we're going to do with what we know."

"What we know *so far*," she corrected, her temples beginning to pound along with her heart.

"So far? You think there's more?"

"I do. And her name was Tiffany Ann."

Chapter 21

The second she walked in the door she could feel a lift in her spirits, a momentary reprieve from a sleepless night spent scrutinizing everything she knew and imagining what she didn't. Troubled thoughts that were still lodged firmly in her mind yet could stand to be set aside long enough to order a cup of hot chocolate and a donut.

Tori cast a precursory glance around Debbie's Bakery for Milo, only to come up short. Which was okay. She needed a sugar boost before planning a course of action that would rattle the town of Sweet Briar to its very core.

"It's good to see you again." Emma Adams popped up from behind the register, a genuine smile lighting her face. "Back for some more black and white cookies?"

"Hmmmm. I wasn't planning on it . . . but okay, yeah, I'll take one—no, make it two of those in a bag and . . ." She studied the glass case filled with mostly breakfast selections—pound cakes, donuts, flavored breads, and bagels. "Do those chocolate-covered donuts have custard in them by any chance?"

Emma peeked through from her side of the case, her head nodding as she pulled the tray outward. "They sure do."

Yum.

"Okay, I'll take one of those and a cup of hot chocolate, too. Only those are for here."

"Gotcha." Emma pulled a plate from the countertop behind the glass case and placed a chocolate-covered donut on top. Setting that on the counter beside the register, she moved with ease toward the drink station. "Whipped cream on that hot chocolate?"

"Yes, please."

"That'll be five dollars," Emma said over her shoulder as she stirred Tori's drink with a red plastic stick. "I just made a fresh batch of whipped cream not more than twenty minutes ago so it should be extra good."

Double yum.

"I'm sure it will be." Tori swung her purse onto the small overhang beside the register and fished out five crisp dollar bills. As she waited for Emma to finish her order and take the money, she skimmed the various photographs that graced the brown pegboard behind the register. Cooper Riley's photograph—dead center just a week earlier—had been replaced by a new one of Jackson Calhoun.

Hmmmm. Trouble in paradise . . .

She felt her lips tug upward at the sight of Milo's reflection in the small rectangular mirror above Jackson's picture, the man's rumpled hair and tired eyes every bit as endearing as they were pitiful. Spinning around, she let the smile play out across her mouth.

"Rough night, huh?"

He ran a hand through his hair and nodded. "You, too?"

"I'm counting on my donut to give me a boost. Otherwise I may fall asleep at the table."

Milo laughed. "Good tip. Otherwise I may have assumed you found me infinitely boring."

"You? Never." But even as she joked, she knew it could never be the case. Milo Wentworth was fun, kind, compassionate, and the kind of man she'd enjoy getting to know on a deeper level.

"I'm glad." He swept his gaze across her face and down her body. "How come you look so good for someone who didn't sleep?"

She felt her face grow warm at his compliment, her hands instinctively smoothing imaginary wrinkles from her white blouse and tan slacks. "Probably because your eyes are more than a little bleary."

"They're not that blear—"

"Okay, here's your drink." Emma reappeared behind the register. With expert hands the girl swapped Tori's drink for the money owed and gestured to the cookie bag and donut plate on the overhang. "If you need anything let me know."

"Thanks, Emma." To Milo, she said, "I'll meet you at our table."

"*Our* table?" A twinkle appeared in his eyes. "That's got a nice ring to it, don't you think?"

"Uh—I—I'll meet you there." As she walked away she mentally chided herself for sounding so foolish. Sure, she was finding it harder and harder to deny the attraction she felt to Lulu's teacher. How else could she explain the butterflies in her stomach when he appeared unexpectedly, or the warmth she felt all over when he first walked in a room? No, that wasn't the issue. Figuring out just how far she did or didn't want it to go was the part that needed to be examined.

But not now.

They had more pressing matters to discuss.

Like how you go about seeking justice for a crime when the perpetrator is related to everyone in an authoritative position? And if everyone in the sewing circle was so reluctant to believe *Dixie* was up to no good . . . then how on earth could she ever expect them to accept *Georgina* as an extortionist?

Not to mention a murderer.

She plunked her cup, bag, and plate onto the table and sank into a chair, the promise of chocolate and sugar no longer holding any appeal. The dots she'd connected during the wee hours of the morning had created a pretty clear picture.

Georgina Hayes had not only broken the law by selling a service she had no right to sell, but she also had a pretty clear motive for yet another crime, one far more sinister and unforgivable than anyone could imagine.

Yet Tori'd imagined it. Again and again throughout the night, her mind unable to find the plot holes her heart was desperate to find. And when she'd looked up potassium cyanide and its potential uses, any hope she was wrong all but disappeared.

The only remaining sticking point was Georgina herself. Women who showed up on your doorstep bearing brownies and an invitation to make friends didn't kill people. They just didn't.

Or, at least, they weren't supposed to . . .

"So, how are you *really* doing?" Milo asked as he set his cup and plate on the table and claimed the empty chair.

She looked down at her donut and simply pushed the plate away. "Not too good."

"I figured that." Gently he scooted her plate back, his brows knitted with worry. "But you have to eat. You're going to need your strength."

"Why? I'm going to lose every last friend I have when the truth comes out." Wrapping her hand around her cup, she waited for the warmth to counteract the growing chill in her body, but it didn't happen. "Georgina is like a *sister* to these women."

He shrugged. "But sometimes you've got to step back and let a family member take their lumps."

"Lumps? Isn't that trivializing things just a little bit?" Tori stared at the donut, her stomach not the slightest bit interested. "I mean she's done something *illegal*. That brings jail time."

Lifting a fist to his mouth, Milo exhaled, his cheeks deflating rapidly before he dropped his hand back to the table and met her gaze head-on. "A *lot* of jail time if she's guilty of worse."

Guilty of worse?

She squirmed beneath his gaze, the sudden pounding of her heart drowning out all noises around them. Did he see it? Did he think it was possible, too?

Gripping her mug between her hands, she swallowed— hard. "Does that mean . . . does that mean you think she may have"—she swallowed again— "she may have killed Tiffany Ann to keep her quiet?"

He reached out, rested his hand on her forearm. "I'd be lying if I didn't admit that's a question I feel awful entertaining. Georgina Hayes is a great mayor and an even better person."

Closing her eyes, she nodded, her voice barely audible to her own ears, let alone anyone else's. "*I know.* I met Rose and Debbie and Margaret Louise *because* of her. And if it wasn't for those three and"—she opened her eyes and looked at him—"you, I'd not only be the lonely outsider, but I'd be the lonely murder suspect, too."

Milo slid his hand down her forearm, sought her hand. with his. "You're not alone. And you're not going to be a murder suspect for long."

She reveled in the feel of his fingers entwined with hers, felt the boost it provided to her confidence. "You're right. I'm not. I just wish my positive didn't have to be someone else's negative."

"I see what you're saying, I really do. But you deserve so much better, and Tiffany Ann's family deserves justice."

He rubbed the top of her hand with his thumb, a ges-

ture that brought the warmth her hot chocolate had failed
to provide.

"Justice," she repeated softly. "Justice for Tiffany Ann."

"That's right. It's the only thing we can—"

The familiar notes of her cell phone interrupted Milo's
words, the sound bringing more than a few perturbed
looks in their direction. Shrugging an apology to her companion and the unfamiliar patrons at nearby tables, Tori
pulled the phone from her purse and checked the caller ID
screen.

Stu Walker.

"I'm sorry, I have to take this," she offered to Milo as
she flipped open the handset and held it to her ear. "This
is Tori."

"Miss Sinclair? This is Stu. Stu Walker. From Ridge
Cove." The staccato cadence to the man's words made her
sit tall in her seat as she pulled her hand from Milo's and
placed it against her free ear. "I don't know who else to
call. I tried the number on the papers but got some daggone
message. I called county but they take forever. Then I
remembered you live in Sweet Briar."

"What's wrong?" she asked, her words causing more
than a few heads to turn in her direction.

"I found Travis. In the creek bed. He's been there a
mighty long time."

Found Travis in the creek bed?

The man's haunted words took root in her mind and
she gasped. "You mean he's—"

"Dead," Stu finished, his dread mirrored in her heart.

"But how-how did it happen?"

"I'm guessin' he was strangled on account of the rope
around his throat."

She closed her eyes in an effort to prevent the table
from spinning any faster. "Strangled?" she repeated in a
choked whisper.

"Sure 'nuff."

"Tori, what's going on?" Milo leaned across the table and touched her face, searched her now wide-open eyes with his own. "Who is that?"

She shook her head as she pulled the phone closer. "You think he's-he's been there awhile?"

"Since that last mornin' I saw him."

Her hand left her ear and grabbed hold of the table. "Why? I mean, how do you know?"

"There's not much left of him. Seems the animals have gotten hold o' him pretty well. But the clothes . . . they're the same."

"Are you sure?"

"As sure as I'm Stu Walker."

Instantly her mind began sifting through everything Stu had told her about that morning, questions firing through her mind faster than she could ask them. "So he handed you back the Sweet Briar contract and then left?"

"He'd already given me the paperwork first thing that mornin' . . . I needed it to show Miss Gilbert when I was givin' her the tour. And I didn't see him leave. The Sweet Briar representative just told me they'd talked and all was well."

"Didn't he have a car?" she asked.

"Nah. Travis just walked through the forest and across the field to get to my place. It's why he liked the setup."

Maybe he'd fallen on the way—

He was strangled.

"You need to call county. Right away," she urged.

"I did. But if it's like normal, they won't be 'round until sometime after nightfall."

"Did you tell them you found a body?" she whispered into the phone.

"Makes little difference with those fellas. That's why I bought the services from Sweet Briar. Though, between you and me, I can't help but feel I just got scammed out of ten thousand dollars."

"Probably because you *did*."

"What?" The man's troubled voice turned to anger. "Wait a minute little lady, are you in on this?"

"No. I just kind of stumbled on it."

"I swear someone's gonna pay for this."

"You're right, Mr. Walker. She is." Slowly but surely any reservation she'd been feeling dissipated, in its place a sense of resolve. Milo was right. Justice needed to be served no matter who got caught in the cross fire. "You focus on Travis . . . wait for county to show up. In the meantime I'll do everything I can to get to the bottom of your contract with Sweet Briar."

She snapped the phone closed in her hand and stared at it. "Milo, why would Georgina sign something like that? Didn't she know she'd get caught? I mean, the first time something major happened she had to know it would come out." She fisted her hand around the phone, the corners of the flat metal handset digging into her skin. "Poor Travis."

"Who's Travis? Who was strangled?"

Words poured from her mouth as her thoughts continued on the same loop. "I mean, why on earth would she sign her name to something like that? She signed her *name*, Mil—"

"I'm beginning to wonder how your Colby, bless his heart, can sign hundreds of books on any given day. Thirty papers nearly did me in."

The phone dropped from her hand as she grabbed hold of the table once again, Georgina's words from that second sewing circle rushing her thoughts. Were *those* the papers she'd been signing?

And *thirty*?

"Oh, Milo," she whispered. "What happens if Ridge Cove isn't the only one she scammed? What happens if she went after some of the other rural towns?"

"Then she's in even more trouble than we realized."

Milo raked his hand over his face, his shoulders tense. "I guess it's a little naïve to hope she didn't know."

"Yeah, ri—"

"Thank heavens I didn't have to read them."

She clapped her hands to her mouth. Was it possible? Really possible?

"I've been signing a lot of paperwork for Thomas the last week or so. He's compiling a few petitions to lobby for the rights of seniors on the state level and he thinks it would help their fight if they had some mayoral signatures. He's hoping my name will carry clout."

"And gain instant trust," she whispered.

"Trust? Trust who?" Milo reached across the table and pried her hands from her mouth. "Tori, what's going on? Please . . . talk to me."

She forced her eyes to focus on the man sitting across from her, a man who'd brought a smile to her face the moment she'd seen his reflect—

His reflection. In the mirror.

In an instant the threads began to come together. Threads that had seemed so inconsequential one strand at a time, yet created an entirely new entity when brought together.

Georgina was no more the key to Tiffany Ann's demise than Tori was, the woman's role as mayor no more a reason to cast blame than Tori's status as an outsider.

"Tori?"

"I saw you in the mirror." She gestured toward the pegboard hanging on the wall behind Emma. "I knew you were standing behind me."

"I figured that but what does that have to do with that call and with Georgina?"

"Tiffany Ann saw him. She knew he was standing behind her and she took off." All the clues had been there from the very beginning, only she hadn't seen them. Until now. "He had time to poison her coffee because she left it behind when she ran out. He, like everyone else, knew her late morning routine. He *knew* she'd be here."

Why hadn't she seen it before?

"*Who*, Tori?"

She hadn't left Stu's parking lot because of a phone call. She probably hadn't even realized the contract was a scam. She'd run because she saw him murder Travis. She was jumpy and nervous because she was scared for her life . . . not because she'd been on drugs as *he'd* insisted. She hadn't told anyone because she feared no one would believe her. . . .

Flipping the phone open, Tori dialed the last incoming number, her heart and mind needing one last round of confirmation for something they already knew to be true.

"Stu, here."

"Mr. Walker, it's Tori Sinclair again. I need to ask you one more question."

"Okay, shoot."

"This representative who spoke to Travis while you were concentrating on Miss Gilbert . . . what was his name?"

"Thomas Hayes."

"That's all I needed to know." She shut the phone inside her palm and rose to her feet. "I need to see Investigator McGuire."

"McGuire? Already?"

Wrapping her hand around the white paper sack of cookies, she planted a grateful kiss on Milo's forehead, the warmth of his skin beneath her lips bringing a much-needed sense of calm to her soul.

"I think the correct word is *finally*."

Chapter 22

She'd envisioned this room for as long as she could remember—the basic details she'd wished for as a child firmly in place, the extra touches she'd dreamed of as an adult bringing it to life in a way she could never have imagined.

Slowly, she turned around and around, her gaze skirting across the child-drawn murals and easy-to-reach shelving, lingering momentarily on the small stage that held the promise of laughter and creativity for years to come, and coming to rest on the overflowing costume trunk. Starting that very night, Sweet Briar children could don clothing worn by a favorite storybook character, adding a whole new dimension to the world of reading—one where alternate endings could be tried and favorite parts could be relived.

But somehow, someway, those assembled outfits meant so much more now. They represented the kind of magic that happened when people worked together for a common goal. They represented what could happen when preconceived notions and outdated stereotypes were laid down in favor of basic human understanding and compassion. And they represented what genuine friendship could accomplish.

"Miss Sinclair?"

Tori spun around, the hem of her black ruffled skirt skimming across her knees. "Yes?"

"Miss Sinclair, I'm not sure if you remember me but"—the twenty-something man bowed his head momentarily before reengaging eye contact—"I'm Nina's husband."

"I know who you are," she answered, her voice even despite the emotions coursing through her body.

"Then you know what I've done." Again his head dipped only to lift high once again. "I realize I need to take whatever punishment comes my way even if it's one I can't bear to face. But"—he twisted his hands inside each other—"please know Nina had nothing to do with any of this. She didn't help. She didn't—and *doesn't*—know."

"Why? Why did you do it?" she finally asked.

"I thought Nina should have gotten Ms. Dixie's job. She worked long and hard for that woman and got nothin' but grief in return."

"You'd never know it to hear Nina talk. She's not had a bad thing to say about Dixie or anyone else since I've been here." She tugged the pale pink sleeves farther down her wrists. "In fact, she may be one of the most positive people I've ever met."

A smile lit his face as he nodded. "Nina is special. I'm a lucky man to have her in my life. I guess I just wanted people to see that. And I figured if you messed up she'd—"

"Look better?" Tori offered.

"Yeah. And then maybe they'd give her a chance." Duwayne toed the floor awkwardly. "I just don't understand why people can't see her for who she is."

She reached out, touched the man's arm. "Some of us do. And we consider ourselves very lucky to have her in our lives . . . don't we?"

He nodded.

"I don't intend to press charges, and I don't intend to tell Nina what you did, but"—she turned her head to the side to meet his eyes—"you need to do something for me."

Surprised, he nodded again, this time even more emphatically. "Anything."

"Have faith in your wife. She'll get where she's going. And trust me . . . when she does, it will mean so much more if she did it on her own. With you cheering her on from the sidelines *believing* she can do it."

"You're amazing, Miss Sinclair . . . just like my Nina says." Duwayne grabbed hold of Tori's hand and shook it gently, his throat moving fast to stifle the emotion she saw glistening in his eyes. "Thank you."

"You're welcome."

And then he was gone, a tiny squeak from his black dress shoes following him down the hallway and into the library.

Glancing at her wristwatch she couldn't help but smile once again. She'd worked feverishly over the past few days trying to get everything done in time, anxious to unveil Sweet Briar Public Library's brand-new children's room. The after-hours event was by invitation only, a sneak preview of sorts for the people who'd contributed to its completion. The fact that some of those people had tried to undermine her job and her place in the community was irrelevant. At least as far as the children's room went.

"Knock, knock." Milo poked his head in the doorway, his eyes sparkling as he took in the room. "Oh, Tori, it's beautiful. Absolutely beautiful." He closed the gap between them with several quick strides, his hands finding hers and squeezing tight. "*You're* beautiful."

"Milo!"

"What? Did I say something wrong?"

She felt her cheeks warm, her hands moisten inside his. "No, but . . ."

He peeked around the room, glanced at the empty doorway. "No one heard."

"*I* heard," she whispered.

"Good." He released her hands and motioned toward the walls. "My students are going to love this."

"Oh, I hope so. This room wouldn't look near as special if they hadn't drawn the pictures for the walls." She brought her hands together and let out a little squeal. "Can you imagine how *you'd* have felt if a picture you'd drawn was painted onto a wall—to stay?"

"I'd have been pumped, that's for sure."

"*Pumped?*" She narrowed her eyes at the handsome man standing in the middle of her room. "Aren't you supposed to say something about fire in Sweet Briar?"

"Fire?" He cocked his head to the side, confusion disappearing from his face as he pondered her words. "All fired up?"

She clapped her hands. "Yes! That one."

He laughed. "I suppose. But I'm trying to feel a little more familiar."

"Familiar? For what?"

"You mean, *to whom.*"

"Okay. So who are you trying to be familiar to?"

"You."

She felt her cheeks redden even more. "By saying *pumped*?"

He shrugged impishly. "Well, I know the southern expressions have to be mind-boggling at times."

Reaching out, she loosened the knot of his tie just a bit and then retightened it against the collar of his white dress shirt. "I can get used to them."

"You can?"

"Maybe even find them endearing."

Now it was Milo's turn to blush. "Really?"

She patted the knot of his tie and then whispered a quick kiss on his chin. "Really."

He reached up and touched his hand to the spot she'd gently kissed, a silly grin stretching from one end of his face to the other. "Cool."

"Yeah, cool." She walked across the room and stopped beside a table stacked with frames. "Come see." The original artwork each student had drawn was featured in a frame, a small gold-colored plaque in the bottom right corner sporting the child's name and date, along with the title of the book they'd chosen to highlight with their illustration.

"Oh, Tori, they're going to love that." He looked from her, to the frames, and back again. "Where do you get the energy for all of this? I mean, to go through the garbage you've been through the past few weeks and still be able to do this . . . with a genuine smile on your face?"

"Mistakes were made. It happens." She scooted the stack to the corner of the table and straightened a small pile of index cards to their left. "The important thing is they were corrected."

He studied her for several long moments, a visual inspection that didn't bother her in the slightest.

"Did he apologize?"

"Whom?" She glanced down at the top card, mentally ran through her opening remarks.

"McGuire."

"He did. He truly had no idea that potassium cyanide can be used to remove tarnish from silver coins. Though, to hear him talk, he was starting to put two and two together."

"And get what? Ten?"

She laughed. "Maybe he's one of those people who use the right side of his brain—like I do."

"Well, the way he settled on you—for no other reason than you were new in town—doesn't bode well for his creativity either."

"Yeah, but he looks good in a uniform." Turning, she leaned against the table and smiled up at Lulu's teacher.

His brows furrowed. "You really think so?"

"No. But Leona Elkin does."

Milo swiped a hand dramatically across his forehead, mock relief on his face. "You had me worried for a mom—"

"Miss Sinclair?"

She pushed off the table and sidestepped Milo. "Yes, Nina?"

"People are starting to arrive."

Looking down at her wristwatch she nodded. "Did you set up the cookies and lemonade?"

"I tried to. But I was shooed away."

She shrugged a question in Milo's direction. "Shooed away? By whom?"

"Your friends." Nina rolled her eyes upward and placed her hands on her hips. "I was informed that there's a right drink and a wrong drink and—"

Tori felt her throat constrict as she recalled lesson number three aloud. "Southerners drink *tea*. Sweet tea."

"That was it . . . word for word. How'd you *know* that?"

She swallowed back the sadness that threatened to emerge for all to see. "Let's just say a little birdie told me."

"Well did that little birdie also tell you that store-bought cookies are not acceptable?"

Uh-oh.

She grabbed Milo's arm. "Can you stop by the bakery?"

"Of course. What do you wa—"

"There's no need, Miss Sinclair. We've got enough food to feed a small nation and not a one is store-bought."

So her sewing buddies had descended in force. She closed her eyes briefly against the tears that threatened to fall. Milo had been right. Things would get better.

"Thank you, Nina. Feel free to send people in as they arrive." As her assistant left the room, she smoothed a hand through her hair, the soft waves she'd added falling gently across her shoulders as she looked at Milo. "Do I look okay?"

"*Okay* is not a word that will ever be used to describe you. *Gorgeous* fits much better."

She stopped her eyes midroll. "I never realized you were such a sweet-talker, Milo Wentworth."

"You were kind of preoccupied."

"Being a murder suspect will do that to you." She flashed a smile at the man as the hallway outside the children's room grew noisy, invited guests making their way toward the reason for the evening gathering. "But no more. This is a fresh start. For me. For the sewing circle. And for Sweet Briar as a whole."

"Then let's get to it." Milo moved to the other side of the room as the first few guests entered, the subsequent *oohs* and *ahhhs* bringing a smile to her heart. She'd pulled it off. She'd taken what had been cast aside as unusable and turned it into a gem no one had ever imagined.

It was just like what happened every time she purchased fabric. A piece of cloth could be anything—a pillow, a hat, a skirt, a shirt, a dress, a wall hanging. And, by the same token, a box-filled storage room could be transformed into a room that would take a child to places they'd never dreamed possible.

Winston Hohlbrook, Lincoln Porter, and James Polk were the first to enter, their enthusiasm for the room more than she could have hoped for—their words of praise reaffirming what she'd hoped was true.

Next came several of Milo's students, their parents in tow. Many were led straight to their child's drawing-inspired mural, others stopped to apologize for their unfair judgment of Tori. All were thrilled with the room.

Then came Lulu, with Margaret Louise on one arm, and her daddy on the other, the child's delighted gasp as she stepped into the room the most touching reaction of all. Sure, Tori'd hoped to make a good impression on the board, and on the town as a whole. But, most importantly, she'd wanted to take hold of something deep inside the children and encourage them to imagine and hope, dream and create. A task she'd accomplished tenfold if Lulu's eyes and face-splitting smile were any indication.

"You should see the dessert table in the library, Victoria. You'll be hard-pressed not to put a few needed pounds on that tiny body of yours," Margaret Louise bellowed, her voice echoing through the room.

"Any Black Forest tortes?" she asked, her gaze still glued to Lulu's look of utter enchantment.

"Tortes? No. Just pies. Lots and lots of pies."

Tori's head snapped up. "Did you say pies?"

Margaret Louise beamed as she patted her handmade purse. "Which means recipes. Lots and lots of recipes."

Tori swallowed over the lump that sprang into her throat. Margaret Louise had been right. People were truly sorry for what they'd put her through.

"Victoria, thank you. For what you've done for my youngin'. She's got a glint in her eye since you came to town." Jake Davis held out his calloused hand and gripped hers tightly. "My Melissa is due back from her mama's tomorrow, and she can't wait to meet you."

Tori felt her cheeks warm with pride at the man's words of praise and admiration. "I'm looking forward to meeting your wife at the next sewing circle, too. And as for Lulu . . . well, she's as special as they come. Truly."

"C'mon, Mee-Maw, c'mon, Daddy. There's a stage! A real stage!" Lulu reached up and grabbed her grandmother's hand, gently tugging the heavyset woman across the room toward the wooden platform and costume trunk as her father followed closely behind. "I want to be Laura!"

Blinking against the tears that hovered just behind her eyes, Tori focused on the door once again, a tall, uniformed man the next to arrive, a police hat tucked under his arm.

Wordlessly, Milo Wentworth appeared by her side as she reached a welcoming hand in the investigator's direction. "I'm so glad you could come."

His steel gray eyes studied her warmly, all hint of accusation gone from their gleam. "And I'm honored to be invited."

Milo looked from side to side and then lowered his voice so as to be heard by only Tori and Investigator McGuire. "How's Georgina holding up?"

"When she comes up for air, I'll let you know. I'll tell you this, though"—he bent his head closer to their ears—"Thomas Hayes is going to be glad to leave the local jail in favor of a lockup farther north."

"She's making it rough on him, huh?" Milo asked, the rhetorical question bringing a knowing smile to Tori's lips.

"*Rough* doesn't even begin to describe it." Investigator McGuire moved farther into the room to allow the next throng of guests to enter, his pleasant and genuine demeanor a welcome change.

"You okay?" Milo asked quietly.

"Yeah. I feel awful for Georgina though. Her whole life has been blown apart."

"She'll rebound. Georgina is strong stock. Always has been. Always will be. Thomas Hayes can't change that."

"I hope you're right." She felt her skin tingle as he touched her arm, a warm and supportive sensation that gave her hope for the future. Jeff's mistake was Jeff's mistake. She couldn't hold anyone else accountable without hurting herself in the end.

Next through the door were friends, women she'd met through a shared passion for sewing, and grown to treasure for their common beliefs and values.

"I'm so very proud of you, Victoria." Rose reached up, her frail and trembling hand pushing an errant strand of curly hair from Tori's forehead. "What you've done in here will touch imaginations for years and years to come."

"Thank you, Rose," she said, her voice raspy with emotion.

She bit back the urge to laugh as Rose guided Dixie Dunn in Tori's direction with a well-placed elbow. "Tell her what you think, Dixie."

Dixie looked around the room, her eyes large and luminous behind thick glasses, her mouth gaping open as she took in every detail of the library's new addition. "The board—the board was right." The woman looked down as she fiddled with a stray string on her sweater. "I . . . I never would have thought of something like this."

Inhaling deeply, Tori squared her shoulders and extended an offer she'd been contemplating throughout the week as she'd painted scenes and reshelved books. "Can I count on you for an occasional preschool story time?"

The woman's head lifted, her cheeks pink with excitement. "Do you really mean that? Even after the things I said and the way I acted?"

Tori shook off Rose's admiration across Dixie's shoulder. "You have things to bring the children, too. I'd be a fool not to see that."

Tears glistened in the elderly woman's eyes as she fell into step with Rose, her shoulders sagging ever so slightly as the retired teacher draped her arm around the former librarian's waist and steered her toward the center of the room.

"Have you seen the pies you have out there?" Debbie leaned forward and gave Tori a hug. "I'm not sure *I've* ever seen that many in one place."

"Margaret Louise has the recipes," she whispered in her friend's ear.

"Then I shall go find Margaret Louise." Debbie walked about two feet only to spin back in Tori's direction. "You're really something special, Victoria Sinclair . . . I hope you know that."

She didn't know quite what to say so she simply smiled, Milo's breath warming her ear with his words. "I know *I* do."

"Mr. Wentworth, come see! They have a Pocahontas costume, too." Lulu's excited little voice carried across the room, causing more than a few smiles to turn in her direction.

"Do you mind?" he asked, as he held the index finger of his right hand in the little girl's direction.

"Not at all. I think I'd like to just stand here a moment and soak it all in."

"Soak away." Milo touched a gentle hand to the small of Tori's back as he stepped around her and headed toward the costume trunk.

Tori inhaled slowly, allowing her senses to soak up everything about this night. The sights, the sounds, the smells. All of it.

"You've done us outsiders proud, dear."

She turned toward the door once again, the familiar voice as much a sense of comfort as it had been her first week in Sweet Briar.

"Good evening, Leona." Tori gestured over her shoulder. "Investigator McGuire is over there somewhere."

The woman shifted a large gift bag from one hand to the other, her chin nudged upward. "I suppose he is, dear. But I'm not here for him. I'm here for you . . . or rather . . . to apologize *to* you."

"Apologize?"

"Lesson number four . . ."

Tori held up her hand. "Actually it's lesson five."

Leona's eyebrows rose upward in an upside-down *V.* "I thought for sure we'd stopped at three."

"We did. I just added one I learned along the way." Tori eyed the package suspiciously, its size and apparent weight making a costume out of the question. Even one that could be slapped together with peel and stick Velcro by a non-sewer like Leona.

"And what lesson would that be, dear?"

"Some questions are actually statements."

Leona rolled her eyes and handed the bag to Tori. "That's a Rose-ism. It's not a lesson."

"Oh." She stared down at the bag, suddenly unsure of what to say or do. "So what's lesson number four?"

"Apologies must always be accompanied by—"

"Wait! I know this!" She glanced across at Margaret Louise as the woman acted out the part of Ma to Lulu's Laura. "Pie recipes!"

Leona simply tapped her foot, her eyes narrowing in disgust. "I leave you alone for two weeks . . . *two weeks* and look what happens."

"Can I open it?" Tori asked, her lips trembling.

"Must *that* be a lesson, too, Victoria?"

"Nah, I think I've got that one." She set the bag on the ground and parted the handles, the tears she'd been holding back all evening finally trickling down her face. "Oh, Leona, you shouldn't have." Tori pulled the wooden sewing box with the horse and buggy carving from the bag and held it close, memories of her childhood tugging at her heart.

"Which brings us to the correct version of lesson four—apologies must be accompanied by something special." Leona lifted the empty bag from the ground and folded it quickly. "And since I couldn't give you to yourself, I picked the next best thing."

"I'm not sure that's a real lesson, Leona."

"It should be."

She swiped at the tears that wet her cheeks, hoped no one in the room noticed. "I miss your lessons."

"Then we must pick up where we left off."

"Can I teach *you* something?"

Leona offered a dainty shrug. "Like what? How to make—lemonade?"

Tori shook her head. "I was thinking more along the lines of sewing lessons."

"Why on earth would I want to learn how to sew?"

"Um, maybe because you're in a *sewing circle*, Leona?"

Leona waved her hand in the air, an amused smile teasing her lips. "Oh. Yes. Well, I suppose I may have overlooked *that* reason."

"That's it," Tori said as she tucked the wooden sewing box under one arm and linked the other around Leona's. "You, my friend, are going to learn how to sew."

Sewing Tips

(As shared by readers of the Gatherings Forum* on ThreadsMagazine.com.)

- Even if you don't sew, it's a good idea to have a pair of sharp scissors designated for fabric, ribbon, and thread. Cutting paper can dull your scissors. Tie a piece of ribbon to the handle as a reminder that they are only for fabric so they will remain sharp.

- Wishing you could sew while traveling by plane but discouraged by the "no scissors" policy? A package of dental floss can be an easy solution as it works great for cutting thread!

- If you scorch wool fabric by using an iron that is too hot, rub a nickel on the scorch mark. Be careful to use a clean nickel on light-colored fabrics.

- To avoid seam imprints on the right side of the fabric, place a strip of brown paper bag between the seam allowance and the garment before pressing.

❧ Anticipate how many bobbins you'll need for a project and wind them in advance. This will eliminate the annoyance of having to stop midseam to rethread your machine.

❧ Keep sharp tools to the right side of your sewing machine so you do not snag the fabric.

❧ Stack your pattern pieces in order of use, after they have been cut out.

❧ Do not put a hot light directly over your sewing machine as it can cause the grease and oil to dry out and freeze up the machine.

❧ Put all the notions, thread, trims, and pre-wound bobbins in a storage baggie for each project so you do not have to stop and search for them.

**Have a sewing tip you'd like to share with readers?
Stop by my website,
www.elizabethlynncasey.com
and let me know.**

Sewing Pattern

Interested in making a pillow similar to Tori's?

An Envelope Flap Pillow

Experience:

Some sewing experience needed.

Materials:

14" pillow form or 12 ounce bag of fiberfill
¾ yard of 45" fabric
Thread
Sewing machine with zipper foot
Sharp scissors
Chalk or marking pencil
Yardstick
Straight pins
Premade piping
Paper
Decorative button or other embellishment, optional

Directions:

Cut two panels of fabric measuring 15" x 15" each.

Create a pattern for the envelope flap by cutting a 16" x 8" paper rectangle. Find and mark the center point of one long side. Then draw straight lines from that center point to each corner on the opposite side of the rectangle. Cut off the excess paper.

Use your paper pattern to cut two triangles of fabric. Pin triangles with right sides together. Sew (½" seam allowance) along the two bottom (shorter) sides of the triangle. Clip the corner. Turn right sides out. Press.

Baste the flap to the top of one of the fabric panels— right side to right side—and machine stitch into place.

Baste piping to right side of the other panel of fabric. Using a zipper foot, machine stitch into place.

With right sides of fabric together, pin front and back panels, sew around all sides, leaving a large opening at the bottom for inserting the pillow form. Clip corners. Turn right sides out. Press.

If desired, hand-sew a decorative button or other embellishment to the pointed corner of the envelope flap, sewing through the pillow front if you would prefer the flap to remain stationary.

Insert pillow form or stuff with fiberfill and then hand-stitch the opening in the pillow closed.